"*I really feel for Neil Fisher, just finding his feet as a new curate. Whenever he trips up, it's in full public glare! But Neil is a man with mission, sincerity and heart, even if his inexperience and natural shyness do land him in trouble now and again, especially with the ladies.*

I love a book that moves you to tears one minute, then has you laughing out loud the next. This book is it!"

Aled Jones, broadcaster and singer

"*Pam's book is a great read! It is a tale of real people who laugh, have fun and love life. I commend it warmly.*"

George Carey, former Archbishop of Canterbury

By the same author

With Hymns and Hearts and Voices

The Dunbridge Chronicles

BOOK 1

FISHER OF MEN

Pam Rhodes

LION FICTION

Published by Lion Fiction
an imprint of
Lion Hudson plc
Wilkinson House, Jordan Hill Road,
Oxford OX2 8DR, England
www.lionhudson.com/fiction

ISBN 978 1 78264 000 4
e-ISBN 978 1 78264 001 1

First edition 2013

Acknowledgments
Author photograph by Jean S. B-C. Mower-Allard

Scripture quotations are taken from the Holy Bible, New International Version Anglicised, Copyright © 1979, 1984, 2011 Biblica, formerly International Bible Society. Used by permission of Hodder & Stoughton Ltd, an Hachette UK company. All rights reserved. "NIV" is a registered trademark of Biblica. UK trademark number 1448790.

A catalogue record for this book is available from the British Library

Printed and bound in the UK, July 2013, LH26

Agent: Lili Panagi, Pan Media, www.panmediauk.com

For Cindy Kent,
Once a curate, now a vicar,
Always a wonderful friend

⇝ Chapter 1 ⇜

*I*t was the spire of St Stephen's that Neil noticed first. In fact, if it weren't for the spire standing head and shoulders above every other roof in the town, he might have needed to keep a closer eye on the map he had balanced on his lap as he navigated round the one-way system which seemed intent on taking him out of rather than into the market town of Dunbridge. Actually, to describe this cluster of houses and shops, some very old, some alarmingly new, as a "town" might suggest more than Dunbridge really delivered. Neil had read that 6,000 people lived here. As he rounded the last corner, he wondered where Dunbridge put them all.

He felt his chest tighten with a mixture of trepidation and anticipation at the sight of the grand old church which stood solidly at the end of the square, looking for all the world as if it were peering down the High Street keeping a benign, unblinking eye on its faltering flock. Neil swallowed hard as he felt beads of sweat spring up on his top lip. Wiping his finger sharply across his face, he firmly reminded himself he had absolutely nothing to worry about. After all, this was just a first visit – to see if the Reverend Margaret Prowse thought he might make a suitable curate in this parish, and to decide if he felt Dunbridge could be a place to call home for three years during his training as a curate.

And wasn't this exactly the moment he'd been working towards for so long? As a soon-to-be-ordained deacon (the ceremony was less than two months away now), those years of longing, of recognizing his call, of study and preparation, had surely all been leading up to this moment – when he finally settled on the parish in which he would start his ministry. Was this the place? Would he become the Reverend Neil Fisher of the Parish of St Stephen in Dunbridge? He rolled the words over in his mind. They had a nice ring to them.

He glanced at the notepad on the seat beside him. "Drive up towards the church, then follow the road round to the right," Margaret had instructed. "You'll find the Vicarage down the first turning on the left. You can't miss it!"

He hated it when people said that. It always made him feel even more of a failure when he proved them wrong.

On this occasion, though, the directions were spot on. A sign on the well-worn gate proudly announced that this was indeed The Vicarage, a large sprawling Edwardian house whose faded glory was camouflaged by a huge wisteria on one side, and a scarlet Virginia creeper on the other. Uncertain whether he should pull into the drive, he decided that it would be more polite to park a bit further up the street, just round the corner from the house, under the arch of a huge horse chestnut. Neil grabbed his briefcase, clambered out and locked the door.

The gate squeaked as he opened it.

"Come round the back!"

The voice came from somewhere above his head. Neil shaded his eyes as he squinted up into the low morning sun.

"Take the path down the side of the house!" came the command again. "The kitchen door's always on the latch. Daft, really, but I like the idea of an open house."

Neil could just make out the silhouette of a round, female face surrounded by thick, neat curls leaning out of the upstairs bay window.

"You must be Neil. You're early! I'll be down in just a sec. Put the kettle on! Mine's a coffee…"

And the head abruptly disappeared.

Getting to the back was quite a challenge. Neil clambered over two bikes, a trailer and a hawthorn bush which had very nearly succeeded in its attempt to straddle the narrow path alongside the house. Finally, he made it to what seemed to be the back door, which was not just ajar, but wide open. Closing the door tidily behind him (he just couldn't help himself), he stepped into a large, alarmingly muddled kitchen in which the table, the worktops and even the hob were piled up with everything from stacks of plates and cutlery to columns of letters, newspapers and magazines. On top of the cooker was a Holy Bible on which was precariously balanced an open copy of the Book of Common Prayer. Neil grinned. Not much doubt a vicar lived here!

Something brushed his trouser leg. He looked down into the calculating gaze of the biggest, fluffiest ginger tom he'd ever seen. He was on the point of leaning down to give the little dear a tickle under the chin when he found himself staring into yellow eyes that gleamed with malevolence. Plainly this four-legged resident didn't take kindly to visitors, as it did a slow reconnaissance figure of eight around Neil's legs. He grabbed hold of a nearby stool and sat on it hastily, clasping his briefcase to him and pulling his knees up as high as he could.

"Frank!"

The same voice, sounding twice as loud, rang through the house from somewhere upstairs.

"Tell him where the tea is, there's a love! I think we're out of biscuits."

Intrigued, Neil looked towards the open kitchen door as the sound of slippered feet padded in his direction. Round the corner came a dapper little man with grey hair but, surprisingly, bushy dark brows. Taking stock of the positions of both man and cat before him, there was a sympathetic gleam of understanding in his eyes as he smiled at Neil.

"Sorry," he said, "my wife's only just got back from an unexpected hospital visit. She'll be down shortly. I'm Frank, by the way. And that's Archie. Quite harmless really, even if he does look a bit fierce. What can I get you? Tea?"

"No, thanks all the same," gulped Neil, not taking his eyes off the feline predator below him. "I don't want to put you to any trouble."

"Oh, the kettle's always hot in our house," smiled Frank. "You'll need to learn that if you're joining the ranks. Your first appointment as a curate, eh? Well, you'll be all right here. Margaret will look after you."

"Frank, have you found him?" That voice again.

"Yes, dear, he's fine. Archie's got him cornered..."

"Oh, for heaven's sake, give the poor man room to breathe, Archie!"

The Reverend Margaret Prowse strode into the room, her arms clasped around a large box full of collecting tins.

"Take these, dear, before I drop them. Why Peter left them here when they should be at the Church Centre, I really don't know!"

There were seconds of confusion while the box was handed over, almost dwarfing Frank, who staggered over to deposit the lot on top of the one pile of papers which was flat enough to perch it on.

"Margaret Prowse!"

Pushing her spectacles further up her nose so that she could peer at Neil a little more closely, she moved towards him, her expression warm and welcoming, her hand stretched out to clasp his.

"How nice to meet you, Neil! Did you have a good journey?"

"Not bad at all. Most of the traffic was going the other way. And I'm very pleased to meet you too!"

Neil became aware that Margaret's attention had diverted from him, as she suddenly stared at the clock on the wall behind him.

"Heavens! Is that the time?" She grimaced towards Neil. "Look, I know this isn't ideal, but you'll soon realize that parish life is never predictable. I hope you won't think me rude, but I do need to pop out for a short while. I won't be long, but I had a call early this morning from Violet, one of our regular congregation members. She's in a dreadful state – bereavement, you know."

"Oh," said Neil, "has she lost a family member?"

"Yes – and no. It's her budgie, Poppet. When you're nearly ninety and your bird is your only companion, then losing that friend is a dreadful shock. Her daughter is coming over at half ten for the ceremony…"

Neil felt his eyebrows shoot up with curiosity.

"Nothing formal. Not even consecrated ground, although a bit of holy water will soon put that right. No, Poppet is destined to rest in peace in the shade of Violet's magnolia tree."

"Have you worked out just what you'll say, dear?" enquired Frank.

"Not really. I'll play it by ear. That's why I was looking in the Book of Common Prayer earlier on, to see if there's anything that might fit the bill. Nothing quite right, I'm afraid. Any ideas, Neil?"

"For the burial of a budgie?" Neil loosened his grip on his briefcase, then lowered it to the ground behind his stool as he watched Archie wander away in boredom. "It's difficult, really, when you can't even give a potted history of the life and achievements of the dear departed, as you would for a normal funeral."

"Quite!" agreed Margaret. "But Violet tells me she's written a poem. That might do the trick. And perhaps a hymn? What do you think?"

"'All Things Bright and Beautiful'," suggested Neil. "That's got a line about God making their tiny wings, if I remember rightly..."

Margaret grinned with approval. "Great minds think alike! Exactly what I came up with. And that reminds me. I've downloaded the accompaniment for 'All Things' on to my iPod. A bit of music might add a touch of atmosphere. Where are those speakers we take on holiday, Frank? You know, the ones that work on batteries?"

"In the upstairs cupboard, I think. I'll go and look."

"Great! Meet me with them at the front door. And you..." Margaret turned her gaze towards Neil, "... might like to take a look around the church while you're waiting. I really won't be long. Sorry I can't take you with me, but I don't think Violet could cope with new faces just at the moment."

"I quite understand. And I'd welcome the chance to take a look around the church while you're gone."

"Go straight out the gate at the end of our garden. You can't miss it."

Not again!

"The door's open, but it's a tight fit. Just watch it doesn't slam shut because it's the devil to open again! Back soon. We can get down to business then. OK?"

Neil nodded, not quite sure which part of the deluge of words he was agreeing to.

But Margaret was already out of the room.

"Frank! Frank, I'm leaving! Where are those speakers? Oh, there you are."

Surprisingly, Neil heard the unmistakable sound of a kiss being planted firmly on a cheek.

"Remember to get those chops out of the freezer. And don't forget you've got to rearrange your dental appointment on Friday. Oh, and the recycling bin needs to go out today. Bye, dear. Bye!"

There was a sudden draught as the door opened, then slammed shut – and she was gone.

"Right," said Frank as he came back into the kitchen. "I've got my marching orders and so have you. The church is that way. Down the garden, through the gate, up the lane a bit – and you're there!"

This time Neil really couldn't miss it. St Stephen's loomed ahead of him the moment he stepped beyond the garden gate. He caught his breath. He'd always loved old buildings, and churches had been a particular favourite even when he was a small boy. That was probably because old churches had been a passion for his father too. There was nothing he'd liked more than coming across a church which he had never visited before. Story books – that's what Dad had called them. Neil remembered so many happy hours when the two of them had wandered around and inside an ancient church, noting a Norman carving here or a Gothic arch there. They would discover masonry marks left by the builders, faces carved in the wooden screen or the christening font, or even at the top of pillars – faces which probably looked very like some of the congregation members in the artist's time; towers hung with bells which had been rung every Sunday for countless generations (except during the Second World War, so his Dad had explained); tapestries and fading medieval paintings telling the Bible stories to congregations who couldn't read or write; even swallows nesting in the eaves, just as they had done for as long as anyone could recall.

Young Neil had listened, mesmerized, imagining the stonemason, picturing worshippers of times gone by, looking up at the great bells which had called the faithful to worship down the years. And to that small boy, it did seem that his father could read the story of each church as if it were a book, noticing details, large and small, which revealed so much of those who'd known the building before them.

"If these walls could only speak…"

Neil could still picture the softening of his Dad's face as he'd said those words.

"… drenched in all that's happened here, those walls are. That's why old churches have such a wonderful atmosphere. They've seen it all and felt every emotion. All the worries, hopes, joys and sorrows of the people who've come here down the years – these walls have absorbed the lot. What a tale they could tell!"

Neil found his pace slowing as he thought again of his Dad. Fifteen years on, and he still missed him. That final illness had robbed him of his zest for life and his dignity too. At least he was at peace now. Neil gave a wry smile. Well, at peace from Mum's sharp tongue, at the very least!

It was often said that Neil looked like his Dad – and he could see the likeness in the thick, wiry hair he'd inherited from his father. Nowadays Neil kept his cropped short, so the tight curls were hardly noticeable – unlike his Dad, who had let his hair grow quite long towards the end, much to his Mum's annoyance, especially as it turned grey. Father and son had also had the same lopsided grin when they laughed, which was often, because they shared a similar sense of humour – but beyond that, Neil could recognize little of his Dad in himself. His broad shoulders and stocky frame came from his Mum's side of the family. Her brothers had both been rugby players "for the county!", as she never tired of telling anyone who'd listen. Physically, Neil was perfect for a scrum half. Actually, the thought of getting anywhere near a scrum was his idea of a nightmare.

The graveyard was nice. A strange thing to think about a graveyard, but he'd always found them fascinating since he'd spent hours wandering around them reading epitaphs as a kid. Taking a quick look at the stones immediately near the path as he walked, Neil was vaguely aware of the church clock chiming noon as he reached the imposing Gothic-arched porch door. In spite of Margaret's warning, one twist of the round metal handle was enough to release the latch, so that Neil could easily push the door wide enough to slip inside.

He hadn't realized how much warmth there had been outside in the late Spring sunshine until he stood for a moment breathing in the essence of the building as he walked along the back pew, then turned to make his way up the centre aisle. There was a quiet coolness about the church, an oasis of tranquillity which didn't entirely cut out the bustle of the surrounding market town. He could still hear traffic noise, children's voices from a nearby school and even gentle birdsong, but it felt as if a blanket had enfolded the building, filtering everything until it seemed distant and removed from him.

Could this church become his spiritual home? He considered the thought as he walked towards the rail and looked up at the huge carved wooden cross suspended above the altar.

Was this it? Would he be able to bring something worthwhile to this community? Would his contribution as a curate in this church make a difference that was beneficial? Could he be happy and fulfilled here?

Like a sigh, he felt a sweep of cold air brush past him – and at that exact moment, caught by the same sudden draught, the heavy church door slammed shut, shattering the peace and shaking the rafters as it echoed round the old building.

* * *

Frank picked up the phone almost immediately it rang.

"Oh, Frank dear, I'm glad I caught you!" Margaret didn't bother to wait for any greeting from her husband before she continued:

"This budgie thing is proving to be a bit more complicated than I thought. Violet lives in sheltered housing run by the council, as you know, and because she wants this ceremony to take place as the body is buried, some 'jobsworth' is saying we need written permission before the budgie can be interred anywhere on council land! Can you believe it? Well, of course you can! Anyway, Violet is bereft, her daughter is threatening to call the local newspaper – and I need to be here for a while to pour oil on troubled waters."

"And perhaps even pour holy water on council land sometime this afternoon!" chuckled Frank. "Oh, you poor old thing. Still, if anyone can get things sorted out, you can."

"It's just Neil, that new curate – well, hopefully *our* new curate, if I can persuade him to join us – must think I'm dreadful to be so tied up when he's come all this way…"

"Well, he'll be getting a measure of how busy it is here, and how much he's needed, won't he!" replied Frank.

"Can you explain and ask him to bear with me? Do you think he'd mind holding on for a bit? Tell him to have a look at the minutes of the last few parish council meetings. Give Peter a ring and see if he'll pop round to talk to him about how involved the churchwardens are at St Stephen's…"

"But he's not here! He went over to the church, as you instructed, around twelve o'clock, and although I know I was out for a while, I really don't think he came back. Just to be sure, I did pop down to the church about two to check if he was there. I stuck my head round the door and called out a few times, but there was no sign of him, so I suppose he must have taken himself off home again."

"How strange! From his letter, it sounded as if he was more interested than that. Oh well, he must have taken one look at the church – and us – and decided it wasn't for him, then!"

"His loss."

"Absolutely."

"Odd, though."

"Certainly is."

"Right, I must get on. Good luck with the budgie, dear."

"Oh, I can handle the budgie. It's the council officials who need to be handled with care."

"They've not met you yet, have they? You'll knock them into shape."

Frank could almost hear her smiling at the other end of the line.

"I'll be back as soon as I can. Bye, dear!"

And the line went dead.

* * *

The main relief was that he'd found the loo. It was now three hours since the door had slammed shut on him, and in spite of shouting, thumping, kicking – and a lot of praying – the door refused to budge, and he was well and truly stuck. Worst of all was the moment about five minutes after the door slammed when he first realized that his briefcase was still stashed behind the stool where he'd been cornered by Archie in Margaret's kitchen earlier that day. In that briefcase was his mobile. Without his mobile, he was lost.

For one hopeful moment about an hour before, he thought he'd heard someone trying the door. He'd been closeted in the vestry at the time, idly looking through papers on the desk and books on the shelves, for lack of anything else to do. He was just opening a hymn-book, thinking that perhaps a verse of "How Great Thou Art" might make him feel better, when he heard something. The sound of footsteps, perhaps – and was it a voice calling his name? He rushed out into the main body of the church and ran back down the aisle, yelling at the top of his voice, then banged his fists for all he was worth on the unmoving old door which had imprisoned him – but there was nothing. No voice from outside filled with relief to have found him. No sound of a key turning in the lock or a shoulder thumping against the door. No sound at all. Zilch.

Exhausted with frustration, Neil staggered back to lean against the old stone font. How come they hadn't missed him? Why weren't they searching for him? Where was Margaret? Hadn't Frank wondered about him not calling back to the house?

What was it Margaret had said about that door? A tight fit? Something about it being the devil to open? Neil slumped down into the back pew, exasperated and exhausted by another bout of trying to pull, prise, cajole, punch or even kick the door open. It simply wouldn't budge.

He ran his fingers through his hair and sat for a while with his head cupped in his hands. He just couldn't understand why no one had come looking for him. Could that have been Margaret or Frank he thought he'd heard earlier? Did they just think he'd taken himself off again without even saying goodbye? Surely they'd see his briefcase? An image slipped into his mind of the Vicarage kitchen piled high with bits and pieces on every available surface. He'd tucked his briefcase behind the stool he was perching on. Would they see it there? Surely they'd find it! He frowned as he wondered if they ever found anything in that muddle. But then there was his car! He groaned out loud when he realized how he'd parked it up the road a bit so that it didn't block their driveway. Margaret and Frank didn't even know that car was his, so why would they take any notice of it?

When might the church be opened again? Perhaps for evening prayers? What time would Margaret think about doing that? Mind you, in a small parish like this one, with only one incumbent, evening prayers were often missed because the vicar was just not available to say the office at the right time. Margaret was tied up this afternoon at the budgie's funeral service. How long would that take? Would she find time to fit in evening prayers tonight?

Neil became aware of a deep rumbling noise, then realized it came from his stomach. He was not a man to miss meals without noticing. He remembered longingly his boiled egg and toast soldiers eaten at eight that morning, and glanced at his watch. He'd been imprisoned in the church for nearly four hours. No wonder his tummy was complaining. He needed food – now! Like a fox out on a night raid, he decided to search every possible nook and cranny for something to munch. There must be some biscuits here, surely. All churches ran on tea and biscuits!

He set off towards the vestry, a man on a mission.

* * *

It was gone six o'clock before Frank heard Margaret's key in the door.

"Mission accomplished," she grinned. "Poppet had a very good send-off quietly after five o'clock, when the council official had knocked off for the day. We sang the hymn and said a few words in Violet's flat, then nipped down and did the deed when he wasn't there to see us."

"Oh, well done, dear. I knew you'd think of something."

"No sign of Neil, then?"

"None at all."

"Odd."

"Very."

"Can I smell those chops in the oven?"

"With baked apple, just the way you like them."

"And roast potatoes?"

"What else?"

"I'm starving! Give me five minutes to sort myself out, and I'll come and set the table."

"How about, as a special treat, having it on our knees in the living room?" suggested Frank. "We can watch the news as we eat."

"Perfect," agreed Margaret, heading upstairs.

Minutes later, when she joined Frank in the kitchen, her nose twitched at the aroma of apples as he dished up the chops and gave the gravy a final stir. Margaret reached down beside the dresser to grab the padded knee-trays which they could balance on their laps as they ate. Suddenly, she stopped.

"Frank, look!"

Following her gaze, his eyes opened with horror.

"His briefcase! Neil left it here!"

"But why didn't he come back to collect it?" asked Margaret.

"Perhaps he just forgot."

The two of them stared at each other for several seconds, obviously registering the same thought.

"Or perhaps," said Margaret slowly, "perhaps he didn't leave."

"He couldn't still be in the church… I went there. I shouted. There was no reply."

"Did you look in the vestry?"

"Why would he be in there?"

"Why not? He might have got cold. Or bored. Or needed the loo. Oh, Frank, he can't still be in there, can he?"

"That blasted door!"

The two of them moved as one, out of the kitchen and down the garden path. It was as they were running through the graveyard towards the church that Frank spotted the light.

"I didn't leave that on!" wailed Margaret. "It must be him!"

Within seconds they ran into the porch, and Frank grabbed hold of the iron ring which turned the latch on the ancient door. Funnily enough, it worked very easily from the outside. Making it work from the inside, however, was a quite different story. It took practice, a lot of practice, to get the knack just right. Why on earth hadn't they made that clearer to Neil?

Practically falling through the door, their calls were greeted by absolute silence. Neil was nowhere to be seen. One small light was on, but the church was quiet and empty.

"Maybe he's in the vestry?" suggested Frank. "I'll go and check."

"Frank." Margaret's voice was practically a whisper. "What's that noise?"

He stopped in his tracks, his head tilted to one side as he listened.

"Whatever it is, it's coming from in here," gestured Frank, looking around the main body of the church. "Down the front there, I think."

"Be careful, dear. It may not be him."

Frank hushed her by putting his finger to his lips, then he began to tiptoe down the aisle, stopping suddenly as he drew level with the row of seating second from the front. Moving silently along the pew, he slowly leaned over to peer down on the seat in front of him.

"Come and take a look at this!" He turned to her with a smile.

What she saw when she joined him made her smile too. They looked down on a peacefully slumbering Neil, snoring loudly, his mouth wide open, his legs curled up along the seat, and his head resting comfortably on a hassock. On the floor below him was an open box of Communion wafers – or at least, what was left of them. He'd apparently found the Communion wine too, because the silver goblet they used in Sunday services stood beside his dangling arm with just a mouthful of red liquid still in the bottom.

"He didn't starve, then," said Frank. "That's a relief."

At the sound of their voices, Neil's eyes shot open, and for a second it was plain he was struggling to remember just where he was.

"Right, then," said Margaret in that no-nonsense tone he would later come to know so well. "It's pork chops for tea. Coming?"

≈ CHAPTER 2 ≈

"I'm your mother, Neil. I know."

Iris Fisher's voice lost some of its impact through the Bluetooth earpiece Neil had attached to his ear while he was driving. He was tempted to turn the volume down, but years of experience had taught him that if he missed one seemingly unimportant fact in her daily monologues, his mother would pounce on his lack of knowledge and blame him for it for months to come.

"Hasty, that's what you are." She was in full flow now. "You never take time to consider your options – and look where it's got you this time! Dumbridge! Whoever heard of Dumbridge?"

"It's *Dunbridge*, Mum, and it's hardly in the back of beyond. It's only a mile from the A1, so it's well signposted."

"On the road to nowhere, just like you. Honestly, Neil, when are you ever going to grow up? A curate in a town no one has ever heard of…?"

"*You* may not know it, but lots of people do – the six thousand people who live here, for a start."

"And what sort of church can it be in a deadbeat place like that? How are you ever going to get noticed there? What about your career? Aren't you interested in your future? If you start off in the backwaters, that's where you'll stay, you mark my words!"

Neil's knuckles glowed white as he gripped the steering wheel and took in a deep, slow breath. Iris, on the other hand, didn't draw breath at all.

"And another thing. Is this what your father would have wanted for you? Have you thought of that? He was a man of calibre and position – a *senior* partner at Hewitt, Manley and Fisher by the time he retired. Whatever would he think of his only son throwing away his prospects to become a vicar, of all things?"

"Actually, I think he'd quite like the idea…"

"Like! Like? I'd give him 'like'! He certainly wouldn't like the idea of his son being anything less than he could be, and you could have chosen so many other more impressive careers, Neil – careers that would have been worthy of you, and your father – and *me!*"

"Mum, I am twenty-five years old. I have a mind of my own…"

"Then use it, Neil! For once in your life, recognize that this idea of yours to go into the church is all very nice, but misguided – and the thought of you rotting away in an insignificant place with a silly name like Dumbridge is just ridiculous."

"It's *Dunbridge* – and the decision is made now. I have the car all packed up and I'm nearly there. In fact, I'll be arriving at my new house in a few minutes."

"Then stop, Neil, stop right now! Turn round, come home and let me sort out a nice accountancy position for you. It's what your father would have wanted."

"Sorry, Mum, the line is crackling. I think I'm going to lose you. I'll ring you tomorrow."

One little white lie, one quick prayer for forgiveness, and Neil decisively switched off his mobile with a sigh of exasperation. The conversation, if you could call it that, he'd just had with his mother was like a long-playing record which she'd played relentlessly from the moment four years earlier when he'd first told her about his decision to follow his heart and his calling. In the face of forceful, tearful, sometimes spiteful and often heart-rending opposition from his mother, he had gone ahead with his application to join the ordination process. Still she had argued, ranted, pleaded, sobbed – and in the end, willed herself into physical decline during which she assured Neil that when she died (which was definitely imminent), it would be all his fault. He had stood firm – and she lived. He went off to interview after interview, meeting after meeting until that wonderful day when news came that he had been accepted for ordination training. He was thrilled, overcome with emotion and a sense of destiny. His mother was at first inconsolable, then decided on the silent treatment for a whole three days, which honestly felt like a godsend for Neil. He knew he *had* to do this, and all the opposition she threw at him could never stop him.

And now, here he was, his faithful Ford estate packed full to brimming, with St Stephen's peering down towards him from the top of the market square in Dunbridge. As his mood lifted, he pulled up for a while to take in the scene. In many ways, he thought, the essence of this square probably hadn't changed in centuries. True, there were modern shops with signs which were familiar in high streets up and down the country, but those businesses nestled alongside other, traditional, stores which looked as if they'd been trading for many years. There was a horse-trough to one side and a coaching inn on the other, which spoke of days when people arrived on horse and cart rather than in the Vauxhalls and Nissans which lined the streets now. Today, with the street market in full swing, and people sitting out drinking coffee around tables in the middle of the square, he was struck by how settled and charming it all seemed. He instinctively felt he would be at home here and, with that in mind, he restarted the car and headed up beyond St Stephen's Church, peeling off to the right to find the property which was destined to be his home for the foreseeable future. 96 Vicarage Gardens, that was the address. Very appropriate for the new curate of the parish.

He'd been told about the house during the pleasant evening he had eventually shared with Margaret and Frank over pork chops and roast potatoes after the embarrassing "church door incident". A week later, he and Margaret had spent the day together, during which they had discussed a whole range of details about exactly where he'd live, what sort of timetable he'd have each week, what duties would be his responsibility and how his training would be organized. His mind had been whirring with facts, names, dates, times and places, so much so that even the notes he'd hurriedly scribbled at the time had later become worryingly blurred and confusing. There was just so much to learn, think about and remember. Anyway, first things first! He reached into his pocket to check for the umpteenth time that the key was there. It had arrived in a letter a few days earlier along with a compliments slip signed by "Peter Fellowes, Churchwarden". So far, so good!

As he turned the corner into Vicarage Gardens, his first impression of Number 96 was a pleasant surprise. It was a newish detached house – probably built in the eighties, he guessed, as it had weathered in well and was surrounded by a mature garden laid to lawn bordered by flowering shrubs. Above the large bay window were two other windows, presumably bedrooms, which looked out over the quiet, orderly, tree-lined avenue. Neil smiled suddenly as he noticed the front door was painted dark purple, the exact shade of a bishop's robe. His mother *would* approve! She'd see it as a sign of things to come for her precious son.

The road was quite narrow, so knowing he had a lot to unload, Neil pulled the car up on the grass verge right outside the house. Not stopping to unpack anything, he jumped out of the car and started down the garden path towards the front door, the key jangling in his hand.

I need to savour this moment, he thought. *This is a momentous occasion…*

"Oy, you! Is that your car?"

Neil turned to see an elderly man in bedroom slippers glaring at him angrily from next door's front garden. Surprised and shaken by the man's animosity, Neil quickly reminded himself about the commandment to "love thy neighbour" before he pinned on his sweetest smile, stretching his hand out in greeting as he moved towards the dividing fence.

"How nice to meet you!" Neil said. "I'm your new neighbour. It's good to be able to say hello so soon. I'm the Reverend Neil…"

"I don't give a monkey's who you are! You can't leave that car there! Move it!"

A little uncertain now, Neil glanced back at the offending vehicle.

"Certainly. I'll move it as soon as I can. I just need to unpack a few heavy…"

"Now! Move it *now*! You're wrecking that grass verge!"

"Am I?" stuttered Neil. "Right, well, perhaps you'd be kind enough to direct me to my parking space, then."

"You haven't got one."

Neil looked up and down the comparatively empty street before turning back to the man.

"But there seem to be plenty of parking spaces available. I just thought the one outside my house would be mine."

"No, it's mine."

"Right," nodded Neil, still confused as he looked at an elderly Volvo standing nearby. "Then whose is that car outside *your* house?"

"That's mine too."

"So you have *two* parking spaces?"

"No. I have one parking space – and the grass verge."

"On which you also park…?"

"No!" was the scornful reply. "Only imbeciles park on grass!"

"So you look after that patch of grass?"

"I look after that patch of grass, and that one, and that one, and all those down there." The man's arms flailed in the direction of every grass strip which lined both sides of the road. "It's called Vicarage *Gardens*, you see, not Vicarage *Garage*! Gardens have grass, and grass is not for parking. So *move it*!"

"Right. Ummm…" Neil looked around, anxiously trying to work out where he could park without causing offence, but still close enough so that he could carry the heavier treasures in his car to the door.

"Alf!"

A woman's voice rang out into the garden from the open front door of the neighbouring house.

"You're not giving our new curate a hard time, are you?"

A slightly built, middle-aged woman appeared at the door, then walked briskly out towards the two men.

"I'm so sorry," she said, "I do apologize. What a dreadful welcome for you!"

"Not at all," replied Neil, unmistakable relief in his voice. "How do you do? I'm the Reverend Neil Fisher."

"Maureen Allen, Alf's carer. I pop in twice a day – but he nipped out just now when I wasn't looking. I hope he wasn't bossing you about before you'd even got the key in the door."

"Oh no! He was just giving me a few helpful directions."

Maureen's voice was firm as she turned to the elderly man beside her.

"You were being all possessive about that darn grass again, weren't you, Alf!"

Alf's expression crumbled in indignant misery.

"Come indoors, you daft old fella. I've made your tea – and how about a piece of your favourite cake to go with it?"

That suggestion definitely caught Alf's attention, and he was already heading off in the direction of the door.

"What about you, Vicar? A bit of Battenberg?"

Neil smiled. "No, thanks all the same. But what about my car? Where should I park it?"

"Exactly where it is. Just ignore him. Bye, Vicar!"

And with that, Maureen disappeared into the house, closing the door behind her.

Neil turned and continued the short walk up to his own front door, a satisfying thrill of accomplishment trickling through his body as he slid the key into the lock to open up his new home and his new life.

What struck him first was the bright hallway before him, lit by a shaft of sunlight which poured through a side window halfway up the stairs. The house smelt of fresh paint and lemon cleaning fluid. Plainly, the church members had been hard at work on his behalf, and he felt touched and welcomed by that thought.

Venturing further down the hall, he turned into a large, pleasant living room which was divided by an elegant archway that separated the lounge area towards the front of the house from the dining room at the back, with its French windows leading out to a small garden. In the left-hand wall of the dining room was a large serving hatch through which Neil peered to see a well-fitted, medium-sized kitchen.

Stepping back into the hall so that he could look round the kitchen properly, he opened a door under the stairs on the way, thinking it might be a downstairs loo, but he was met instead by a collection of practical items such as a vacuum cleaner, a mop and bucket, and an airing frame. They seemed to have thought of everything. It was all immaculate, with many thoughtful touches, like the row of starched tea towels and dishcloths that hung on hooks, and the cutlery drawer filled with neat rows of knives, forks and spoons. There were cereal bowls, serving dishes, sparkling tumblers and brightly coloured egg-cups.

There was even a flowering pot plant on the windowsill, on which was propped a card blazoned with the word "Welcome!" in large red letters. Touched by their kindness, Neil inwardly registered that with his gardening skills, he didn't give the pot plant more than a couple of months before, in spite of his best efforts, he'd manage to kill it off.

Leaving the kitchen, he made his way back to the bottom of the stairs where, to the left, was a door which led into what was obviously a study, complete with mahogany desk and bookshelves, and a matching two-seater settee and comfy armchair in which he could already see himself having heart-to-heart chats with parishioners.

At the top of the stairs he found the master bedroom, painted in a tasteful shade of beige. Next door was the main bathroom which, to Neil's fascination and slight alarm, was dominated by an outsized, cream-coloured jacuzzi corner-bath, complete with an impressive array of controls and taps.

There were two more rooms – the largest kitted out as a spare double bedroom, and the other containing both a fold-up bed and a desk, suggesting that Neil could, if he chose, make this either another spare room, or perhaps a more personal office, less public than the study downstairs, which was likely to play host to a stream of church visitors.

He couldn't wait to start settling in, and after several trips to the car, he pottered about, trying to find a place for everything. It helped when he realized that he actually had his own garage at the end of the back garden, and it was in there that he found a corner to stash his fold-away bike, a multi-gym he'd only used twice but thought he should bring anyway, and the stack of empty plastic boxes in which he'd brought everything he'd unpacked so far.

He decided to put his "reading for pleasure" books (including his complete set of Bernard Cornwell novels) in the lounge, his inspirational and reference books in the study, while his personal papers and folders were neatly stacked on the shelves of the upstairs office. He hung his everyday clothes in the master bedroom wardrobe, then put his clerical robes in the longer wardrobe in the spare room. He laid his shoes out in pairs in a line on the wardrobe floor, saving the last space for the trainers he was actually wearing. His washbag was emptied out into the bathroom cabinet, and his electric toothbrush safely attached to the socket.

An hour later he sank down on to the bottom stairs with satisfaction, knowing that his home was organized and orderly, just the way he liked it.

Two brisk rings on the doorbell abruptly broke his thoughts. He opened the door to reveal a silver-haired, tall, distinguished man smiling at him.

"You must be Neil. Welcome! I'm Peter Fellowes, churchwarden. Just wanted to make sure you're settling in OK."

Neil shook his outstretched hand warmly. "Lovely to meet you, Peter. I think I have you to thank for this wonderful house. I can see you've put a lot of work in here."

"Well, not just me. It was a team effort. The PCC formed a sub-committee. We're good at that."

"And I," said a melodious female voice from somewhere behind the flowering honeysuckle that framed the front door, "I prepared your welcome pack for you!"

Peter was firmly pushed to one side as a woman stepped into view, filling the doorway with her presence. Neil's gaze took in her elegant high heels, her expertly coiffed hairdo, the tailored cerise jacket which barely covered the neckline of a blouse which seemed, even to Neil's inexpert eye, surprisingly low for a lady "of a certain age".

"Glenda Fellowes," she drawled, her eyes locked on Neil's. "I hope you have all you need. Bread, milk, cornflakes, sugar…"

She rolled the last word round until it sounded almost like a term of endearment. Then, before Neil could see it coming, in two quick paces she was across his threshold, enveloping him in a smothering bear hug. It was an experience he would remember for many years to come, as he found himself firmly clamped against her, almost choking on her heady perfume as his face was squashed down against her generous folds.

"Welcome, dear Neil," she whispered huskily into his ear, "on behalf of us all at St Stephen's. And if you need anything…"

She untangled him then and held him at arm's length.

"… anything at all…"

Her eyes were burning into him.

"… just ask. My wish is your command."

Mesmerized, Neil felt that his feet were rooted to the ground. A slight cough to one side broke the mood.

"Right," said Peter, a note of impatience in his voice. "Let the poor man get on. I'll probably see you tomorrow, then, Neil, at Morning Prayer. In the week, we only open up the church for the Daily Office on a couple of weekdays, and although there's just a handful of us, I rather enjoy it."

His eyes still fixed in horrified fascination on Glenda, Neil could only manage a nod of his head in Peter's direction.

"Come on, Glenda!" Turning on his heel, Peter set off down the garden path.

And with one last, lingering gaze, Glenda held up her long-nailed hand to pat Neil's cheek, then tiptoed daintily after her retreating husband as fast as her stilettos would allow her.

* * *

It took Neil a mug of sweet tea and a couple of hours to recover from the encounter with Glenda, but at last, as sunset descended around his new home, he felt calm enough to settle down for his regular evening worship. He thought carefully about where it would feel most appropriate to say the familiar words, read his Bible and pray, and finally decided on the study, with its comfortable armchairs and peaceful air. He considered which words from the Bible would suit the occasion best, and found himself turning to one of his favourite passages, John 14. He read:

*In my Father's house are many rooms… I am
going there to prepare a place for you…*

And he did feel that Christ had gone before him to bring him here to the neat, welcoming rooms of this clean, shining house. This was the culmination of more than just a physical journey with its destination here in Dunbridge. This was a spiritual odyssey begun in the heart-warming times he'd shared as a child with his father in churches they had both loved; continued through his struggle to find a role in life which was a vocation rather than just a job; and decided when he recognized at last that God was calling him, and giving him the strength to face whatever lay ahead.

Theological college had been a joy for him. He loved studying the Scriptures, and the hot debates between students on spiritual and moral issues which their Bible study threw up. He grew confident in the shared fellowship of mission and worship. He began to believe that he had the faith, intellect and instinct he would need to minister to others, and to support them in the ups and downs of their own Christian journey.

He also recognized his limitations. He didn't imagine he would ever get a night's sleep before having to give a sermon, and the thought of actually leading a complete service himself still made him feel very queasy – but every day brought him nearer to his goal, and nearer to God.

So tonight, on the eve of starting work in his first parish, Neil lowered his head in thanks for simply getting there – and prayed with humble fervour that he could cope with whatever tomorrow might bring.

≈ CHAPTER 3 ≈

*H*is first full day in the job started with worship too, though this time it was shared with the Reverend Margaret and Frank, who met him at the church gate at half past eight so they could say Morning Prayer together. Neil watched anxiously as the Vicar unlocked the heavy church door which had caused him so many problems on his first visit to St Stephen's. Noticing his discomfort, she grinned at him before leading the way down the aisle and towards the vestry, taking time on the way to point out where to find whatever he might need whilst in the church. By the time they reappeared, Neil was pleased to see they had been joined by a few other worshippers. Churchwarden Peter, thankfully without his terrifying wife, waved acknowledgment from where he was standing next to a slightly built, middle-aged woman who was smiling warmly up at him as they chatted quietly on the far side of the church. As Neil made his way over to the small side chapel where the Daily Office was usually said, he noticed another new face, an elderly man whose blue eyes twinkled kindly beneath bushy eyebrows and a shock of matching white hair.

"Harry Holloway," he said, walking forward to meet Neil. "Welcome to St Stephen's!"

"Nice to meet you, Harry," replied Neil. "You're an early bird!"

"Habit of a lifetime," smiled Harry. "I was a milkman for forty years. Can't stay asleep once it's light. I've been up since five this morning, so this feels like lunchtime to me."

"You're a regular at Morning Prayer then, are you?"

"Whenever there's an early service like this, yes, I usually come – but I've always liked my time in this church. It brings back so many memories of my Rose, and I can't sit here and not think of her. You know, we were married right here in this church fifty-one years ago. She didn't quite make our Golden Anniversary, which was a shame, because I planned to take her to Rome. She'd always wanted to go there and throw three coins in that fountain…"

"The Trevi Fountain?"

"That's the one. She liked Frank Sinatra singing the song about it." He chuckled. "You're too young to remember that record."

"I do know the one you mean. It's a track on the Sinatra compilation CD I bought for my Mum a couple of Christmases ago."

"Well, Rose thought that was a really romantic idea, and she was always moaning at me because she said I was never romantic at all. Well, you aren't, are you, when you've been married as long as we were?"

"Oh, romance isn't everything," agreed Neil, hoping he sounded like an authority on the subject when, honestly, his track record with relationships had been bumpy, to say the least. "It's the love between you that matters…"

Neil stopped mid-sentence as he noticed Harry's blue eyes were glistening with tears.

"Well, that's the other thing that keeps me awake at night."

Harry's voice was barely above a whisper. "I loved her, of course I did. She was my world – but I never told her, you see. I thought she just knew how I felt about her. Why else would I work all hours to keep food on the table? Why else would I constantly be doing little jobs to improve the house? I loved her. She should have known that."

"But now you're not sure she did?" asked Neil softly.

"At her funeral, her friend Elsie – they'd known each other forever, practically grew up together – told me that Rose had been upset for years that I'd never said I loved her."

The old man took a neatly ironed white hankie out of his pocket and discreetly dabbed his eyes and nose. Neil watched in silence, uncertain what to say.

"So I come here most days just so that I can sit in this church where we both sat Sunday after Sunday. Then when I'm praying, I ask God to make sure she's OK and give her my love. He can do that, can't he?"

"Absolutely," agreed Neil.

"I miss her so much."

"How long ago did you lose her?"

"It'll be two years next month – and you know, I feel as raw about it now as I did then, perhaps more. She's buried in the churchyard, at the back near the gate above the river. That's where I'll be one day, and, honestly, I long for that time when we'll be together again. I can put things right then, can't I? Tell her what I should have said every day when we were together."

"When you're ready, Neil!"

Neil looked up to see that Margaret had already taken her place in her stall.

"Shall we get started?"

Glancing in Margaret's direction, Harry gave a wry grin.

"That's women for you! Make you feel guilty even if you've done nothing wrong. Rose was good at that too."

"And you have done nothing wrong, Harry. I'm sure she recognized your loving care in her own way, even if you never actually said the words."

"Neil! Are you joining us?" There was something in the tone of Margaret's voice that reminded Neil of a headmistress he'd once had.

"I'm coming!" Neil called back.

"So is Christmas!" retorted Margaret with a definite twinkle in her eye. "Do you think you could make it a bit quicker than that?"

Harry grinned to see the red hue of embarrassment that spread upwards across Neil's face as he rushed to take up his position in the reader's stall.

Neil had always found the experience of dedicating the coming day to God reassuring and encouraging. To be speaking these familiar words on the first day in his new role felt personal and special, and by the end of the short service, Neil's mood was buoyant and confident about whatever this step in life might bring his way. He had hoped to have another word with Harry before he left, but it seemed the older man had slipped away immediately. Instead, the person intent on having a word with Neil was Margaret.

"Right!" she barked. "I've got an appointment to see a parishioner who is going through family problems at the moment. It's all a bit sensitive, and I think she would be happier if I went alone, for the time being at least. I will introduce you properly in time – in fact, I'll introduce you to everyone on Sunday morning. We should have a good turnout because, now you've finally arrived, most of the congregation are planning to come and give you the once-over."

"Oh," sighed Neil, whose natural shyness made the prospect of being assessed and found wanting by this group of fellow Christians very daunting. "I hope they're not disappointed."

"Well, that's up to you!"

Neil was relieved to see that a soft smile had crept over Margaret's face, in spite of her curt reply. She was right, of course. His life was what *he* made it. Hadn't that been the whole point behind the journey he'd already travelled to bring him to this place? A vision of his mother's face with that familiar expression of exasperation and disappointment suddenly shot into his mind. Straightening up his shoulders, he pulled on his jacket.

"What would you like me to do while you're busy?"

Margaret glanced at her watch. "It's nine fifteen now. The playgroup will be starting in the church hall at half past. Ask for Barbara. She's in charge. Go and say hello. It will be a good way for you to meet some of our locals. Then come back over to the house for a spot of lunch. I'll get Frank to rustle up a sandwich. We can take a look at what's happening this week and work out a schedule for you. Right?"

"Right!"

Once the dreaded porch door was safely shut and locked, Neil started to follow Margaret up the path.

"Neil." Margaret's voice was deliberately patient. "I'm going this way because my house is in this direction. You're going to the hall – and that's over there!"

He felt her hands firmly grip his shoulders, turning him around to face the opposite way completely.

"Down that path, the big building on the right with the leaky roof and the windows that need painting. You can't miss it!"

And with that, Margaret strode off purposefully. Neil set off too, but at a much slower pace, taking time to glance at the gravestones on either side of the path. Most of them dated back a century or more, but his father had taught him to imagine the stories behind the short, formal words carved in stone. He stopped for a while to consider the fate of the family of William Stephen Allard who had been laid to rest in 1868, three short years after his young wife Mary had died in childbirth. Mother, father and child had been laid in the same plot, together forever. Neil wondered what had caused William's death. A common illness of the day – or a broken heart? Neil's heart was touched with compassion as he moved on.

Shafts of sunlight dappled through the row of beech trees with their boughs of green and red leaves arching over the left-hand side of the path. Glancing beyond them, Neil realized that the ground fell away, probably sloping down to the river which Harry had mentioned earlier. Rose's grave must be over there somewhere – and it didn't take long for Neil to spot it. It was a blaze of colour, adorned with cheerful polyanthus which had almost certainly been planted there by Harry. It was clear that the imaginative arrangement and obvious care of this plot had come from more than a simple sense of duty or habit. This spoke of dedication. It was for his Rose. The plants here were rooted in love.

Neil's thoughts were interrupted by the sound of the church clock chiming the half hour. Turning quickly, he hurried back to the path towards the wrought-iron gate that led through towards the hall. The gate had obviously seen better days, because when Neil undid the latch and tried to push it open, it stuck fast. His first attempts to push it gently developed into a series of sharp thumps with the palm of his hand, followed finally by a kick loaded with all the frustration he felt – which made no impact on the gate whatsoever.

"The other way!"

Neil turned sharply to find himself the object of a cool stare from the greenest eyes he'd ever seen. They belonged to a slightly built, spiky-haired young woman in gumboots who was watching him with detached interest as she leaned over the garden fork she'd plainly just been using on one of the churchyard flowerbeds.

"You're pushing it the wrong way. It opens inwards."

"Oh!" mumbled Neil, flushing scarlet as the gate opened with obliging ease the moment he pulled it towards him.

"You must be the new curate," continued Green Eyes. "I heard you've got a problem with locks and latches."

"Not really," retorted Neil with as much dignity as he could muster. "I'm on my way to the church hall."

"Through the gate, then go right. The side door will be open." Her face was suddenly transformed by an impish grin. "Mind you, it probably won't be if it's *you* that tries it. Do you want me to come with you, just to make sure you can manage it all right?"

"I'll be fine, thank you," Neil replied stiffly. "Good morning."

And as he walked away with what he hoped was an air of confidence, he could just picture the look of amusement on her face as she watched him go.

In the end, getting in through the side door of the church hall wasn't the problem. The challenge was to get anywhere once inside. The door led into a wide entrance hall lined with coat-hooks and benches – at least, that's what Neil thought he could see through the throng of chattering, occasionally wailing, youngsters and their mums, who bore expressions which ranged from besotted to berating as they prised their excited offspring out of their coats and outdoor shoes, then into their plimsolls and brightly coloured overalls.

"Quietly now! Don't forget to put your name sticker on so that everyone knows who you are!" A voice of authority rang through the chaos. "Joseph, you want to start in the sandpit, don't you? Go and find Debbie, then. She's in charge of sand play today. Phoebe, don't do that, there's a good girl! Look, Amy's over there, waiting for you. In the Wendy house, see! Oh, I'm glad to see you, Mrs Howard. Your subs are a bit behind, did you know? Any chance of making it up today? See Christine. She's got the books. Yes! Can I help you?"

Neil became aware that the short-haired, loud-voiced woman who had been issuing instructions to all around her was now looking pointedly at him. As the crowd shifted between them, her face broke into a smile as she spotted his dog collar.

"Ah, we meet at last! You must be the new curate."

"Neil Fisher." He grinned. "Do I need a name sticker too?"

"Not a bad idea. I've got one!" She pointed in the vague direction of her overalled bosom to the large sticky label with "BARBARA" written on it in bold red capitals. Before Neil could draw breath, she had whipped out a felt-tip pen and slapped a label saying "NEIL" on the lapel of his jacket.

"Right, are you any good at making tea? Jan, who normally mans the kettle, has got her ante-natal this morning. The urn should be hot by now. Turn it down to 2 when it starts to boil. Mugs are in the top cupboard, sugar and biscuits down below – oh, and can you go and fetch some milk? Get two two-litre packs of full-fat for the children – and we'll need a carton of semi-skimmed for the grown-ups. And some Hobnob biscuits… Now, Daniel, I've told you before about doing that! Give that doll back to Kylie immediately! Where are her clothes? Why have you taken the dolly's clothes off? She'll be freezing…"

And Barbara was gone, disappearing through the door into the melee of small bodies and noise.

Three hours later, Neil had made the decision that he would never have children of his own. He thought it might be because he was an only child, but the awesome prospect of being responsible for one of these demanding, illogical, needy little people was too terrifying to contemplate. Of course, there were exceptions. He'd taken quite a shine to a little angel with a mane of bouncing golden curls who had climbed up on to his lap when he was deep in conversation with one of the mums, popped her thumb into her mouth, then instantly nodded off to sleep.

"That's Chloe," explained Barbara as she scooped the sleeping child into her arms with a look of real tenderness. "Her Dad's left. Mum's not coping very well, and I think Chloe's missing a father-figure around the place. You must look dependable and comforting…" Barbara's eyes surveyed him critically, "… to Chloe, at least. Oh goodness, look at the time! The mums will be arriving to collect the little ones for lunch any minute. Help Debbie clear away the sandpit and finger-paints, will you, Neil, there's a love!"

When Neil was finally free to leave, he shouted out his goodbyes to the staff he'd met, and headed towards the side door through the hallway, where the rush to take off overalls and plimsolls and put on outdoor clothes was, thankfully, beginning to subside. Nevertheless, his eyes were drawn to the nearest corner of the hallway where one mum with her back to him was displaying a very shapely figure in pale-blue jeans as she bent over to buckle up her little boy's shoes. He didn't realize his gaze had stayed on her until, seconds later, the apparition stood up and stared back at him, her green eyes blazing.

"Are you trying to find the door?" she asked coolly. "It's just over there. If you need help opening it, do let me know."

"I was just going to say hello…"

Toe-curling embarrassment was sending blood coursing up Neil's neck.

"Best to say it to my face then, don't you think?"

"Of course," said Neil, striding across towards her, his hand outstretched. "We met in the churchyard, of course, but seem to have got off on the wrong foot. How do you do? I'm Neil Fisher. The Reverend Neil Fisher."

"Oh, I know who you are." Her eyes scanned the length of him as if she was deciding whether he was worth bothering with. Apparently not, because without another word, she smiled down at the little boy, then holding hands, they both walked through the door, closing it firmly behind them.

Neil, his hand still outstretched, stared at the door in dazed confusion for several seconds before he stuffed his hand into his pocket and turned on his heel so that he could leave the hall by the door he hoped he'd find at the front of the building. To be honest, *any* door would do except the one that had just been slammed in his face.

* * *

By the time he turned the key in the front door of Number 96 at the end of his first day on the job, his mind was a muddle of things he should remember and moments he'd rather forget.

Had it been a good start? In some ways, yes, with one notable exception…

Had he enjoyed it? On the whole, definitely – but was he really cut out for this type of work?

With a sigh, he caught a glimpse of himself in the hall mirror. He certainly looked the part, with his neat shirt and jacket starkly black against the gleaming white of his clerical collar. Looking right wasn't enough, though. How long would it be before he could feel confident in the role? Was he really the sort of person who could be alongside others in the ups and downs of their lives and faith? Was that possible when he remembered how out of depth he'd felt at times that day – and how he had blushed bright red at the slightest suggestion of upset or embarrassment? He was twenty-five years old, for heaven's sake! There had been times today when he'd felt like a kid who knew absolutely nothing.

He needed to pull himself together. This was only the first day, after all. Suddenly he turned to stride up the stairs, two at a time. It took him minutes to change into jeans and a sweatshirt, and head back down again. He hadn't had time to do a proper supermarket shop yet, so possibilities for supper were very limited, and from past experience he knew that angst and stress always made him ravenous. Food! That's what he needed, hot and cooked by someone else. It was time for him to find his way round Dunbridge – and he'd start with the nearest pub with a good bar-snack menu. He'd noticed several pubs in the old market town, some of them advertising their own real ale, which he'd enjoy sampling. If there was one place for a newcomer to meet the locals, it would be in the busiest pub in town.

It was called The Wheatsheaf, and he found it tucked down an alleyway leading off the main market square. One glance at the list of dishes on the blackboard outside the door made the choice easy. Bangers and mash! His mouth watered at the thought of it. Once inside, the range of beers displayed on the pumps brought a smile to his face. If the mash wasn't lumpy and the gravy was half decent, The Wheatsheaf might well become his local.

"Bangers and mash, please," he asked the bartender who came to take his order. "And a pint of Bishop's Finger to wash it down."

"Do you know," said another man who was propping up the bar next to where Neil stood, "that they only ever brew that beer on Fridays?"

"Really?" Neil turned with surprise to take a proper look at his companion, a thirty-something man with a round face to match his definitely rotund body. "Why?"

"Some ancient charter says they have to – and they can only brew up in the antique Russian teak mash tun they have there."

"Where's that?" asked Neil.

"Somewhere in Kent, I think. I don't know. I just remember reading that somewhere. If ever I see an article about beers, I read it."

"Like beer, do you?"

The man raised his half-full beer tankard with a look of pure love. "When it's real beer, like this, I most certainly do." He patted his tummy affectionately. "It's made me the man I am! I'm Graham, by the way – Graham Paterson, Deputy Head of the Maths Department at Dunbridge Upper School by day, and a sociable beer drinker by night."

Laughing, Neil stretched out to shake Graham's hand. "Neil Fisher, Reverend."

"You're joking!"

"Afraid not. I'm the new curate at St Stephen's."

"Ah, well, I wouldn't know that, being a heathen."

"No real ale lover could ever be a complete heathen," grinned Neil. "You don't happen to like bangers and mash too, do you?"

"Love it!" said Graham. "They do a good one here."

"That's a relief. I've just ordered it."

"A sound choice. I wouldn't expect a curate to have to buy his own dinner, though. Haven't you got all the ladies of the parish wanting to cook for you?"

"No such luck – not yet, anyway. This is my first day."

"A tough one, was it?"

"You could say that."

"Beginning to think you've chosen the wrong job?"

"No, the job's OK – at least it *will* be. It's just been a bit overwhelming today – lots of new people to meet and so much to learn about what goes on here in Dunbridge."

"Not a lot, believe me. You'll cope."

"How long have you lived here?"

"Man and boy. I went down to Brighton for my teacher training, which was a laugh – great for the beer – but I came back here to take up where I left off. I still go round for my Mum's Sunday roast every week. I even ended up teaching at my old school, Dunbridge Upper School, except it was the Boys' High School in my day. At least the little blighters have girls to dribble over during lessons these days."

"I think I'm supposed to be taking an assembly at the Upper School some time in the next few weeks."

Graham raised an eyebrow.

"Got body armour, have you?"

"Oh, don't say that. I'm scared enough at the thought of any public speaking, but a school full of teenagers – well, that's enough to give me nightmares."

"But you're a curate. You have to give all those sermons and take funerals and things. Isn't speaking in public part of the job?"

"Unfortunately, yes."

Graham put his tankard carefully down on the bar so that he could take a long look at Neil.

"Why become a priest, then?"

"It's a calling. I felt called to do it."

Graham's eyebrows shot up

"By God," continued Neil. "I felt called by God to take up the ministry."

"How did he call you? What did he say?"

"Well, it wasn't a face-to-face conversation. I didn't have a vision, or anything like that. It was just a feeling that sort of crept up on me – a certainty, really, that this is what I'm meant to do."

Graham stared at Neil curiously for a second or two, before turning back to study his beer.

"Does it pay well?"

"Not really – but I do get my own house while I'm here."

Graham grinned. "Well, there *is* that. And I'm told that women love a man in uniform. Where's yours, by the way? Haven't you got to keep your dog collar on at all times, just so that all the rest of us know to mind our language?"

Neil chuckled. "My collar was chafing a bit after today. I was glad to get back into civvies."

"Do you find, when you're wearing your collar, that people want to pour out their problems to you? You know, a bit like a doctor, when everyone wants to tell them about their aches and pains…"

"If it happens, then honestly I welcome it. That's probably one of the main reasons why I wanted to become a priest in the first place, so that I could be there for other people when they have concerns or worries."

Graham snorted as he tipped up the tankard to down a long gulp of beer.

"I've never had a problem yet that didn't seem a lot better after a pint or two," he said, returning the tankard to the bar with a bang. "A game of darts helps too. Fancy a game before your bangers and mash arrive?"

"I must warn you," laughed Neil as he rolled up his sweatshirt sleeves ready for action, "that I was undisputed Darts Champion at theological college."

"And I must warn you that if I don't feel I'm winning, I'm not above cheating a little!" retorted Graham. "Let battle commence!"

≈ CHAPTER 4 ≈

"*C*an you sing?" asked Margaret the next morning.

"A bit," replied Neil. "I sang in the choir at college."

"Perfect! What are you? Bass? Baritone? Surely not a tenor?"

"No," smiled Neil. "Probably a bass, I should think."

"Can you read music?"

"Passably well, providing I've got someone who can really do the job beside me."

"That's good enough. Our choir will be delighted! Obviously, you can't be with them during services, but if you're able to hold a harmony line wherever you are in the church, you'll be a great asset – especially as I'm so dreadful at singing! By popular request, I try to look prayerful and keep my mouth shut during congregational hymns. Our hymns always seem to sound better that way!"

Neil chuckled. "Actually, I'd quite like to go along. It's a good way to meet people anyway. When do they rehearse?"

"Well, if you're up for it, there's a rehearsal tonight at half seven in the church. It will be good for you to learn the sung responses we use at St Stephen's, because our organist Brian Lambert wrote them himself. They're quite good, actually.

In fact, he's *very* good – and so's his wife, Sylvia. She's our choir leader, which makes them quite a formidable pair. Or perhaps I should say a talented trio! Their daughter, Wendy, teaches music at our church primary school. She has the most marvellous voice, plays the keyboard and the flute – and, quite frankly, our music group would grind to a halt without her. Well, she started it all, because she brought along a few friends who play guitars and drums – and even a saxophone every now and then, when Gordon manages to get up in time on Sunday mornings."

"Half seven tonight in the church," nodded Neil, searching for his pocket diary.

"They're desperate for men. They'll be very glad to see you. Perhaps you can come up with something special for your Welcome Service on Sunday. Everyone will be dying to meet you, so it would be good if you could be involved in the choice of music."

Neil was still scribbling the details down in his diary when Margaret abruptly stood up from her desk.

"Heavens, is that the time? We need to get on the road for the Eucharist run. Four calls, six communicants – all of them too elderly or infirm now to get along to church. Grab the bits and pieces! The travelling Holy Communion set is on top of the cupboard. The water and wine is all ready, right there on the table. Don't forget the wafers! I'll just nip up to grab my papers and meet you at the car."

* * *

Neil saw a different side to Margaret that morning as she greeted her elderly and sick parishioners in their homes with a tenderness, familiarity and concern for their well-being –

mind, body and soul – that was deeply moving. This was why he had chosen the ministry! One day he hoped he would be able to bring as much Christian comfort and fellowship as he saw in her that day.

Their first call was to Queenie Draper, an elderly widow whose mind was plainly as sharp as a pin, in great contrast to the frailty of her body, which was racked with painful arthritis. It was clear that her friendship with Margaret spanned years of conversation and shared thoughts. Margaret asked after each member of her far-flung family with knowledge and interest. Queenie wanted to be brought up to date on the goings on and gossip at the church. Over a cup of tea which Neil had been dispatched to the tiny kitchen to make, the old friends chatted, laughed and finally prayed together. In the silence of Queenie's cluttered front room, the three of them took bread and wine as the much-loved words of the Eucharist were spoken in an intensely intimate and holy atmosphere. The hairs on the back of Neil's neck bristled with a sense of God's presence, and he struggled to stop his eyes filling with tears as he recognized how this quiet moment epitomized everything he hoped for in his own ministry, and brought him a compelling sense of arrival and fulfilment for what lay ahead.

The neat little cottage owned by Mr and Mrs Brownlow was the next port of call. Mary Brownlow was well into the late stages of dementia, and it was clear that she no longer related to or registered much of what was going on around her. Her long-suffering husband, John, was coping valiantly, chatting away to her constantly even though her expression and total lack of reaction was heartbreaking to see. Margaret managed to persuade the exhausted man to sit down for a few minutes while Neil made them all a cup of tea (*another* cup – would his bladder cope with all this liquid?), and when he came back to the living room carrying a tray of steaming mugs, Neil's heart went out to this dignified and devoted husband overcome with embarrassment as his eyes filled with tears of sadness and frustration.

With Margaret gently touching his hand, his voice choking with emotion, John explained the pain he felt to see the essence of the woman he'd loved for nearly forty years fade away until all that remained was someone who looked like his wife, but had none of her personality or characteristics.

"It's as if her life has been sucked out of her. You remember, Margaret, Mary always had such a wonderful sense of humour."

Margaret nodded in agreement. "Most definitely. She's always enjoyed hearing people laugh – but then I think that's because Mary loves people. She'd do anything for anyone – totally devoted to helping others."

John's face creased into a smile. "You're right! Mary has a loving heart. She really cares for people. Never stops." He looked over towards his silent, expressionless wife. "Well, that's how she used to be. It's hard to tell what's at the heart of her now."

"Dementia is such a cruel condition," agreed Margaret. "It robs us of the ability to connect with those around us, or communicate how we feel inside. The Mary we have always loved is still here with us. She just can't express herself as she used to."

"It's a pity you didn't meet her a couple of years ago, Neil," John said, anxious that the newcomer should understand how his much-loved wife had changed. "She's a hard worker, always willing to muck in when help is needed. She's been a churchgoer all her life, from the day she was christened. Well, we both have. I first met her right here in Dunbridge, in St Stephen's, when we joined the choir, and that must be almost fifty years ago now. Being in church, taking part in services, reading the Bible, praying together – that's been our life since we married."

"And now the services come to you, like this?" asked Neil. "Do you ever manage to get to church yourself?"

"Well, until about a year ago, I used to take Mary along, but she was so unpredictable. Often she would call out when she wasn't supposed to, and even got quite angry, because, I think, she was really frustrated. The saddest thing was that she didn't recognize old friends in the congregation she'd known for years. It was so upsetting for them – and me. And because I was always worried about her wandering off or saying something inappropriate that would disturb the worship of everyone else, I finally decided it was kinder to our fellow churchgoers, and to us too, if we didn't go any more."

"And that's been really tough on you, hasn't it, John?" Margaret said quietly. "Mary may not notice the change in your routine, but you certainly have. Sunday mornings must feel so different for you now."

"Oh, I've really missed it. I've always loved being there alongside all the friends and neighbours I've worshipped with for years. I miss singing the hymns, and going up to the altar rail to take Communion. And I especially love that time when you get back to your seat, and there's the chance for your own private prayers. The choir are usually singing quietly in the background. I've not sung in the choir for a while now, but I still love to hear them."

His eyes filled with tears again.

"And Mary is missing out on all that too," he continued. "Her relationship with God has always been at the heart of who she is – and because of this awful condition, she's lost that connection completely. She doesn't pray. She doesn't even know what prayer is. The comfort that she should be getting from her faith is no comfort at all. And if I'm honest, I question God about that. Here I am, watching the woman I love – and *he's* supposed to love – suffering in such a cruel way! So much for him being a *loving* God! It's just shaken me, shaken everything I've always believed in."

"How much help do you get with looking after Mary?" asked Neil. "Do you have carers coming in during the day?"

"No," said John firmly. "Mary doesn't need carers. She's got me. I'm always here for her. For better or worse, in sickness and health – that's what I promised, and I will keep that promise."

"I know you will," said Margaret. "What worries me, though, is who is taking care of the carer? You look worn out. Is there anything we can do? Anything at all?"

"No, I can manage," came John's stiff reply.

"But if someone came in to give you a bit of a break, you wouldn't love Mary any the less, would you?"

"No…" John acknowledged reluctantly.

"There you go, then! Because we don't want you caving in from exhaustion, do we? What would happen to Mary if you got ill as well?"

Fear flashed in John's eyes at the thought. "She's not going into a home!"

"No, no, of course not!" Margaret soothed him. "I didn't mean that. Of course you'll keep Mary here with you for as long as you possibly can, in your own home where you both belong. But, you know, I can't help thinking that you'll be more able to take care of her here if you have a bit of help now and again – don't you think?"

"I don't need help." John reached out to clasp his wife's hand. "*We* don't need any help."

Margaret held his gaze for a while.

"Well, if ever you *do* feel you could use another pair of hands around the place, just to make caring for Mary a little easier for you both, you will talk to me, won't you? Promise?"

"Promise," agreed John.

"And I know there are lots of people at the church who would like to pop round and see you, but they're worried you might think them a nuisance."

"I don't want people coming to gawp!"

"Of course not, but these would just be a few old friends who've known you both for years. You surely wouldn't mind if they popped in? In fact, they've been talking about whether they could organize a rota to come and sit with Mary, just so you can get a bit of peace and quiet yourself."

"I can manage."

"You have always managed brilliantly, John, everyone knows that – but it's hard work. Wouldn't it be nice if every now and then you had a couple of hours to yourself, knowing that Mary is well cared for by people who love her? You could get out in the garden for a bit. You've always loved that, and the garden is usually such a picture. I bet you'd enjoy the chance of a bit of time out there, wouldn't you?"

The anxiety in John's expression gave way to interest, as he was clearly tempted by the prospect of getting to grips with the garden again.

"I'll think about it. I will," he said at last.

"Well, let's pray together," said Margaret, changing the mood, and they all bowed their heads, except for Mary, whose unblinking eyes stared resolutely at the patterned wallpaper across the room.

Both Margaret and Neil were lost in their own thoughts as they drove from John and Mary's house to the edge of town, where two sisters lived in a small, neat, ground-floor flat. Elsie and Lily were gracious hosts, so chatty and sprightly that Neil imagined them to be in their late seventies at the most. When he heard that Elsie was ninety-six while her big sister was only a few months off receiving a telegram from the Queen, he was really surprised.

In fact, the sisters rarely left the flat now, both feeling they'd travelled enough over the years to merit the chance to put their feet up a bit. They had remained unmarried, devoting their lives to missionary work in Africa and the Far East on behalf of the Church Army. Over a piece of Elsie's home-made Madeira cake, Neil had the chance to look through some of their albums of mostly black-and-white photos showing the sisters surrounded by the people whose lives they'd shared over the years. He felt humbled in the face of such faith; they had devoted their whole lives to God's service.

As Margaret began the familiar words of the Eucharist, the sisters reached out to join hands with their two visitors, so that the four of them were in an intense, God-filled circle, the memory of which Neil knew he would always cherish.

Elsie insisted on filling Neil's pockets with more Madeira cake and a couple of scones when finally he and Margaret dragged themselves away to make their last call of the afternoon.

Bert Overington had worked hard all his life. He'd been a lorry driver, making every penny he could to support the family he adored – his wife and three daughters. But his wife had died five years before, soon after the last of their girls had left home to bring up a family of her own. Bert's quiet life had been shattered when he was diagnosed with lung cancer less than a year ago. He'd been a smoker, of course. What lorry driver of his generation wasn't?

Living alone now – although regularly visited by his youngest daughter, Sue, who lived in the next road – Bert struggled with the pain and exhaustion that months of chemotherapy and radiotherapy had brought. He felt tired, old and he missed his wife. He was ready to join her.

In these last months, as he was simply waiting to die, his faith had become more precious than ever to him. As he'd explained to Margaret many times during her past visits, he hadn't been much of a Christian during his lifetime. Even now he wasn't exactly sure what he believed. He just felt there was something there, and that the connection was becoming stronger as he neared the time of his death. So every week, Margaret came to bring him Communion, and he joined in the responses with his breathless, rasping voice full of emotion.

Just as Neil and Margaret were about to start the Communion, they heard a key turn in the front door. In walked the sandy-haired woman that Neil had seen talking to Peter, the churchwarden, at Morning Prayer on his first day. Margaret greeted her with affection.

"Val! How nice to see you! Is this a work call or pleasure?"

"Both," smiled Val, looking warmly at Bert. "Bert's my favourite patient, and he knows it. I always spend twice as much time here as I'm meant to."

Bert's face brightened in spite of the unnaturally pale hue of his skin.

"Is it all right if we just say Communion with Bert, then we'll get out of your way?" asked Margaret.

"Tell you what," said Val as she put down her bag and took off her coat. "Can I join you? It's been one of those days, and an oasis like this is just what I need."

And in the quietness of Bert's front room, with the clock ticking loudly beside them, the four of them prayed together.

"She's a real comfort, you know," said Margaret fifteen minutes later as she and Neil made their way back to the car. "Val is so good at being with people at the stage of illness Bert has reached now. She's a palliative care nurse attached to the local hospice."

"But she works in the community?" ask Neil.

"Well, nowadays they recognize that people want to be in their own homes for as long as possible. In fact, many patients make the choice to die at home where their family can feel comfortable around them."

"Is that what Bert wants?"

"Yes, most definitely, with his daughters at his side towards the very end. He doesn't want to be a burden to them, though, when they all have young families of their own, so as long as he can manage with Val and other carers coming in, he feels well looked after."

"Presumably Val's job means that she has to be on hand just when she's needed, day or night," said Neil. "That must be a bit hard on her own family. What do they think?"

"Her son and daughter have left home now. Her daughter has followed her into nursing – she's a paediatric nurse at Great Ormond Street children's hospital in London, and Val is so proud of her. Her son is a solicitor, I think. Sad to say, Val lost her husband to cancer when their children were still very young, so she has real understanding of what her patients and their families are going through. I guess it was quite a challenge bringing up a couple of youngsters as a widow."

"And her own experience of bereavement must make her very compassionate company at such difficult times," added Neil thoughtfully.

"It certainly does. Oh, I know nurses are supposed to have a professional detachment from their patients, but one of the nicest things about Val is that she doesn't find professional detachment comes easy to her. Sometimes she's with patients for weeks, even months, so when they do finally pass away, it's really upsetting for her. I think that's why she tries to come to church whenever she can."

"Does she often join you for Morning Prayer?"

"Yes – whenever she can fit it in with her shifts, but usually a couple of times a week." Margaret turned to look at Neil. "You might find it interesting to talk to her some time. She's a woman whose faith underpins every aspect of her life. It's the motivation for all she does, and gives her the support and comfort she needs to do her job really well."

Neil nodded slowly as he took this in.

"Val lives with the dying and the bereaved every day of her life," continued Margaret. "Our role as priests means that we often spend time with people when they are facing their own death, or perhaps trying to cope with the loss of someone they love dearly. I must say I've found it really helpful to talk to Val – and you might too."

"I will," agreed Neil, "I certainly will."

* * *

When he walked into the church at half past seven that evening, Neil was pleasantly surprised at the number of people who had turned up for the choir rehearsal. A few faces he recognized. He noticed Val straight away, as she stood taking off her coat in a pew near to the door. Val didn't see Neil because she was looking across to where churchwarden Peter was sorting out piles of music books. As if he could sense her gaze, Peter looked up to smile at her – then, just that moment, Neil's view was obliterated by Peter's daunting wife, Glenda, who was heading straight for him with her arms outstretched. Neil braced himself as he disappeared into another of her smothering embraces.

"Neil, darling," Glenda gushed, "I had no idea you could sing. How wonderful!"

She looked coquettishly up at him through her unnaturally long eyelashes.

"I bet you're a bass. A man like you *would* be a bass." She sniffed delicately as she added, "Peter's a tenor."

"OK, choir! It's gone half past! Let's get started!"

"Oh my goodness!" wailed Glenda, "I must powder my nose before we start. I came straight from work, you know."

"Really? Do you work locally?" enquired Neil politely.

"Oh no!" Glenda's nose creased as if offended by a bad smell. "There's nothing worth doing here. Dunbridge really doesn't offer the kind of opportunity that I need to stretch my mind and use all my training and ability. No, I travel into London every morning. Mayfair, that's where I'm based. I manage the office at a *very* exclusive fashion house."

"Gracious! That sounds glamorous."

"Oh, it is – most definitely!"

"So do you have to go to fashion shows and organize models, things like that?"

"I go everywhere my CEO goes. Roland Branson! You might have heard of him?"

"I have to admit that I'm not very up on the world of fashion, as you might guess if you saw the contents of my wardrobe."

Glenda looked Neil's attire up and down, and plainly found it lacking as she nodded in complete agreement. Suddenly, to Neil's alarm, she reached out to run her hands up and down both sides of his body.

"Turn round!" she commanded. He was too surprised to do anything other than what he was told.

"I could do a lot for you, you know. Your basic body shape isn't bad. Not good, but I could work with it. You obviously do need a few lessons in fundamental fashion!"

"Well, thank you," said Neil, stepping back beyond her reach, "but I don't really need much fashion skill to dress for my job. It comes with a standard uniform, you know…"

"You'd be foolish not to take advantage of the offer. I've learned *so* much from Roland. He's inspirational. Mind you," she giggled as she leaned forward to touch Neil's arm, "he says he's learning a lot from me too. I've worked in the very top echelon of business for years, you know. I bring a lot of experience to the table – and Roland recognizes that."

"Places please, everyone!"

A dark-haired, bespectacled lady wearing a smart knitted jacket stopped shouting instructions as she suddenly noticed Neil. She put her music down on the stand and moved towards him with a friendly smile of welcome.

"Margaret said you might be popping in tonight. And she said you've done a bit of singing in the past."

"Well, not that much," grinned Neil sheepishly. "I thought I might just come along and listen this evening, if that's OK with you."

"Oh, grab a book and join in!" replied the woman. "If it's not your cup of tea, you don't have to come next week. We know you can't actually *join* the choir, but to have a minister keen enough to come along and learn parts will go down extremely well with our congregation."

"Sylvia, are there any more copies of this sheet music?" It was Peter who asked the question.

"Brian's got some over near the organ, I think. And a few

others need copies too, so can you hand them out pronto?"

She turned back to Neil. "Sylvia Lambert, choir leader. My husband Brian is our organist. I'll introduce you properly later – but for now, it's really good to have you here. The basses are over there, all two of them! Can you hold a harmony line?"

"Maybe," said Neil with a wry smile. "We'll all soon find out, won't we!"

Before he could move, Sylvia clapped her hands together to get everyone's attention.

"Listen up, everybody! For those of you who haven't already met him, this is Neil Fisher, our new curate."

There was a murmur of approval and greeting around the room, and Neil pinned on his best smile even though he knew his face was reddening with embarrassment.

"As you know, we have a special service for Neil on Sunday to welcome him to the parish – and what could be better than him joining in wholeheartedly with the singing?"

There was a smattering of applause at this suggestion. Sylvia turned to Neil.

"Neil, we do have a couple of pieces in mind which we plan to rehearse tonight – but have you any favourite hymn or anthem you'd particularly like for your special service?"

"Um, well, let me think…"

"Do you prefer traditional hymns – or is your taste more modern than that?"

"Well, honestly, I like both," mumbled Neil, aware that he was the object of a great deal of speculation and curiosity as he felt twenty pairs of eyes inspect him. "I'm quite fond of Stuart Townend's work."

"An excellent choice!" beamed Sylvia. "What's your favourite?"

Thankfully, Neil had no problem with his answer. "'In Christ Alone'. The theology is sound, the poetry wonderful – and the music a delight to sing."

"Perfect!" agreed Sylvia as others nodded in agreement. "We'll need more than just the organ for that. Music group, can you take your places, please? Oh, Wendy, over here for a minute!"

The girl who started to make her way towards them was a younger, slimmer version of Sylvia. Her shiny dark-brown hair swung freely over her shoulders, and she looked both neat and casual in black trousers and a long, crisp, white blouse over which she wore a pale-pink waistcoat.

"May I introduce my daughter, Wendy?" smiled Sylvia. "She's the leader of our music group. Wendy has a degree in music, and she teaches at the local school here."

As Wendy stretched out her hand towards Neil, her eyes sparkled with warmth and interest.

"Welcome, Neil! I hope we'll be seeing a lot of each other – especially as it seems you enjoy music and singing too."

Her smile was so engaging, and Neil found himself transfixed by the flash of hazel light in her eyes. What a charming girl!

"Right, everyone," shouted Sylvia, "let's get started."

Friendly hands ushered Neil towards the back row of the right-hand choir stalls where he joined the basses, making them up to a grand total of three voices. Opening up the sheet music before him with some trepidation, he cleared his throat, ready to start.

What he didn't see was Wendy's return to sit at the electronic organ to the side of where Sylvia was standing to conduct. Wendy squeezed past Dan on the guitar and her best friend Debs on the flute.

"OK?" asked Debs as she noticed the pink flush across Wendy's cheeks.

"Oh, I'm fine," replied Wendy as she took her seat. "In fact, I'm more than fine. I've just met the man I'm going to marry!"

And with that, she turned towards her mother, ready to start the intro of "In Christ Alone" the moment the baton was raised.

CHAPTER 5

y the time Neil was singing "In Christ Alone"
during his Welcome Service the following Sunday,
his mind was almost overwhelmed by all the people
he'd been introduced to throughout the week. So many faces
– and all those names to remember! He'd taken to carrying
around a small notebook in his pocket, so that whenever he
was able, he found a quiet moment to jot down the odd name
or fact to help him recall all he'd been told.

Slowly, though, faces were becoming familiar to him.
He'd now met the other churchwarden, a down-to-earth
grandmother called Cynthia Clarkson, who chuckled
delightfully as she explained that "everyone calls me Cyn!"
She was the matriarch of a Dunbridge dynasty. She'd brought
up four children of her own, who had all stayed local enough
to provide her with a brood of grandchildren who plainly
adored her. Theirs was a staunchly Christian family, and the
Clarksons, old and young, filled up more than three rows of
pews in the church every Sunday.

He'd seen Harry Holloway several times that week too,
but not only at church. It was when Neil was walking back
to Number 96 late one afternoon that he spotted Harry in
the front garden of Number 80, doing a bit of obviously

skilful pruning in a garden which was a mass of colour from beds, baskets and barrels all overflowing with a profusion of flowering plants.

"My goodness, Harry, you've got green fingers! I didn't even realize we were neighbours. Your garden puts all the others in the shade. It's a picture!"

"Well," beamed Harry, who plainly appreciated the compliment, "I'm pretty good with plants. I'm not so good on my pins when it comes to digging and grass-mowing these days, though. My great-niece helps me when she can. She's a good kid."

Neil thought how nice it was to hear that a "kid" would take an interest in gardening in order to give her elderly uncle a hand, especially when most youngsters preferred computers for company nowadays.

"I started growing flowers in the garden so that I could give Rose a bunch to put on the sideboard twice a week. Even in the winter, I managed to keep that going."

"She must have liked that."

"I hope so," said Harry wistfully. "She seemed pleased."

"I'm sure she recognized the love that went into growing them," added Neil gently.

Harry's eyes clouded slightly.

"I hope she did. I really do hope so."

Neil recalled that conversation as he caught Harry's eye during the singing of "In Christ Alone". He'd noticed that the older man had sung all the traditional hymns with enthusiasm. This modern song Harry would probably describe as a "happy clappy", and it was clear from his expression that it really wasn't quite to his taste. He was determined to give it a try, though, and by the third verse, he was singing along quite competently.

Neil remembered with a mixture of appreciation and horror the way in which Margaret had introduced him to the congregation that morning while she was giving notices before the service began.

"Well, he's here – at last!"

Her first words were followed by a small cheer and a ripple of friendly applause.

"As you know, this is a busy parish, and we have been in need of extra pair of hands for some time. I am absolutely delighted that Neil Fisher has agreed to join us as our new curate. He's making himself at home at Number 96, where I am sure the kettle will always be on if you fancy dropping in for a chat and a cuppa."

Neil felt all eyes in the church on him, but their expressions were kind and interested – from the group of small children who were standing to one side, ready to disappear with the Sunday School teacher (who he understood was called Brenda, although he'd still to meet her properly); to the mums and dads, some of them sitting in the pews alongside their older children; and on to the more elderly congregation members (the ones who would definitely *hate* "happy clappy"!) looking at him with wary fascination.

"So I'll be teaching Neil the ropes over the coming year until he is priested – and even after that we hope he will enjoy Dunbridge enough to want to stay on for another two or three years, until he decides he's ready to take on his own parish."

There was a general reaction of nodding heads and smiles.

"But Neil is quite capable of speaking for himself, so let me introduce him now – our new curate, Neil Fisher!"

An enthusiastic round of applause rippled around the congregation, as Neil felt blood flush to his cheeks and a trickle of cold sweat course its way down his back. It was the "public speaking" part of his role as a priest that worried him most. Perhaps he was just naturally shy. Perhaps he had been overshadowed and hushed up by his mother for so long that he'd hardly dared venture his own opinion for all too many years. Recognizing, though, that speaking to congregations was very much a part of the role he'd chosen, he steeled himself to move to the centre of the church and smile out at the crowd who were now greeting him in friendly welcome.

"Well," he began somewhat hesitantly, "thank you for your greeting. I know I'm going to love my time here in Dunbridge. I liked the town from the moment I first saw it, and I've enjoyed meeting so many new friends and neighbours here, even in the short time since I arrived. More than that, I recognize that St Stephen's is the Christian heart of this town, and that the sense of fellowship and care for one another is rich and strong. I look forward to joining your worship. I look forward to supporting and encouraging you in your individual journeys of faith. I look forward to being here for you not just at the important milestones of your lives, but week by week as we praise God together. I know I will learn from you all, and that is a delightful prospect. And yes, whenever I'm at home, the kettle is definitely on, and I'd love visitors. I have a well-stocked biscuit barrel – so please know that you are very welcome."

With relief, Neil acknowledged that the reaction to his speech was warm with approval. Seeing that a couple of people on the front row were standing up to shake his hand, he quickly rubbed his dripping palms on his surplice as he moved to greet them. It was encouraging to see the wide range of ages and characters who made up the congregation of St Stephen's. He had a strong sense that this well-established Christian family had a fellowship of genuine care and concern, and a lot going on which brought them into the church not just for services but throughout the week too. Neil saw family groups and couples, and many others too, both elderly and younger, sitting alongside a friend or just peacefully alone. They greeted each other with real affection during the Peace, wandering from their places to shake hands with fellow worshippers right over on the other side of the church. They waited in the middle aisle to let their neighbours out of each pew on their way to take Holy Communion – here and there offering a supporting arm where old age had brought frailty and made walking alone too difficult. As the last communicants were taking bread and wine, and Margaret placed a consecrated wafer into each humbly waiting hand, the music group led the choir gently into "Make Me a Channel of Your Peace". At that moment, Neil found himself overwhelmed by a warm sense of belonging. This was it! This was his spiritual home for the next few years. This congregation, which was mostly just a group of strangers to him now, would become his Christian family and his good friends. This was why he had longed for ordination. This was what he'd trained for. This was the true start of his ministry – and the emotion of that thought had him dipping into his pocket for his hankie so that he could discreetly give his nose a good blow.

Coffee and biscuits in the church hall after the service proved a noisy, haphazard affair. Neil soon realized that there was no shortage of volunteers to man the teapot and spoon out the coffee. In fact, there were almost too many willing hands! The good-humoured chaos which had everyone snaking down the hall as they queued for a cuppa, was caused by what could best be described as "too many Indians and not enough chiefs". Not that Neil got anywhere near the queue! He found himself surrounded by groups of people all clamouring to introduce themselves and have a chat with him. After twenty minutes of constantly changing conversation, he looked up to catch Wendy's eye over the shoulder of the elderly man who was regaling him with the prowess of the Dunbridge Cricket Team.

"Coffee?" she mouthed silently.

He nodded gratefully.

"Milk?" Again, her mouth shaped the question without her actually speaking.

Another nod.

"Sugar?"

He held up one finger.

She winked at him so cheekily that it was hard for him to keep a straight face as the man talking to him went on to discuss in very sombre tones the water-drainage problems of the local cricket pitch. Five more minutes elapsed in which others came up with invitations for him to join the local Amateur Dramatic Group and take up tango lessons – and then he sensed rather than saw Wendy slip a cup of coffee with a couple of ginger biscuits in the saucer on to the table beside him. With a flick of her long dark hair, she turned and moved away, leaving Neil wishing that he'd had a chance to thank her properly for her thoughtfulness.

After the service, Margaret and Frank had invited him round for Sunday lunch. He was particularly looking forward to joining them for a proper home-cooked meal because he was quickly discovering that his culinary skills weren't up to much. Twice that week he had resorted to having a meal in The Wheatsheaf, which on both occasions had led to him spending a couple of pleasant hours playing darts with Graham. On one of the other nights he'd heated up a frozen fish pie in the microwave, but it was so small that, having eaten it, he felt he could devour it again twice over! Next time he must remember to get some frozen vegetables and perhaps potatoes to make the pie go further. He knew he had a lot to learn…

So having gone home to change into "something a little more comfortable" after the service, he worked his way down the garden path of the Vicarage to enter by the kitchen door, as instructed by Margaret. The kitchen looked as muddled as ever, with piles of papers and boxes balanced precariously on every flat surface – and across the room he could just make out the figure of Frank standing at the sink chopping up cabbage.

"Hello, Neil. Mind Archie's bowl as you come across. I think he's left another half-eaten mouse beside it. Drives me mad, even though I know it's the nature of the beast. I have to forgive him because he thinks he's bringing us a loving gift."

As Neil bent down to pick up the mutilated mouse, he came eyeball to eyeball with Archie, who was sitting under the table, his yellow eyes narrowed and staring with malice. Neil dropped the mouse instantly, stood up very slowly, then backed away as fast as he could.

"Something smells good!"

Margaret came striding into the room, touching Neil's shoulder in greeting as she went over to join Frank at the sink.

"Can you chop that a bit smaller, dear? And don't forget to cut all the stalk out. You usually leave far too much on."

Frank carried on chopping without comment.

"Have you made the Yorkshires yet?" asked Margaret.

"Pudding mix is in the bowl. The tray is ready and heating in the oven. Dinner should be on course for half an hour's time," said Frank, glancing up at the clock, which hung at a slightly skewed angle above the mantelpiece.

"Good! Can you set the table then, Neil?"

Neil looked across at the kitchen table, which was covered in a tottering mountain of bits and pieces.

"No, not *that* table," retorted Margaret, following his gaze. "The one in the dining room. Here's the cutlery drawer. The table mats are on the sideboard. It's beef, isn't it, dear?"

Frank nodded that it was.

"Horseradish, then!" she announced, stretching up to a wall cupboard to hand down salt, pepper and a jar of sauce to Neil. "And if you'll excuse me, I'm just going to call our daughter Sarah, as I usually do at this time on a Sunday. She and her husband Martin have provided us with our first grandchild, haven't they, Frank?"

Frank nodded in agreement as Margaret barely drew breath before continuing.

"Edward Francis. Named after his grandfather! His second birthday will be coming up soon – and he's already *so* advanced for his age! I'll give them your love, Frank, and tell them you'll probably ring later."

Margaret was almost out of the kitchen door when she suddenly turned round.

"And I think we should break open a bottle of red, don't you? See you at dinner!"

With a flourish, she was gone, leaving the two men in a room which felt suddenly empty without her larger-than-life presence.

"I know," said Frank at last. "You wonder why I put up with her, don't you?"

"She's a very positive personality..." replied Neil carefully.

"We've been married a long time. There's a lot of shorthand in a relationship like ours. Sometimes she's got so much on her mind that she doesn't give any thought to how her comments come across. She might sound abrupt, but I know how to read between the lines."

"You're retired now, are you, Frank?"

"I used to work for British Rail. Reached sixty-five and was pensioned off with a gold watch nearly four years ago. I was in the accounts office, which wasn't the most stimulating of work, but it paid the bills and I had some good friends there."

"Do you miss it?"

Frank's hand hovered above the cabbage as he gazed out the window.

"Sometimes," he answered at last. "I don't miss working in London, though, and all that commuting at each end of the day."

"How long have you been here in Dunbridge?"

"We came here soon after I retired. This is Margaret's second parish, and you can see what a good job she's making of it."

"Did she have another career before she started training for the ministry?"

"Well, she'd brought up our two children, so didn't go out to work when they were young – but by the time they'd left home, she was itching to get involved with something really fulfilling. And she felt *called*. She'd had that sense of vocation for several years, so I knew it was only a matter of time before she realized for herself that being in the ministry was the route she must take. And she's doing so well, even though there's far too much work for just one minister here. She's wonderful with all the parishioners. She makes time for everyone, and is always willing to go the extra mile. Oh, I know she may not be the most organized of people…"

Frank stopped when he saw the smile that crossed Neil's face.

"You're right!" he laughed back, "and Margaret would be the first to admit that she's a nightmare when it comes to tidiness and keeping track of things. But when it counts, she's on the button. You'll find that while you're here, Neil. There are so many claims on her time, she's torn in all directions – so although she may not always be right by your side, you will have her solid, unfailing support and encouragement. She'll train you well – perhaps not in record keeping or where to find things – but how to listen, how to read between the lines, how to get alongside people when they're hurting or fearful, how to show the love of God to those around you – that's the sort of thing you will learn in abundance from my very dear wife!"

"And I'm looking forward to that. But what about you, Frank? After all, she's the one with the official position here, and yet it's clear it would be very hard for her to accomplish all she does without your support and help."

"I'm like the Vicar's wife, aren't I!" said Frank with a grin. "Tied to the kitchen sink, dinner always in the oven. I'm her backroom boy, and I am glad for that. There's too much for her to get through on her own."

"But didn't you have your own thoughts about what you might like to spend your time doing in retirement? Were you going to build a model train set or take up travelling?"

Frank turned to look at Neil.

"My greatest love is Margaret. She's like a steamroller sometimes, but there's more to her than most people see."

"Of course," nodded Neil.

"Besides," added Frank with a smile, "she's a lousy cook! Heaven help us if we relied on her for meals!"

"Frank!" Margaret's voice echoed down the stairs from her upstairs study. "Where's the phone number of that couple who rang this morning about getting married here?"

"On the pad by the phone, dear. Do you want me to bring it up to you?"

"Oh, would you? That will be a great help! And a cup of tea would be nice…"

Frank dried his hands, flicked down the switch on the kettle, then turned towards Neil with a wry smile. "You see, I'm a great help – and that's OK with me."

"Well, now I'm here, hopefully I can be a great help too," replied Neil – and he picked up the knife to take over the cabbage chopping from where Frank had left off.

* * *

It was gone seven, after Evensong, when Neil finally made his way home, his mind reeling at the events of the day. Images of the many people he'd met at the morning service; lunch with Frank and Margaret followed by hours of very constructive chat about his role in the parish team and how his training would be organized – and finally, the warm fellowship he'd felt as he worshipped with the small group who gathered in the church for Evensong. Already, he could feel himself relaxing into this community as he learned more about the role he was called to play. There was so much to learn, such a lot to do – but he instinctively knew that this was where God wanted him to be, and it was up to him to rise to the challenge.

He was lost in thought as he walked up Vicarage Gardens towards Number 96, until he noticed Harry was still hard at work in his own front garden. This time, though, he was not alone. He had a very small, fair-haired assistant, a little boy who looked oddly familiar. It was when Harry called Neil over to introduce the two of them, and the youngster looked up at him with pale-green eyes, that Neil remembered with a sense of dread where he'd seen the boy before. So, when Harry had mentioned "the kid" – the niece who helped him with his garden – the girl he actually meant was…

"You're staring again!"

Neil felt rooted to the pavement as he found himself once more under the disdainful scrutiny of the young woman he'd met in the graveyard, the one whose attractive rear view he had inadvertently been admiring in the church hall. Well, she *was* very attractive in an unusual sort of way, even in the old jeans and baggy T-shirt she was wearing at that moment. Her naturally pale skin was tanned from the outdoor life she plainly enjoyed, and her cropped sandy-coloured hair curled rebelliously around her face as she stood up from the flowerbed she was weeding to put her arm protectively around the boy's shoulders.

"Oh!" said Harry with a smile, "so you know each other? Well, of course, you do – through the church! Claire looks after the church grounds, Neil, but you probably already know that."

"Ah," started Neil hesitantly, "we have met once or twice, but we haven't really been introduced."

"Well," continued Harry as he slipped his arm round the girl's waist, "this is my niece…"

"*Great*-niece," corrected Claire.

"Great-niece," agreed Harry. "Her grandfather was my older brother, Arthur, God rest him."

"And my name is Arthur too," interjected the boy. "Samuel Arthur Holloway. She's my Mum!"

Neil smiled down at the earnest expression on the young boy's face.

"And are you usually called Samuel? Or just Sam?"

"It depends. When Mum's mad at me, she calls me Samuel. I like Sam best, though."

"So do I," agreed Neil, "and I am really very pleased to meet you properly, Claire."

She didn't reply, but turned instead towards Harry.

"You've been at this for ages. Are you ready to stop for some tea now?"

"Great idea!" replied Harry. "Fancy a cuppa, Neil?"

"Oh no, don't worry." Neil's voice stuttered slightly with embarrassment. "I don't want to intrude, and I've got work to get on with tonight."

"It's Sunday, the day of rest!" replied Harry. "Come round the back and sit on our patio for a while before the sun goes down. We've got one of those seats that swing, you know. I can never sit on it for more than five minutes before I'm nodding off."

Neil grinned. "Sounds like my kind of chair!"

"Then I can show you the pond Claire built from scratch for me last summer. She went to agricultural college to study horticulture, didn't you, love? She's very talented."

"And we've got fishes," enthused Sam, "big red ones, and a black one with goggle eyes!"

"Goggle eyes?" Neil struggled not to chuckle as he looked down at Sam. "Surely not! That's something I have to see!"

And as Sam grabbed his hand to take him round the back, Neil tried to ignore the resigned sigh from Claire before she left them to it.

With Sam and Harry leading the way, Neil was towed around the side of the house until they all emerged into the most glorious back garden he'd ever seen. It was longer than he expected, and appeared to stretch further still into the parkland beyond. It was a picture of colour, shape and texture, with graceful shrubs and bushes arching over vibrant beds of flowering plants interspersed with gravel paths and patches of forest bark. Right at the centre, a series of ponds sparkled with water that leaped and tumbled through reeds and water lilies.

"They're here!" exclaimed Sam excitedly. "There's Goggle Eyes! Over there, see?"

Harry settled himself on one of the rustic benches to the side of the largest pond, and watched them both with an indulgent smile.

"Claire did all this, you know. It took her months last summer, but look how it's matured in just a year."

"She's obviously very talented," agreed Neil, who was genuinely impressed by the skilful planning and planting which must have gone into creating the garden's crowning glory.

"And Mum and I think that Goggle Eyes is a bit lonely because he's the only black fish. We're going to find a girlfriend for him."

"I bet he'll like that," said Neil gravely. "Where will you go to get Mrs Goggle Eyes?"

"Where will we go, Mum?"

"To the big fish centre, Sam, where we got the others, do you remember?" Neil hadn't realized until that moment that Claire had come through the kitchen to join them – or more likely, to keep a wary eye on him!

"Are we going to get her now?"

"Not right now," replied Claire. "It's nearly your bedtime."

"Tomorrow, then?"

"Maybe. We'll see."

"Can *you* come?" Sam asked Neil.

"Well," replied Neil, very conscious of Claire's disapproving stare, which challenged him to do anything but turn down Sam's invitation. "I have a lot of work to do, and I may be busy when you and Mum are able to go…"

"Well, Grandad's coming too, aren't you, Grandad? We could all go together. Mum would like that, wouldn't you, Mum?"

"Tell you what," ventured Neil, "I'd love to have a look round the rest of your garden. Will you take me, Sam?"

The little boy's face lit up.

"I could show you the greenhouse. I found a caterpillar in there. It had yellow stripes and sticky-up hairs!"

"Oh dear, I don't suppose your Mum wants caterpillars crawling over her plants in the greenhouse," smiled Neil.

"Why not?" asked Sam with a puzzled expression.

"Because they'll eat all the leaves!" said Claire.

"When? I haven't seen them eating leaves!"

"Well, believe me, they love them – for breakfast, dinner and tea!"

"They'll get very fat," replied the little boy, his face troubled.

"They'll be very *flat*, if I have anything to do with it…" murmured Claire under her breath, and when Neil caught her eye, he thought for just a moment she almost smiled.

"Tell you what, Sam," interjected Harry with a laugh, "as it's nearly your bedtime, how about you show Neil the greenhouse another day? If you get into your pyjamas nice and quick, I'll give you a game of Snap!"

Caterpillars forgotten, Sam began to run towards the house, calling over his shoulder to Neil, "Do you want to play Snap too?"

"Oh no, you've all got things to do. I don't want to be a nuisance…"

"You'll only be a nuisance if you're too good at Snap and don't let Sam win every time," muttered Harry.

"Do you mean *cheat?*" Neil's face was a picture of mock outrage.

"Exactly!" agreed Harry.

"That's OK, then. I'm good at that!" And Neil grinned as he caught up with Harry to walk back into the house.

* * *

One hour and five games of Snap later, Sam was clearly struggling to keep his eyes open.

"Come on, little man," said Claire quietly as she scooped him up into her arms. "Time for bed!"

"Can I have a story?"

Sam's voice was drowsy with sleep.

"If you stay awake that long," whispered his Mum as she started to carry him up the stairs.

Both men watched them go – and almost as if Harry had read Neil's unasked question, he said, "Claire and Sam live here. They have done since she knew she was expecting."

"And Sam's Dad?"

"In Australia. I mean, he is an Australian. Ben was here for a gap year before he went back to university. He and Claire were joined at the hip for the ten months or so that he was here – but he still went back home, even though he knew Sam was on the way."

"How caring and responsible of him!"

"Well, they were both so young – and I think there was quite a bit of pressure from his parents for him to go back and get on with his studies."

"Did they know about Claire? About their grandchild?"

81

"They don't keep in touch at all, so possibly not."

"And Ben? Does he support his son?"

"Claire hasn't heard from him for years."

"Does she mind?"

"She did in the beginning. He broke her heart. She's not got a very good opinion of men at all now."

"I noticed!"

Harry grinned. "You too, eh! Well, you're not alone. To be fair, I think she's got her hands full, what with Sam and working all hours too. That's why it's good for the two of them to be living with me. I can look after Sam when she's busy – and she can look after me in return!"

"I can see it works really well."

"Well, Rose and I were never blessed with children of our own. We had a tragedy early on in our marriage when Rose got pregnant. We were so excited when we found out she was expecting, but then our son was born premature and stillborn. Rose never really recovered from that. It was a sadness that stayed with her – with both of us, really."

"So what about Claire's parents? Do they live near here?"

"Her Dad, Trevor, was a Navy man. He married my niece, Felicity, after a whirlwind romance. Now, let me think, they got married after Christmas – in '84, that must have been. She got pregnant really soon. Turned out, though, that he was also promised to a woman up in Faslane, and that's where he disappeared off to one night. Felicity tracked him down eventually and went up there to see him, taking Claire with her – but he wasn't interested. It turned out he already had a three-year-old son by the other woman. Felicity didn't want him when she knew how much of a creep he really was. She wouldn't even keep his name and reverted to her maiden name as soon as the divorce came through. That's why Claire and Sam are Holloways, like me."

"So Felicity brought Claire up on her own?"

"Like daughter, like mother! Yes, Felicity was a good Mum. They lived down the other end of the town, so Rose and I saw them often."

"And is she still there?"

"Well, Felicity's story has a happy ending. She didn't marry for years. Then, when Claire was at agricultural college – she would have been about nineteen then – Felicity met a lovely fella called David. She worked in the offices of a big insurance company that's based near here, and he's a financial advisor up in Yorkshire who used to talk to her on the phone several times a week. They must have got to know each other quite well during their calls, because when he finally drove down to meet her, it was love at first sight! He proposed within a couple of months, and not long before Claire's twentieth birthday, David married Felicity and whisked her off to live in Scarborough."

"How did Claire feel about that?"

"Delighted! She wanted her Mum to be happy, and it freed her up to get on with her own life."

"And then along came Ben?"

"That's right, a couple of years later – and he scarpered back home as soon as Claire told him she was pregnant."

"Poor Claire…"

"Do you know, I think, whatever reservations she had at the time, Claire would say now that Sam is the best thing that's ever happened to her. She's a great Mum. She's happy, I think."

"She gets all the hours she needs as a gardener?"

"Well, Margaret has been good to her. She gets paid for all the work she does at the church. And people see her out digging and notice how nice the flowerbeds look since she's been giving them a bit of attention, so a few more jobs have come in on the back of that. She does all right."

"And she still finds enough puff to work in the garden here! I'm exhausted just thinking about all she does..."

"He's off!" said Claire, as she came down the last few stairs to join them in the living room.

"Well, so am I," said Neil. "This has been an unexpected but really delightful end to the day. Thank you, both of you."

"I'll show you out."

Neil checked he'd got everything, then, waving to Harry, he followed Claire out towards the front door. He turned to face her as he stepped outside.

"Your garden is lovely."

"You're a pretty good loser at Snap."

"I'm sorry about when we met before..."

"You were a git."

He grinned sheepishly.

"I was – but I honestly didn't mean to be. Do you think we could start again?"

They looked at each other silently for a moment, neither of them sure how to continue.

"Well," she said finally as she stretched out her hand towards his. "Hello, Neil Fisher. It's nice to meet you."

"Hello, Claire," he replied, taking her hand, his gaze fixed on her pale-green eyes. "It's good to meet you too."

"See you, then," she said.

"See you...."

And as he turned away, Neil didn't realize that the smile creeping across his face exactly matched Claire's own.

CHAPTER 6

"Neil, mate, I need a favour."

Graham's voice was unmistakable, even through Neil's rather elderly mobile phone.

"Ask away! What do you need?"

"You're not free tonight, are you?"

"Could be. The Wheatsheaf?"

"That'll be great. I've got something I want to show you. I'll bring my laptop."

"Sounds intriguing."

"I'm doing something. Well, I've done it really, and now I have, I'm not sure I should've."

"Is it you who's confusing – or me that's confused?" asked Neil.

"Look, I teach maths to over a thousand spotty teenagers every week. Of course I'm confused!"

"Point taken. Eight o'clock OK?"

The offer was cut short by Graham's voice booming so loudly that Neil had to hold the phone away from his ear.

"Richard Robinson! Pick that up!"

There was the sound of movement and a muffled response from someone, presumably the boy in question.

"I don't care!" was Graham's bellowing reply. "Don't drop litter – and don't be where you shouldn't be when the bell's gone! Where's your next class?"

Another muffled response.

"Well, you're late! Get going *now!*"

Neil could hear footsteps pounding away from the phone.

"Eight's fine," said Graham, his voice now absolutely normal.

Neil chuckled. "Remind me never to get on the wrong side of you. You're terrifying!"

"No, I'm not. I'm a big wimp. That's why I need a bit of encouragement and advice from a good and truthful mate this evening. Right?"

"Right!"

"Just come when you're ready. Hang on…"

His voice shot up several decibels again. "The Art Room is *that* way. I'm *watching* you!"

Neil clutched the phone for a moment in stunned silence – then, in the most friendly of tones, Graham's voice returned.

"See you tonight then! Bye!"

And the phone went dead.

Neil still had a grin on his face remembering that conversation as he headed through the churchyard on his way to the hall. After two months in Dunbridge, it was a relief to realize just how familiar the town was beginning to feel to him. His arrival at the end of July had been at the start of the holidays, so he had immediately been thrown into a heady mix of responsibilities which ranged from manning the Wet Sponge stall at St Stephen's "Grand Summer Fete" (and even ending up being the target for a soggy throw or two); arranging an OAPs' summer tea party (although, to be fair, Wendy from the music group had been an immense help in organizing that, and she'd been very generous with her time when it came to the two of them getting together to plan everything so that the party was a great success on the day); helping out at several of the weddings which were a feature of practically every weekend; taking funeral services at the nearby crematorium (well, to be fair, he had only just started to take them on his own, because previously he had always been there to observe and help Margaret so that he could learn the ropes); and dodging Glenda Fellowes, because Neil always felt she stood too close and hugged him too tight for comfort whenever she had the opportunity, much to his acute embarrassment.

How quickly the weeks had flown! He had arrived when the gardens and churchyard were full of summer colour. Now, even he, who knew nothing about plants and gardening, could see the gold and red hues which were creeping across bushes and trees wherever he looked.

The playgroup was in full swing as Neil stepped into the hall which echoed with the deafening sound of excited children and commanding adults. Across on the other side of the room, he could see Sam busily playing with a group of small friends in the Wendy house. Claire was nowhere in sight. Well, she wouldn't be, not on a bright Autumn day. She'd be out in her wellies, digging someone's garden.

Barbara caught Neil's eye the moment he walked across the hall, indicating that she'd like a chat. She guided him through to the kitchen where two of the mums were preparing brightly coloured cups of squash and plates of apple slices and grapes for the children's "elevenses".

"Just wanted a quiet word," she said, pulling him to one side of the open hatch through which they could look out on to the hall without really being seen themselves.

"You see over there in the corner, in the boots and brown jacket? Linda? Do you know her?"

"I don't think so," replied Neil thoughtfully. "Is she new?"

"She's been quite a few times before, but not on a regular basis. She's got twin boys, Nathan and Jake. They're playing in the sandpit."

"I see them."

"Well, it wouldn't be a bad idea for you to do a bit of your pastoral stuff in her direction. Keep it subtle, because I don't know her that well and I'm not sure if she's got any religious beliefs or anything. I just happen to know she's going through a tough patch and could probably do with a good listener."

"Can you give me a clue?"

"Husband trouble, so I've heard."

"Aah," said Neil, thinking he was hardly the best advisor on how to be a good husband. "I'll do my best."

Grabbing himself a cup of coffee, Neil worked his way round the edge of the hall, chatting to helpers, mums, and a few of the youngsters on the way, until at last he found himself standing alongside Linda, who was half perched on a table, keeping a watchful eye on Nathan and Jake playing in the sandpit a few feet away.

"Twins! I bet they're a handful!"

Linda looked round at Neil, obviously surprised that he should be speaking to her when they didn't know each other. He smiled.

"I'm Neil, the curate here. I think the vicar thinks it's character-building for me to help out at this playgroup at least once a week. In fact, it may be enough to put me off fatherhood forever!"

She laughed.

"And what does your wife think about that?"

"Heavens! Do I look married? I always thought I seem far too scruffy and disorganized for that."

"No sign of Miss Right just yet, then?"

"Well, I've not noticed anyone beating a path to my door."

Neil watched as the smile which initially lit up her face faded with sadness.

"That may be just as well."

"What makes you say that?" he asked gently.

She looked directly at him for a second or two, as if weighing up in her mind whether or not to continue the conversation. Then she turned to gaze at her boys before speaking.

"Marriage isn't always what you imagine it will be."

"That sounds like the voice of experience. Have you been married long?" Neil asked.

"Seven years now – and I'd known John for three years before that."

"You two must have your hands full with two lively boys to look after."

"You can say that again. I love it, though. When Jake and Nathan came along, I felt complete, as if by being born they made me what I was meant to be – a mum."

"And does John enjoy being a dad too?"

"It's different for men, isn't it? John works long hours. He's a civil engineer, and his company has several bases around the country. He can be away all week sometimes."

"That must be tough for you. Never getting a break from looking after the boys – and however much you love them, I guess that sometimes you just need a breather."

His words must have hit home because she turned towards him as if anxious to continue talking.

"I do! John doesn't understand that. He thinks because I'm at home all day with just the boys to look after, life must be a doddle for me. He gets quite annoyed if I say I'm tired, or try to tell him how the kids have been driving me mad." She sighed. "It's not that I'm moaning, because I *do* love being a mum – but I'm on my own with them so much, I sometimes don't speak to another grown-up all day. I've even started to wonder if I'm capable of having a conversation with anyone over the age of three!"

"You are," he chuckled. "I'll vouch for that!"

"And…" She hesitated before going on, as if considering how much she should say.

"And," she said at last, "It's not all work for him when he's away. He stays in nice hotels, has lovely meals that the company pays for – and often he's not alone…"

"He travels with colleagues, does he?"

"Well, I suppose a *colleague* is one way to describe her. He says she's his PA – although I never knew the duties of a PA were supposed to include tucking her boss up at night…"

"Oh." Uncertain whether she would say more, Neil waited quietly for her to continue.

"I've never been the jealous sort – never thought I needed to be suspicious – but I came across a hotel receipt in his pocket when he asked me to take his suit to the cleaners. The room was in his name, but it was a double room with *two* people in it."

"And it couldn't have been someone else? A male colleague he was working with?"

"Not when they were booked in as Mr and Mrs!"

"No, I see your point. Did you challenge him about it? What did he say?"

"Not a lot at first. He shouted at me that I had no right to go snooping in his pockets – and honestly, I wasn't. I had no idea there was anything to find. Then he said it was just a one-night stand. It meant nothing, just someone he met up there and would never see again – as if I was supposed to think *that* made it OK! He was full of apology, said it was a mistake, that he loved me and the kids, and he'd make it up to us…"

"And did he?"

"Actually, the only thing he was making up was his story as he went along. It wasn't a one-night stand at all. And he wasn't with someone he'd just met by chance. I hate myself for it, but for the first time in my life, I found myself checking up on him."

"Well, no one would blame you for that."

"I went through his briefcase, read his emails, listened to his phone messages – and eventually I found it all there. Messages from her that left no doubt about their relationship. I was able to hate her – and only her – for the family-wrecker she is, until I came across the messages he'd sent her! He was so sure of himself, and of me, that he didn't even bother to delete them. It wasn't her who wrecked our marriage. It was him."

"Who is she? Are they still working together?"

"Her name is Trish. She started work in his department just over a year ago, and apparently they've been carrying on since the drunken kiss they had at the office party last Christmas. Didn't take her long to get her claws into him, did it!"

"So where does that leave you?"

Her eyes filled with tears as she looked at him.

"Leaving him – or at least that was my first thought. The second was that it shouldn't be me who leaves, because the boys need the security of our home, so if anyone moves out, it's got to be him."

"Does that mean he's still living at home with you at the moment?"

"Yes."

"And he's still involved with the other woman?"

She gave a wry smile.

"No, I don't think he is."

"And how do you feel about him in the light of that?"

"I'd probably feel better if it were John who'd made the decision for them to break up – but it didn't happen that way. Trish disappeared very quickly when she found out about what else is going on with him at the moment."

Neil noticed that Linda had been picking absent-mindedly at a loose bit of skin on her thumb until it started to bleed.

"He's ill." Her voice was so low, he wondered if he'd heard right.

"Seriously ill. It started as a bruise at the top of his arm that wouldn't go away. Then another just like it appeared near his hip."

She scraped her fingers under both eyes to brush away the tears which threatened to roll down her cheeks.

"It's cancer of the bone. He's only thirty-five – and he's got cancer in his bones."

"But he's still a young man. Surely they can do something…?"

"They say it's early days. He only got the diagnosis a fortnight ago. He's had one set of scans and they're talking about others."

"Is he feeling very unwell?"

She looked at him.

"Honestly, I think he's felt unwell for months. I just put it down to exhaustion because he was travelling all the time. He was always tired, always stressed. When I found out about the affair, I gave up feeling sorry for him because I really couldn't care less that he'd probably just worn himself out trying to keep his sordid little relationship secret. But now he's got cancer. Now everything seems different again. Now I don't know what I feel or think..."

"What's his reaction to the news?"

"He's scared, really scared. The other night he cried in my arms like a baby. He's terrified he's going to die. He's been reading up as much as he can on the internet, and he's certain that he's in for a lot of pain and treatment which will leave him old before his time, and eventually kill him."

"It sounds as if he's going to need a lot of help and care."

"Yes." Her voice had a bitter edge to it. "And I'm his wife. People will expect me to provide all the care he needs."

"Whatever other people think, it's how you and John feel that matters."

"What I feel is *cheated*. Cheated by the man I loved and trusted, and who let me and his sons down without a thought for us at all. Now he's ill. Now he needs me. Now he's begging me not to break up the marriage – as if it's *my* fault we've got to this point, and it's nothing to do with him having an affair at all. How *dare* he try to make it *my* fault?"

She fell silent, picking angrily at her thumb.

Neil mulled over his thoughts for a while before saying, "I suppose there is one really important question you need to answer before you can decide anything. Do you still love him?"

"Am I in love with him? No. I never will be again. That's gone, along with any trust I ever had in him. But do I still feel some sort of love for him?" She thought for a while. "Yes, I probably do. Is that enough for me to stay with him, knowing what lies ahead? Honestly, I'm not sure. I really don't know if I can nurse him through this, and put the kids through it too, after all that's happened. He took a sledgehammer to my feelings. He didn't care about me when there was someone more exciting around. Now he's ill, he's suddenly declaring deepest love for me. I don't think it's love he feels for me though. It's *need*. He needs me. He knows that I'll have to find a lot of love for him if I'm to give him the care he needs, and he's scared I'll walk out on him and leave him to deal with his illness alone."

"And will you?"

"I wish I knew. What I *do* find myself remembering is that we got married in church. That seemed important to both of us at the time."

"Because of the vows you were making?"

"I certainly thought so – but he seemed to forget his promises soon enough when Trish laid it on a plate for him."

"But what about you? How do you feel about those vows you made on the day you married him?"

"Where in the marriage vows does it say anything about sticking with your husband when he's a cheating, selfish adulterer? He chose to have an affair, so surely that allows me a choice too? If he wasn't sticking to his promises, then why should I?"

"But in those vows, you also promised to stand by your husband in sickness and in health…"

"And that's the problem, isn't it? I *did* promise that – and I can't see that I have any choice but to keep that promise, because he didn't have a choice about getting cancer."

"And what are you most scared of? Is it your lack of feeling, or your lack of confidence that you'll be able to cope?"

"Both, if I'm honest. On all levels, I'm terrified I'm going to make a mess of things."

At that moment, Nathan came over to ask his Mum to help him put together a cart-and-horse toy he'd been struggling with. Her face was full of love as she looked down at her son, chatting softly to him before running her fingers through his hair and sending him happily on his way back to the sandpit.

"Tell me," Neil began again, "did you want to get married in church because you felt that God was part of the contract you were making – that you were inviting God to be a constant presence in your marriage?"

"Probably, but it didn't do much good, did it? Where was God when John was playing Mr and Mrs in hotel rooms with some other woman?"

"And for you? Is having God in your life important to you?"

She turned to look at him as she considered her answer.

"I'd like it to be, but I don't feel God's done me any favours lately."

"The trouble is that, as human beings, we are both blessed and cursed with our own free will. God doesn't make our decisions for us. He leaves that to us – and what a mess we get ourselves into!"

"Well, John didn't decide to be ill. That wasn't down to his free will, was it? It wasn't his fault – and I certainly don't hold with that daft idea that illness is some sort of punishment. If John needs any punishment for what he's put us through, then the boys and I are the ones with the right to decide on that. But honestly, I don't think he's being punished and I don't think it's his fault – or mine. So, if there is a God, it must be down to him!"

"It seems to me," said Neil, "from the little I know, that cancer is very much an illness of our time and lifestyle. Of course it's not John's fault – but I don't believe it's God's fault either. It's just one of those dreadful things that happen. No warning, no blame..."

"And apparently no hope either!" she finished bitterly.

"Is that what the doctors have said?"

"No, not really. They wouldn't be that black and white, would they? But John's done a lot of reading, and so have I. The future doesn't look very rosy right now."

"Well," said Neil gently, "I think that it's when life doesn't seem fair, when we're hurting and lost and in despair, that God is right there with us. You may not agree with that right now, but from all I've heard from other people and all I've learned along the way, I really do believe that's true."

"I hope so." Her voice was barely a whisper. "I do hope so, because if God is real, and if all we're taught about him loving us is true, then I need him to do his stuff for us right now. We need a miracle."

Her eyes shone with tears as she spoke. "So if you've got a hotline to him, let him know that, will you? We need a miracle, and we need it now."

* * *

"I need a woman in my life."

Graham took a gulp of beer, then set the glass down.

"I'm thirty-one years old, and if I'm ever going to be in my prime, then *this* is as good as it gets!"

"Are you talking about finding a life partner – a wife?"

Graham grinned at Neil. "Well, given my track record, anything lasting more than a few weeks will seem like a life partner to me! I'd like a deeply meaningful relationship, of course – at least that's what I'll put on the application form – but honestly, any half-decent girl who's prepared to spend an evening in my company would seem pretty meaningful to me right now!"

"Application form?" queried Neil, taking a mouthful of his own beer.

"On the internet. I've found a site that looks quite good. *Dream Partners*, that's what it's called."

"I think I've seen the advert for that on telly. Is that the one that doesn't just go on appearance, but looks for deeper compatibility?"

"Nothing deep about it. It's free, that's why I like it. And it's a looker I'm after. Can't be doing with all this compatibility rubbish! Either we fancy each other or we don't!"

"Then you're probably talking to the wrong friend here. It's the compatibility bit that I'd advocate, along with the 'loving and cherishing till death do us part'."

Graham nodded with understanding. "Yes, you're a man of the cloth, so I knew that's what you'd say – but I'm a man of the world, and I could do with a good mate who's not listening with his dog collar for the next five minutes."

"OK, try me."

"Well, this bird has sent me a message – and I don't know what to say."

"Had you contacted her, then?"

"Yes – well, not exactly *contacted* her. I saw her picture, so opened up her profile online. Apparently, that flags up to her that I've been showing an interest – and she's practically bitten my hand off! That must mean she's keen, mustn't it?"

"I reckon so. What did she say?"

"She said her name is Gemma, she's twenty-three…"

"So quite a bit younger than you."

"… but she sounds very mature, and I think I'm young for my age, don't you?"

Neil chuckled into his beer.

"She's a beautician," Graham continued. "They're always gorgeous, aren't they? She works in one of the big department stores in Oxford Street."

"Where does she live?"

"About ten miles from here, that's all. Nothing, really!"

"So? Are you going to meet up with her?"

"Look, I've printed off her profile sheet so that you can see for yourself."

He pulled out a neatly folded piece of A4 from his inside pocket, and spread it with a flourish on the pub table.

"Feast your eyes on that!"

A man of the cloth he might be, but Neil's eyes practically popped out on stalks when he saw the glamorous, scantily clad girl who posed provocatively in the picture.

"Wow!" he said at last. "I don't think she's a girl you'll be taking home to meet your mother."

Graham picked up the paper to peer at the picture closely. "Looks to me like she'd have a good bedside manner."

"Have you replied to her yet?"

"No! That's why I need your help. What should I say? Should I play it cool? Should I spin her a line to make myself sound more interesting?"

"You are interesting. You are a highly intelligent and respected member of the teaching profession…"

"I'm thirty-one years old, two stone overweight, and my hobbies are drinking real ale, playing rugby and watching cowboy films."

"So tell her that. If she doesn't like what she hears, you can keep looking online to find a girl who *does* want someone just like you."

"Look, Neil, you know what they say about a bird in the hand. This girl has shown an interest in me. *This* is the girl I'd like to meet."

"So what does she know about you?"

Graham's expression was suddenly sheepish. He pulled

another piece of paper out of his pocket and slid it towards Neil.

"But this picture looks nothing like you!"

"It *is* me – well, it *was*! That photo was taken five years ago at my sister's wedding."

"But you were five years younger then…"

"…. and a stone lighter!" finished Graham. "Neil, mate, can you imagine a bird like that taking a second look at me as I really am? Slightly balding, pot bellied, with a taste for takeaway kebabs and curries. So I just spiced up my description a bit…"

"Interests," quoted Neil, "Reading, youth work, films and sport."

"I do play rugby and I enjoy a good DVD."

"Reading? Youth work?"

"I read the riot act to the little blighters at school, and if you don't call sorting them out 'youth work', then I don't know what is!"

"Non-smoker," continued Neil.

"I can take it or leave it. Well, I could probably leave it for a few hours while we went out. She probably wouldn't notice."

"Income bracket – sixty to eighty thousand pounds?"

"I'll get that if I ever decide to become a headteacher."

"Have you applied to be a headteacher?"

"And be buried in paperwork? Not likely!"

"Hello, Neil! How nice to bump into you like this!"

Both men looked up with a start as a warm, amused female voice cut into their conversation. Neil smiled to see it was Wendy Lambert from the music group.

"Wendy! What a pleasant surprise."

"Come on, let's go and sit over there by the window."

The girl who spoke was carrying two glasses of white wine as she appeared beside Wendy. She stared good-naturedly towards Graham as she went on, "I get enough of my next-door neighbour at home without having to spend time with him down the pub too."

"Neil, you know Debs, don't you?" gushed Wendy. "She plays the flute with the music group whenever she can get to church on Sunday mornings."

"I'm in the police," explained Debs. "Shift work."

"And you were making a right noise starting up that bike of yours at the crack of dawn yesterday morning!" moaned Graham.

"I have to be on duty at six."

"Can't you get a nice quiet car, then – or a push-bike?"

"Need your beauty sleep, do you?" teased Debs, sitting down beside him. "Go on, shove up! I've changed my mind. We're joining you."

Neil's nose twitched as Wendy's sweet, musky perfume drifted in his direction as she eased herself into the seat beside him.

"What's that?" said Debs, grabbing towards the internet details Graham had been showing Neil.

"It's nothing!" snapped Graham, snatching the paper up and stuffing it into his pocket.

"Give it here," demanded Debs. "I want to see it."

"Look, it's nothing to do with you, so mind your own business!"

"You're trying internet dating, aren't you?"

Debs' eyes danced with humour as she looked at him.

"Well, you're going to have to spruce yourself up a bit. You didn't say what you really look like and what your personal habits are, did you?"

Graham squirmed with embarrassment. "Debs, you're a pain! Push off and take your drink somewhere else!"

"You didn't tell them how you still live with your mother, never walk anywhere, only shower every other day…"

"How do you know that?" asked Graham indignantly.

"Because you sing in the shower. No, I take that back – you *bellow* in the shower – so I guess the whole street knows you only shower every other day. To be honest, we couldn't cope with any more."

"You two sound just like my brother and me," interjected Wendy.

"Our families live next door to each other," agreed Debs. "Our mums always looked after each other's children without thinking too much about who actually belonged where. So Graham feels as much like a big brother to me as my real brother, Darren, ever did."

"You're still living at home too!" accused Graham.

"I'm twenty-four, and saving up for a deposit on a house. You're thirty-one – and you're drinking your deposit."

"Perhaps," suggested Wendy, "he's looking on the internet for a sugar mummy who will provide him with a roof over his head, and see to all his worldly needs?"

"Nothing wrong with that," grinned Graham.

"And what about you, Neil?" asked Wendy as she gazed at him fondly. "Are you looking for love too?"

Neil's cheeks immediately reddened. "Ah, not really – I mean, not at all. Well, I wouldn't mind if I came across some nice girl who was willing to take me on – but I'm not really looking…"

"You look terrified!" laughed Debs.

"Aren't we all?" agreed Graham. "You women *are* terrifying."

"Well," said Debs, "if you're serious about wanting to find the girl of your dreams, we're going to have to give you a helping hand."

"A haircut." Wendy nodded in agreement as she looked Graham up and down. "And a new wardrobe. A fitness regime, a strict diet – and eyebrow shaping. Your brows practically meet in the middle!"

"I'm not going on a diet," said Graham moodily.

Debs took his chin and turned his head towards her so that she could look at him in critical close-up.

"You're a mess, Graham – but with a bit of work, there may be hope for you."

"Thanks a lot," was the grumbled reply.

"And I can start right now," said Debs as she rummaged around in her enormous handbag. "Ah, here they are!" She held up a pair of tweezers with a triumphant flourish.

"Get off me!" Graham was laughing as he pushed her away.

"Internet dating!" snorted Debs as she put the tweezers back into her handbag. "You'd have to be desperate to resort to that!"

"It's the modern way to make friends, though, isn't it?" said Neil. "When people have such busy lives, it's a way of widening their circle of friends beyond just those they work with or live next door to."

"Would you ever go on internet dating, Wendy?" asked Graham.

Wendy looked thoughtful before replying. "I've honestly never thought about it, but then I have a large circle of friends already – some I went to school with here, others from university, and now quite a lot through work. I don't think I'd ever need to meet people that way."

"But do you have an image of your ideal man?" Graham went on. "Because if you knew someone like him in your present circle, presumably you'd have snapped him up already. So what's wrong with a little help from modern technology when it comes to finding Mr Right?"

"My ideal man...." continued Wendy dreamily. "He'd be about twenty-five years old, not too tall, certainly not skinny – in fact, quite broad-shouldered would be rather nice. Dark hair, curly perhaps, not too long. A good listener and well educated. And I like a man with depth of character – you know, someone who has passion and commitment. After all, we'll be partners for life. I'm not really interested in anything less."

Debs looked at Neil. Neil said nothing as his face became redder.

"Come on, Wendy!" said Debs. "We came out to catch up on the gossip, so let's leave these boys to finish their drinks in peace and quiet."

And with a whiff of perfume and a friendly wave, the girls moved away.

Neil and Graham sat in silence for a while, sipping their drinks.

"You're in there, you know!"

Neil raised an eyebrow in surprise.

"That Wendy fancies you."

"Oh no," spluttered Neil. "She's the leading light of the music group. We have to work together quite a bit..."

"She's certainly working on you, that's for sure."

Not knowing how to answer, Neil fell silent as he picked up his glass. He wasn't used to girls "fancying" him – and Wendy *was* a particularly lovely and talented girl. There was no way that he would hold any interest for a cultured and capable young woman like her!

But still, he allowed the possibility to roll around in his mind for a minute or two, because if it were true, then he couldn't quite decide if he was pleased – or scared witless.

≫ CHAPTER 7 ≪

"*I*'ve rung you three times. Why haven't you rung back?"

That was his mother's opening line when he answered the phone. No niceties. No "Hello, dear." Not even an enquiry about the weather.

He took a deep breath to calm his reaction to her before he spoke.

"Hello, Mum. I'm sorry. I've just been busy, that's all."

"So they're over-working you, are they? I told you this wasn't the job for you…"

"No, not over-worked, just busy in a very challenging and enjoyable way."

"You have a very odd understanding of enjoyment, Neil."

Neil's breath hissed through his teeth. There was no reasoning with her, so he wouldn't bother to try. Instead, he changed the subject.

"And how are you, Mum? Is your sciatica still playing you up?"

"It will *always* play me up, Neil. You could never understand the pain I go through. No one could," she ended with a dramatic sigh.

"Have you been to see Dr Jones again? What does he say?"

"Nothing. He took early retirement, right out of the blue. Can you believe it? Broke my heart! They've handed me over to a whippersnapper who's barely out of junior school. And it's a woman! When it comes to doctors and newsreaders, I want a man!"

"But don't you need more medication? You'll have to find at least one doctor in the practice you'd be prepared to see."

"Oh, I'm dealing with it, Neil. I've made my feelings *very* clear to the Practice Manager!"

Heaven help them, thought Neil.

"How's your dandruff?" she enquired sharply. "Are you buying that shampoo I told you about?"

No, he thought. "Yes," he said.

"And are you avoiding dairy products after that very suspicious rash you developed last year? It must have been painful, bearing in mind where on your body it was…"

"That was just stress, Mum. I was taking my final exams."

"Cut out dairy products. It always works for me, and you and I must have the same metabolism."

His silence at that point brought this line of conversation to a swift end.

"Anyway," she said petulantly, "it shouldn't be me having to ring you. A boy should want to ring his mother. A fine son, you are! Got time for all your new friends down there in Dumbridge, I've no doubt, but when it comes to remembering the people you should be grateful to, you just can't make the effort…"

Her voice faded into the background as Neil's attention was suddenly diverted towards his front garden. Surely that was his lawnmower he could hear? He pulled back the net curtains just in time to see Claire giving him a cheery wave as she walked past the window pushing the electric mower. Whatever was she doing here? This was a nice surprise!

"… Saturday morning. I'll let you know the train time. And I don't want any lumps in the mattress. You know how I suffer with my back."

"What?" asked Neil, suddenly realizing, as he caught the last few words of his mother's monologue, that it sounded as if she was planning to visit him – soon.

"Sorry, Mum, can you just recap on that again? This line isn't brilliant."

"Next Saturday, Neil. I'll be at Paddington at midday. You can pick me up from there."

"You're travelling alone?"

"Of course! I wouldn't think of dragging anyone else to the pits of Bedfordshire. Besides, I won't be alone once you get there."

"And how long are you thinking of staying?"

He held his breath as, with a sense of dread, he anticipated her answer.

"Oh, not a moment longer than I have to!"

Neil let out a silent sigh of relief.

"I'll stay with you on Saturday night and travel back on Sunday morning."

"That will be lovely, Mum – although of course, I won't be able to take you back to Paddington on Sunday morning."

"Why ever not? That's the most convenient train, and I don't want to be travelling after dark."

"I know the nights are drawing in, but it's still light until seven o'clock at least. But the reason that time is difficult for me is that I have two services on Sunday morning."

"Can't the Vicar do them?"

"She does really, because I'm still a deacon until next July when I'm priested, so I can't take the Eucharist service completely on my own yet."

"Good. Then you can take me to the station."

"No, Mum. It's my duty to be there. I'm the curate. Besides, It's more than a duty, it's a devotion that's important to me."

"Huh!" she snorted. "Well, I suppose it would be interesting to see you in action. I wouldn't mind having a word with that vicar of yours while I'm there. A woman, you say?"

It was clear from her tone that it wasn't only doctors and newsreaders who, in her opinion, should only ever be men.

"Margaret is an excellent priest, and I'm sure she and Frank will make you very welcome."

"Well," she said in a way that made it clear she was very put out, "my train gets into Paddington at noon sharp. Be at the end of the platform so I can see you clearly."

"That will be lovely – and you've picked an interesting day to come. We've got the Harvest Supper in the church hall that evening."

"Supper?"

"Yes, the ladies of the parish have been planning the menu for weeks – home-grown vegetable soup, lasagne and salad, and a selection of fresh-fruit puddings."

"Well, I have to say that sounds a great deal better than anything you might cook for me, Neil. I agree to go."

"Thank you," said Neil, hoping he sounded suitably grateful when actually he was appalled at the thought of his mother let loose among the congregation he was still trying to impress.

"Right, must rush. I'm due at the Bridge Club. Till next Saturday then, twelve o'clock sharp! Don't be late!"

"Looking forward to it!" he lied – but he spoke to the dialling tone because she had already hung up on him.

He leaned back against the sideboard drained, mulling

over the thought of his mother being here next weekend. It would be appalling. She would embarrass him in every possible way.

His thoughts were interrupted by a knock on the window-pane. The sight of Claire trying to catch his attention certainly lightened his mood, and he went immediately to open the front door.

"Mowing my lawn, eh? Have you run out of gardens to work in?"

"Well, apparently you haven't been doing much mowing yourself – or dead-heading or pruning…"

"Now you're talking technical! I own up to a complete ignorance of anything that's needed in the garden – except a deckchair and a cool beer, I suppose."

She laughed. "Cyn and Peter both thought you might need a hand – and this is church property, after all."

"Thank God for our very thoughtful churchwardens!" smiled Neil. He thought how pretty she looked, even though her cropped hair was definitely doing its own thing and her skin was flushed with exertion.

"Fancy a cold drink? I've even got some ice cubes, I think."

"You're a life-saver – but I can't stay long. I have to be in Maple Avenue by four."

"Another lawn to mow?"

"Much bigger than this one, so it will take me at least three hours. I'd like to get it done before the light goes."

Neil considered her slight build having to cope with the heavy-duty work she was called upon to do.

"You must be exhausted by the end of each working day."

She laughed. "Not by the gardening. I really love it. I turn on my iPod, plug in my earphones and get lost in a world of my own. It's quite relaxing, really – certainly compared to looking after Sam when I do get home in the evening. Harry is wonderful, of course. He still loves cooking, and often he's got a meal organized for us all by the time I get back – but I do worry about him doing too much. He's been like a father to me. Sam even calls him Grandad!"

"He does seem to be a very special and caring man."

"He is. What about you? Are you close to your Dad?"

"I was, very. He died almost sixteen years ago now. I'm probably quite a chip off the old block. I'd like to think so, anyway."

"And your Mum?"

He groaned. "Ooh, my Mum. That was her who just rang. She's planning to visit next weekend."

"That will be nice…"

She stopped as she saw his pained expression.

"Or perhaps not so nice?" she finished.

"The thought of her being here fills me with horror. To say she's overbearing is an understatement. In fact, she's more like a steam-roller, and I always seem to end up deflated, flattened – in fact, well and truly squashed by her!"

"Is she still a widow, or has she married again?"

"Marry! Who'd have her? I can't imagine why Dad asked her in the first place, although I'm glad he did, of course – for me, if not for him!"

"What do your brothers and sisters think?"

"Only child, I'm afraid. Nowhere to hide. No one else to take the flak along with me."

"She's probably just being protective of her baby boy."

"Over-protective, you mean. Dominating. Interfering. Opinionated. Bigoted. Selfish. Hypochondriac. Do you get the picture?"

"But you've escaped! You must have been at college for what, three years? And now you're here, you're not in reach of her tentacles any more."

"Don't you believe it! She rings most days, although I try only to answer one day in three. She may live a hundred miles away, but she would still like to know exactly what I'm eating, who my friends are, whether I'm up to date with the housework and if my vest's tucked in!"

Claire giggled. "And now she plans to visit Dunbridge?"

"She's arriving next Saturday morning and staying until Sunday afternoon."

"Not too long, then."

"That's a matter of opinion."

"Well, what damage could she really do? Who is she likely to meet?"

"Everyone. I'll have to take her to the Harvest Supper on Saturday night."

"And church the next morning?"

"Not that she's really interested in the service. She'll just want to weigh everyone up and find them lacking. She's making vague threats about having a meaningful chat with Margaret…"

"I pity your Mum. Margaret is capable of wiping the floor with anyone – nicely, of course, but she doesn't put up with any nonsense. That's one of the things I like most about her."

Neil sighed.

"I just don't want Mum to hurt anyone's feelings. I don't want her to look around Dunbridge and complain about everything she sees. And I don't want her to talk about me to anyone. In fact, I don't want her to talk at all – especially not to me!"

"Have you ever told her how you feel?"

"Couldn't get a word in edgeways. No point even trying."

"Come on, Neil, you are a professional listener – and a pretty good talker too, if what I've seen is anything to judge by. You must be able to sit her down and let her see that her little boy is a grown man who is respected for doing a good job around here."

"I am? Do you really think so? I still feel I'm such a beginner..."

"Now you're fishing for compliments! I've not seen much of you at work in the church, of course..."

"You never come. Why is that?"

"I don't believe in God. Seems like a stupid idea to me."

"Oh," said Neil, taken back by her bluntness.

"Does that mean you'll take back your offer of a cold drink? Do you serve atheists?"

He laughed. "I serve all of God's children. Come through and I'll sort it out."

She looked down at her muddy boots.

"I'll see you round at the back door, then."

Minutes later, she downed a pint of iced orange squash without stopping once.

"Thanks," she smiled, handing back the glass. "I can return the compliment on Saturday night."

"Oh?"

"The Harvest Supper is made from local ingredients – in other words, the vegetables I've grown in various gardens belonging to congregation members. I'd love to see whether my veg goes down well, so although I'm not doing the cooking, I've said I'll help out as a waitress, serving drinks and things."

"Then you will have the pleasure of meeting my mother."

"I certainly will," she agreed. "I'll make a point of it."

* * *

"Here you are, Neil, a job for you. Could you pop over this morning to see Mrs Davis – the address is on the card. Her husband, George, died at the weekend and she's booked a service for him next Tuesday at the crematorium. She's made it pretty clear that, in her opinion, such an occasion should be led by a man – and you're the nearest thing we've got to that! Anyway, it will be my day off, and you are quite confident leading funerals now, so it's good for you to get the experience of doing some on your own. I'm here if you need to ask about anything."

"Thanks Margaret," grinned Neil. He looked down at the note. "Joan Davis, 14 Keats Avenue. And the appointment is at eleven." He glanced at his watch. "Heavens, I'd better get going!"

Keats Avenue was on the relatively recently built Poets Estate, so called because all the roads were named after famous British wordsmiths. Neil turned down Yeats Drive, went left into Wordsworth Lane and found Keats Avenue not far up on the right-hand side. Number 14 was a typical modern three-bedroom detached house with an integral garage and neat box hedging surrounding a tidy cropped lawn. Neil rang the bell and waited, gazing down at two stone lions who sat, like guarding soldiers, on either side of the door, which was promptly opened by a thirty-something young woman with a row of rings of various sizes in each ear, and a tattoo on her wrist as she stretched her hand out to welcome him.

"Mum's in the living room. Go on in. Tea?"

"Coffee, white, one sugar please, if it's not too much trouble."

Neil found Joan Davis sitting in a wide, comfy armchair which was covered in a large, flowery print. She wore a cardigan embroidered with a row of brightly coloured flowers, and a skirt which was a mass of blue and gold blooms. It was difficult to tell where her skirt stopped and the chair cover started so that, all in all, the effect was of one great big bouquet. She didn't get up, but held her hand out to him with a forlorn expression on her face.

"Thank you for coming, Vicar. Excuse me for not getting up. It's the shock, you know. It's knocked me for six."

Neil settled himself on the sofa opposite her, opening his briefcase as he said, "I am so sorry to hear about your loss, Mrs Davis. Had George been ill for long?"

"No," she replied. "He'd always been a very fit man – got a lot of exercise, you see. His heart attack just came out of the blue. It was a great shock for everyone."

The girl with the earrings came in then carrying a tray on which tea and coffee was served in flowery china mugs, alongside a plate of neatly arranged shortbread fingers.

"This is my daughter, Tracey."

"We've met. Thank you for the coffee, Tracey. I'm sorry to be meeting you under such sad circumstances."

She shrugged. "These things happen." She glanced towards her mother. "We'll cope."

"And are you George's only daughter?" Neil asked. As Joan started to reply, she was interrupted by a coughing fit which suddenly afflicted Tracey.

"Sorry," she said, her face red as she tried to clear her throat. "I've had a cold."

Neil smiled sympathetically, and took out his pen, ready to take notes on their conversation.

"Tracey's my youngest," Joan began again. "Then there's

Shane. He's with his partner, Kylie, and they've got a couple of youngsters of their own now. He's done well for himself. Got his own tyre centre on the London Road. Do you know it?"

"Oh yes! That's your son, is it?" replied Neil, hoping that his lack of familiarity with the area didn't show too much. "And no other children? Well, let me take down a few details about George, just so that I've got a clear picture of him. Have you got plans for any members of the family or perhaps old friends to pay a tribute to him during the service?"

"We would prefer you do it. We'll be much too emotional to say anything on the day," said Tracey.

"Of course," said Neil, pen poised above his pad. "Let's start with some general notes about his life and achievements."

Neil scribbled like mad for the next twenty minutes as George's life story unfolded. He had worked for a local manufacturer most of his life, finally reaching the grade of foreman of the factory. His seemed to have been a simple life. He played football for the local town team as a young man, although when his son Shane came along, he continued his interest from the sideline where he loved to cheer his son on. As a member of the local Working Men's Club, he was Captain of the Darts Team, which had enjoyed a measure of success each year in the county league championships. He'd apparently enjoyed DIY projects too, like woodwork and decorating.

"Right," said Tracey, suddenly very business-like. "We've put together a few notes too. There are some things we definitely want said about him. We'd appreciate it if you didn't change the wording of this bit. Just read it as it is here. Is that all right?"

"Of course," agreed Neil, glancing down at the sheet. He could immediately see phrases like "good with his hands", "a lover not a fighter", "he enjoyed mixing with people in all walks of life", "loved by one and all", "always ready to help out a neighbour".

"This is excellent," he commented, as he flattened the sheet tidily into his pad. "Now what about hymns? Have you thought of any favourites that might be appropriate?"

Mother and daughter looked at each other for a moment, before Joan said, "We've come up with a couple. 'He's Got the Whole World in His Hands' – that was one he liked. And there's another old one we think is appropriate – 'Who Would True Valour See'. Do you know it?"

"The one based on the words of John Bunyan's *Pilgrim's Progress*, you mean? Yes, I know it. Mind you, most people sing the more modern version of that nowadays – 'He Who Would Valiant Be'. The words are a little less archaic."

"What's the difference?"

"The old version has a line about 'hobgoblins' and 'foul fiends'."

"That's the one we want."

"Really?"

"Dad sang it when he was at school," was Tracey's quick reply. "That's how he remembered it, so that's how we'd like to remember him."

"And there's a piece of music we think should be played as the curtain closes," said Joan. "It's an old hymn called 'Seeds of Love'. Have you heard of it?"

"Can't say I have."

"Well, we'll bring a recording. And we've chosen a couple of tracks for him, one for when he comes in, and another for when we all leave. We'll put them on the CD too."

"OK," said Neil, "just give that to the undertaker some time before the service, and they'll organize everything according to your instructions. Now, there are just a few more points I need to check…"

Several minutes were spent sorting out the details of the undertaker, the time of arrival and the arrangements for flowers. After that, Neil gathered together his things, and stood to say goodbye to Joan and Tracey.

"It's important to us," said Joan, looking directly into his eyes as if to make sure he heard every word, "that everything is exactly as we'd like it. We want to get it right, and make sure he gets the send-off he deserves."

"Of course," agreed Neil. "And I wonder if you would like us to share a prayer before I leave?"

"Probably not," was Tracey's immediate reply. "Mum's getting tired. Shall I show you out?"

And as Neil found himself bundled out the front door, he mused on the fact that bereavement affected everyone in their own individual way. This family was grieving, no doubt about that – and as he drove off, he said a silent prayer for them anyway.

* * *

"It's a bit of a box."

Neil's mother twitched her nose dismissively as she looked around his home.

"I like it. It's not too big to keep tidy, but large enough to fit in everything I need."

She wandered through the lounge and then into the kitchen.

"Who chose the decor? Not you, I hope!"

"The churchwardens, I suppose. It was all newly decorated when I got here."

"They were preparing your new home ready for your arrival, but they didn't think to ask you about your choice of colour scheme?"

"I like the colour scheme."

"Of course you don't, Neil. No one could like a house where every room is in varying shades of putty!"

"It's beige – and I like it. I find it restful."

"I find it boring," she retorted as she peered out at the garden through the window of the back door.

"The garden's a bit small."

"I'm a curate, not a gardener. If I had no garden at all, I'd be quite happy."

Neil followed as his mother let herself out the back door so that she could inspect the offending garden in closer detail.

"You seem to have found time to mow the grass. Not much more, though, as far as I can see…"

"The church gardener deals with this garden too, as the house is church property."

"Is he an old man? He hasn't put a lot of energy or thought into those flowerbeds!"

"*She* is not old – and *she* doesn't spend much time here because *she* is busy elsewhere. And I think what she does is fine. I appreciate that she comes at all."

Iris sniffed. Obviously gardeners should be men too! Her glance strayed over to the garage which ran along one side of the back garden.

"What's in there?"

"Do you want the list? Lots of stuff – my bike, that fitness equipment I bought and never used, empty boxes that I've unpacked…"

"You mean you don't keep your car in the garage! Surely that's what garages are for?"

"Actually, I don't know anyone who keeps their car in the garage. They've usually got too much junk in it to have room for a car."

"May I remind you, Neil, that I helped you buy that car? It may have little value to you, but I can assure you it was a very large undertaking for me!"

Neil saw little point in answering. His mother immediately assumed his silence was an admission of guilt.

"Do you get the car regularly serviced?"

"Of course."

"And valeted?"

He stared hard at her.

"No."

"Surely you have a position in the community to consider now, Neil! Whatever will people think of you if you can't even keep a tidy car?"

"My car wasn't untidy when I picked you up from Paddington."

"Cleaned it out this morning, did you?"

"Don't you go picking those flowers!"

A man's voice cut across both the conversation and the garden with a suddenness that surprised them both. Neil's face softened.

"Hello, Alf."

"Don't you let that fat woman pick those flowers!" Alf repeated from the next-door garden, staring pointedly at Iris.

"I *beg* your pardon!" she spluttered with indignation. "How dare you speak to me like that!"

"Well, you *dare* pick those flowers, and I'll… I'll…"

Alf frowned as he tried to think of the worst thing he could inflict on her if she didn't do as he asked.

"I'll tell Maureen!" he announced with triumph.

"Tell me what, pet?"

Alf's carer, Maureen, came up to slip her arm through his as the two of them looked across the garden fence at Neil and his mother.

"I do apologize," she said with a smile. "Alf is very protective about flowers. Not just his own – anybody's!"

"You could hardly call a spindly shrub or two and a handful of dahlias *flowers*!" retorted Iris, her voice brittle with coldness. "And I suggest you confine your interest to your own rather pathetic garden display before you start criticizing the achievements of others."

Maureen's smile didn't drop, but Neil almost laughed out loud as he realized that, with her experience, the carer was more than capable of summing up Iris accurately.

"Oh, this has got nothing to do with the real state of the garden, either yours there or ours here. Alf just likes to see things neat and tidy, that's all."

"Flowers are for gardens!" announced Alf. "You shouldn't pick flowers from gardens. Flowers belong in gardens."

"Quite right, Alf," agreed Neil, ignoring with a degree of pleasure the look of sheer annoyance shooting at him from his mother's direction. "How are you today?"

"I'm drawing a picture. I've got coloured pencils."

"What's in the picture?"

"Flowers!" replied the old man, who obviously thought Neil was very daft not to have worked that out for himself.

"Shall we go inside and do a bit more drawing then, Alf?" asked Maureen gently. "And I'll make you a sandwich…"

That certainly caught Alf's attention.

"With ham in?"

"Uh-huh," she nodded.

"And butter?"

"Yep!"

"And brown sauce?"

"Lashings of it."

But Alf was already on his way up the path to his kitchen door. With an apologetic wave and a smile, Maureen turned to follow him.

"What's that? Care in the Community? Fancy them putting you next door to a mad old man like him!"

"Alf isn't mad. He's beginning to suffer from the effects of dementia, but in fact he's always been a highly intelligent and well-qualified man – an architect, I believe. That's why he likes drawing so much. And Maureen – she's his carer – she's endlessly patient and imaginative with him."

"But a man like that could become a real danger. He shouldn't be allowed to live right next door to decent people."

An angry red flush shot across Neil's face.

"Alf is a perfectly decent neighbour. In fact, he's a Neighbourhood Watch scheme all on his own!"

But Iris was bored. She turned to walk back towards the house.

"Which is my room?"

"I've put you in the quiet room at the back."

"I hope the curtains are backed. I'll never be able to sleep in a room where the curtains are too see-through."

Neil watched his mother disappearing from view for a few seconds before he could muster the enthusiasm to follow her. This was plainly going to be a very long weekend…

⪼ CHAPTER 8 ⪻

"M adam."

Harry bowed slightly as he took Iris' hand.

"It is a pleasure to meet you. Neil has told us so much about you."

"Has he, now?" asked Iris suspiciously, although Neil could tell from the way her face had flushed that she was rather enjoying such a gracious greeting.

"Mum, this is my very good friend and neighbour, Harry Holloway."

"And I have come, my dear lady," continued Harry, "to escort you to the Harvest Supper. Neil has to be there much earlier than either of us, so he suggested that, as we have to walk past my house on the short journey to the church, you might do me the honour of taking a stroll around my garden for a while first."

"Harry's being modest, Mum. His garden is absolutely beautiful!"

Neil could see Iris was torn. Was she infuriated that Neil had apparently "fobbed her off" with a total stranger – or was she charmed by the gentlemanly offer Harry was making? And his effort to impress didn't stop with his words. Harry was dressed in his best suit, with a crisp white shirt, shiny black shoes and a striking red rose in his lapel.

"And whether or not you choose to accept my invitation," continued Harry, "I have a little gift for you."

He laid into her outstretched hand an exquisite corsage of dainty roses, their petals apricot-coloured with a splash of deep red frilling around the edges. The buds had been woven into a delicate bed of silver and dark-green foliage. It was plainly made with great skill and care. Claire, thought Neil. I bet that's her handiwork.

Iris melted as she looked at the blooms – and the two men glanced at each other in silent relief.

"Mr Holloway, how very kind of you. Did these roses come from your garden?"

"Of course," replied Harry with a smile.

"Then I will be delighted to accept your offer. Run along, Neil. Go and do whatever it is you have to do, and we'll see you there."

The church hall was buzzing when Neil arrived a few minutes later. The edge of the stage and the window-sills were draped in golden garlands of leaves and fruits, and on each table, surrounding large candles which glowed inside glass bowls, was a display of conkers, nuts and pine cones. Soft orange and gold lights discreetly placed around the hall gave the whole room the feel of Autumn.

"This is an absolute triumph!" Neil said to Cyn, who had volunteered to be in complete charge of the Harvest Supper arrangements. "The hall is transformed. It looks wonderful!"

Cyn beamed with pride. "That's one of the blessings of being the matriarch of such a large family," she said. "I sat them all down, told them what I wanted and left it to them. This is what they came up with! Not bad, is it?"

"The cooking smells good too," said Neil, his nose twitching to identify the warm aromas coming from the kitchen.

"Ah well, Frank is in charge of that. Margaret detailed him off for the job, and he's loving every minute of it. He's got a bevy of beautiful assistants peeling the spuds and doing the washing up. He's in his element!"

Neil laughed. "Well, I'm in charge of background music, so I'll go and sort out the sound system."

"For heaven's sake, you're far too young to be in charge of music for a Harvest Supper! Don't you go putting on any heavy metal or songs with inappropriate language, will you?"

"Cyn, I have to admit that when it comes to music, I am the child of my mother. The Rat Pack and 'Songs from the Shows' were her favourites – and sad as it is, I know the words to just about every song that falls into that category!"

"Right." Cyn looked doubtful.

"But I've called in the help of a few folk at the church who know a lot more about everyone else's taste than I do, and together we've compiled a CD that has got a lovely selection of music on it – all quite well known from the radio, the odd hymn or worship song – a nice mix, really. I think you'll approve."

"No second helpings of pudding for you if you get it wrong!" she warned with a grin. "By the way, did I hear that your mother is coming this evening?"

Neil grimaced. "I'm afraid so."

He saw the look of surprise on Cyn's face.

"Oh, don't get me wrong. She can be charming..."

He struggled to know how to continue, as Cyn's expression changed to one of understanding.

"You're an only child, aren't you?"

"Uh-huh."

"And is she pleased at your choice of career?"

"Not exactly."

"And this visit is to check you out – and probably us too?"

"That's about the measure of it, yes."

Suddenly she stepped forward to envelop him in an affectionate hug.

"Don't you worry, Neil. We promise to be on our best behaviour. We'll take very good care of her, just you wait and see!"

Someone called Cyn's name from the other side of the hall just then, and with a wink she turned, leaving Neil wondering whether the small amount of relief he felt after her words was any match for the knot of dread which sat in the pit of his stomach every time he thought of his mother being here, amongst these people who were becoming very dear to him.

"You made it out the door, then?"

Claire laid down a tray full of glasses on the table beside him.

"Harry worked his magic on her!" returned Neil with a grin. "You should have seen him, all dressed up and so gallant as he gave her the corsage. I assume that *was* your handiwork?"

"It took minutes," said Claire dismissively.

"Well, it was a lovely thought and Mum was plainly charmed by it. Thank you, Claire. And I assume that a lot of these garlands and table decorations are your work too?"

"I enjoy it. Anyway, we all did it together."

"Well, it's clear that a huge amount of work has gone into getting everything ready for this evening."

"It's been fun."

"And no Sam tonight?"

Her face lit up as she thought of her son. "He's very excited because he's having a sleepover across the road at the house of the couple he calls Auntie Jan and Uncle Paul. Their boy, Brendan, is a bit older than Sam, and Beckie is about a year younger, so they've grown up together, really."

"I bet he'll love that."

"Neil, there you are!"

Wendy smiled directly at Neil as she approached, completely ignoring Claire.

"The music group are all here now. Where would you like us to set up? And am I right that you want us to play for about a quarter of an hour after the meal has finished?"

Claire discreetly moved away, leaving them to it.

"That would be lovely, thank you."

"And because timing is everything, I've arranged to sit next to you on your table. That way we can make sure everything runs smoothly."

She smiled warmly, aware that she was looking particularly pretty that evening in a slightly sparkling gold-coloured top that perfectly complemented her gleaming brown hair and hazel eyes.

"What a good idea," replied Neil. "I'll just go and sort out the background music, and see you at the table later."

Neil made his way up on to the stage where he began plugging in and checking the sound system. Looking up to survey the busy scene in the hall beneath him, the sound of laughter from the far corner caught his attention. Peter Fellowes was taking direction from Val in the art of laying out place settings, and their heads were almost touching as they shared something that had made them both laugh.

"I know what you're thinking," said a familiar voice to one side of him. "They look very comfortable together, don't they?"

Margaret had joined him as they looked towards the churchwarden and the palliative care nurse who plainly enjoyed each other's company very much.

"They are both such nice people," said Neil carefully.

"And Glenda is a nightmare!" was Margaret's curt response.

"I have to agree with that."

"Poor Peter," said Margaret softly. "He's had a rotten time for years, yet he never complains."

"So it's good that he has such a friend in Val."

"Speaking as their friend rather than their Vicar, I can't help thinking it would be even better if they could be the couple they were meant to be."

Neil turned to look at her. "But he's married!"

"He is, and he never forgets that. There's nothing going on there. They are far too committed to their faith to overstep the mark. They are both very decent people – but I do feel for them."

"Do you think Glenda notices anything?"

"Does Glenda ever notice anything that's not about her? She's so full of that job of hers."

"It sounds very glamorous! She runs the office of a big fashion house in London, she was telling me…"

"Well, she answers the phone and makes the tea. And her boss is the only other person in the office."

"But he's quite well known in the fashion world, isn't he? She seemed shocked that I hadn't heard of him."

The expression on Margaret's face as she turned to answer him was one of disbelieving indignation.

"He sells ties! She's talks it up, but the truth is that she works for a tie salesman, nothing more."

Neil struggled not to laugh before the sadness of the situation struck him.

"Peter works too, though, doesn't he?"

"He's retired now, which is why he's able to help out so much as our churchwarden. He ran his own estate agency here in Dunbridge for years, but sold out to one of the big chains several years ago. He really struggled to get used to not having the responsibility of the business any more. It had claimed so much of his energy and time that he was like a duck out of water when he first sold up. Being churchwarden has really filled the gap. I used to worry that he was putting in far too many hours, but now I realize that's the way he wants it."

Neil looked across to where Peter and Val were companionably setting tables together. Following his gaze, Margaret said softly, "That's where his heart is."

"Will he do anything about it, do you think?"

"Break up his marriage? No, I don't think he would ever be the one to do that. It would be against everything he believes."

"And Glenda? Can she possibly be happy with a situation like that?"

"I honestly don't think Glenda will ever be truly happy, and Peter is very useful as someone to blame for all the wrongs in her life. To her mind, her husband is little more than a failure – and yet I know him as one of the most sincere and sensitive people I've ever met. He's a friend I'd trust in every situation, a good man through and through."

"How sad that Glenda doesn't recognize that."

"I honestly don't think she cares enough about Peter to notice. She's the one who needs all the attention in their marriage."

"They loved each other enough to marry. If their vows are important enough to them to keep them together in spite of everything, then perhaps they could rekindle that love. Counselling, perhaps?"

"Maybe," replied Margaret thoughtfully, "but I doubt Glenda would see the need for that. I spend quite a bit of time with her one way and another, and I don't detect any element of doubt in her mind that Peter is to blame for the demise of their marriage. For her, that fact doesn't merit further discussion."

"Poor Peter."

"Indeed. I do pray for them."

"I'm glad. What do you pray for?"

"Oh, a happy ending, I suppose…"

"For who? Peter and Glenda?"

"In a way, yes. I can't help hoping for an outcome which brings fulfilment and happiness to all three of them – Val too. You only have to watch her and Peter together to see what happiness they find in each other's company. I hope God can see a way to help them out of this unhappy situation – but then, I'm a Christian minister, and I shouldn't really advocate that, should I? But I can't help thinking that at the heart of the God I know and worship is love – and how can you have love unless it goes hand in hand with forgiveness and compassion? Not everyone will agree with me – but strictly between ourselves, that's what I hope for."

Neil gazed across towards Peter and Val until Margaret suddenly broke the mood.

"Come on, the hall's beginning to fill up. I need to go through tonight's programme. Coming?"

And with a shared smile of complete understanding, the two of them rejoined the crowd below.

An hour later, the Harvest Supper was in full swing. Neil was sitting on a table of eight, with his mother to one side of him and Wendy on the other. His mother was in surprisingly good spirits, and for that Neil knew he had to thank Harry, who was simply charming the socks off her. They arrived looking like old friends, especially as Harry introduced his mother to various members of the church community in a suitably gracious way. Iris held her hand out to each of them in turn as though she were a dowager duchess, smiling and chatting briefly before moving on to the next face. A cold trickle of fear coursed its way down Neil's spine when he thought of the snippets of wisdom about her beloved son which Iris was no doubt imparting to Harry and anyone else who would listen. Still, there was nothing he could do about that this evening, so with resigned relief, he left Iris in Harry's capable care. In the end, as one of the "hosts" of the evening's event, Neil's supper was interrupted several times by calls for him to talk to someone about this, or deal with that. On every occasion, when he made his way back to the table, he could see that Iris and Wendy were talking animatedly across his vacant seat. It was nice that Wendy was taking the trouble to keep his mother company.

"Did you know that Wendy made these pavlovas?" asked Iris as he pulled out his chair to sit down.

Neil looked admiringly at the shiny pink meringue topped with raspberries and whipped cream, then turned to smile at Wendy.

"Heavens! Where do you begin making a masterpiece like that? They're magnificent! I had no idea you enjoyed cooking so much."

Plainly pleased at the praise, Wendy's cheeks flushed prettily. "Oh, they're not as hard as they look – and I've always loved baking. I've been on a few cordon bleu courses in London."

"I can see that!" enthused Neil. "You are plainly very talented – and not just at cooking. You'll be hearing Wendy playing with the music group after supper, Mum."

"So she was telling me," beamed Iris. "I'm looking forward to that."

At that moment, another parishioner, who was on the opposite side of their table, claimed Neil's attention. Seconds later, Wendy felt a touch on her left arm as her best friend, Debs, who was sitting beside her, leaned closer to whisper in her ear.

"What's that they say about the way to a man's heart being through his stomach?"

With a smile, Wendy's head bent towards her friend so that no one could overhear their conversation.

"That's very true," she agreed, "but I also think that the way to *this* man's heart may be through his Mum!"

Debs laughed as Wendy turned back towards Neil and Iris.

"Oh, I see the coffee's arrived," said Wendy. "Shall I be mother?"

* * *

Thankfully, apart from saying how much she'd enjoyed the Harvest gathering, Iris was quite reserved in her opinions about the Dunbridge church community when they got home that night. Neil realized with some surprise that the evening had tired her out. She had always been a larger-than-life presence for him, determined to control his every action and decision. He just assumed she was, and always would be, full of energy, and yet the weariness in her face showed plainly as she said goodnight. She'd never admit to being sixty-six years old, but Neil thought for the first time that she was beginning to look her age. That shocked him. Malevolent she may often be towards him, but he couldn't imagine a world without his mother in it. With unexpected fondness, he hugged her as he wished her sweet dreams. She looked as surprised as he felt, and they both stepped back from the embrace, slightly embarrassed by the unusual show of emotion.

She looked a lot brighter the next morning as she made her way into church for the Harvest Festival Family Eucharist. Neil had left much earlier that morning to take part in the first service of the day and, ever the gentleman, Harry once again stepped into the role of companion for Iris, arriving to accompany her to the later service in good time for its 9.30 start. The church looked wonderful – a feast of orange and gold. Window-ledges, pillars and archways were decked with boughs of autumn leaves, and heaps of grasses and sheaves of corn combined with gleaming fruits and nuts to fill every corner with colourful displays. The overall effect was warm and welcoming, and Iris seemed charmed by what she saw as she made her way down the centre aisle, chatting cheerily to people she'd met the evening before with responses which ranged from a majestic nod of the head to a gracious shaking of hands. The warmest greeting was reserved for Wendy, and Neil watched in amazement as the two women hugged each other fondly. Mind you, he thought, Wendy had such a friendly, positive personality that no one could fail to be drawn to her – even his mother!

He was nervous that morning. The wording and flow of the service was second nature to him – but his mother's presence tied his stomach in knots, just as it had throughout most of his life. In Dunbridge he was his own man, respected and accepted because of his contribution and ability. Iris being here complicated all that. He was right to be nervous. Intuitive as ever, Margaret recognized his reaction straight away as they walked towards the vestry to join the choir for a few moments of prayer before the start of the service. Wordlessly, and with complete empathy, she squeezed his arm. She understood – and he was glad.

In fact, the service went seamlessly, as everyone joined in the traditional Harvest hymns with gusto, and felt their hearts warmed by the sight of the children – some still in their parents' arms – taking their contributions of tins, packets and home-grown produce up to the altar to be blessed, before it was distributed to where it was needed most in the local community. To the strains of "We Plough the Fields and Scatter", the clergy and choir proceeded down the aisle and back into the vestry, where they quickly de-robed, ready to join the rest of the congregation who had gathered in the church hall for coffee.

Neil found himself looking around fondly at this motley collection of people who were becoming so dear to him. From the elderly ladies who sat chatting at the edge of the hall to the youngsters who darted around dodging coffee cups, grown-ups' feet and their parents' disapproving looks, he was beginning to feel part of them all. One after another, members of the congregation came up to chat to him – and for Neil, an only child who had often felt very alone in a home dominated by someone like Iris, this new experience was a revelation. It felt almost as if he was beginning to belong to a warm-hearted, extended family who welcomed him with open arms and caring friendship.

Listening to a funny story told by Barbara, who ran the playgroup, he noticed his mother in deep conversation with Frank on the other side of the hall. *Well, that's good*, he thought. In his role of "Vicar's right-hand man", Frank was likely to give a good account of Neil's contribution to the parish. Certainly, his mother seemed very interested in what Frank had to say, and although Neil was consumed with curiosity to know what they were discussing, his attention was claimed by one of the mums who regularly helped out at the playgroup, so it just wasn't possible to get across to join his mother, even if his instinct told him that damage-limitation was probably needed.

In fact, Iris seemed uncharacteristically quiet and thoughtful as they made their way back to his house after the service. They weren't planning to stay long, as her train from Paddington left in just over two hours. Her bag was packed and ready at the front door, so they were in the car and on their way down the A1 towards London within a quarter of an hour of leaving the church. Her unnatural quietness unnerved him, so Neil held his breath, waiting for the comments that were sure to come. In the end, only ten minutes or so from Paddington Station, she finally spoke.

"How much longer will you be a curate?"

"The rest of this year, then at least two more years after that."

"And you plan to stay in Dumbridge?"

"*Dun*bridge!" he corrected. "Yes, I'd like to."

Seconds of silence ticked by.

"I approve," she said eventually.

Neil almost smiled, but his expression was more of surprise.

"You do?"

"But you have to make the most of your time here – pack in as much experience as you can, do a bit more studying, get involved in eye-catching projects, make sure you're noticed…"

"By whom?"

"Everyone who matters. Have you met the Bishop yet?"

"Briefly."

"And have you followed up the contact?"

"I'm just a curate, Mum. I've still got a lot to learn."

"Yes, you have to learn. You also have to impress. Use your initiative. Come up with your own ideas…"

"Why? I'll just come across as pushy, and that's really not me."

"Make it you! Frank was telling me that, above all, Anglican bishops have to be good businessmen these days. You spent that year working in the accounting firm your father started. With that background, you are just what the church needs…"

"Mum, stop! I didn't apply for ordination because I am interested in business. This is a spiritual journey for me…"

"Fine. That's all well and good, but God also gave you talents, didn't he? Isn't that what you believe?"

"Of course, but…"

"Well, use them! You are good at figures and paperwork. Make yourself useful. Move up this organization as fast as you can. Take every chance you can get."

Neil sighed, knowing that reply, let alone argument, would be completely useless.

"And another thing…"

Neil kept his eyes on the road, not bothering to look in her direction to find out what other pearls of wisdom she was going to impart.

"That nice girl, Wendy – do you know what her father does?"

"Yes. He plays the organ at St Stephen's."

"That's his hobby. It's his *job* that's really interesting."

Iris seemed oblivious to the deliberately bored expression on Neil's face.

"He's an accountant! He has his own highly successful business."

"And?"

"And your father was an accountant with his own extremely successful business too."

"Why should that matter?"

"You and Wendy have so much in common! And she's such a clever girl herself – extremely talented too, when you consider the first-class honours degree she has in music."

"Stop it, Mum!"

"She's a teacher, so she plainly loves children…"

"Mum, please just stop thinking that putting two and two together makes a couple."

"And she can *cook*."

He turned angrily towards her then.

"So can I!"

Iris spluttered in amused disbelief.

"She's a cordon bleu chef!"

"And I'm a very straightforward guy who enjoys simple food."

"That's right!" Iris was triumphant. "Simple food – simple man! Wake up and smell the coffee, Neil!"

"Which means what?"

Her expression became suspiciously warm and caring.

"You're twenty-six years old, Neil. I won't be here to look after you for ever! You've got to sort yourself out and settle down some time."

"And you think Wendy would be…"

"… the perfect partner for you!" Iris sighed dramatically, rolling her eyes with exasperation. "At last! Simple you may be – but the penny's dropped *at last!*"

❧ CHAPTER 9 ❧

The driveway up to the crematorium was lined on both sides by banks of flowerbeds, mostly faded now with the autumnal nip in the air. There was obviously a service already taking place, as Neil had difficulty finding a corner in the packed car park, but as he walked towards the chapel, he saw that quite a few people were already gathering outside the entrance in good time for the service for George Davis. Neil slipped in by the side door, and went into the room where he could robe up and sit for a few minutes going over his notes. During the first few months of being in Dunbridge, Neil had simply observed Margaret as she took the services. Later, she'd been at his side to supervise as he led the proceedings. Now, she had enough confidence in him to let him lead cremation services himself. This would be his fourth, and he still couldn't help feeling that Margaret had more confidence in his ability than he had. Margaret had drummed into him that to the bereaved family and friends, it was the detail that mattered most of all – getting the facts and figures of the life story correct, and being able to talk about their personality and achievements with a sensitivity that suggested the minister had known the departed well.

With that in mind, Neil glanced down at the paragraphs given to him by George's widow, Joan, and their daughter Tracey. The two women had been adamant that he should read this piece exactly as they'd written it. Mindful of Margaret's instruction that it was essential to get every detail right for grieving relatives, Neil felt his stomach knot with anxiety. It occurred to him – not for the first time – that a man who had chosen a vocation which involved constant public speaking should surely feel more at ease when speaking to any gathering. On the contrary, just the thought of having to make a speech at a function like this, where accuracy and sensitivity were of utmost importance, simply filled him with dread. His mouth was dry, his palms clammy, and his hands shook so much that he could hardly read his notes.

He became aware of voices beyond the frosted window, so he could tell that the previous service had ended as the mourners now moved into the Garden of Remembrance to look at the floral tributes. That was his cue to go into the chapel to find Clifford sitting at the organ, which was tucked just behind the curtain on the opposite side to the minister's lectern so that he could always see exactly what was needed and when. Clifford greeted Neil with his customary theatrical kiss on both cheeks. He was a very gifted musician who, at the height of his career, had conducted a string of West End musicals. Latterly, he divided his time between playing keyboard at end-of-pier summer seasons and pantomimes, and being pianist at the rehearsals and performances of several local amateur operatic societies and dance classes. In addition, he made a tidy packet each week by providing the music at crematorium services. In fact, he not only played the organ. He also played the *part* perfectly. His camp banter and *risqué* comments could cause offence, but Clifford was wise enough to know when to change his expression to one of sad, respectful grief.

"Odd choice of hymns and music," he said, looking down at the list Tracey had given him. "Family favourites, so his daughter told me."

Neil nodded. "Have you got the CD with the tracks we need as he first comes in, and then when the congregation leaves? And they've chosen a recording of a very old hymn for when the curtains close on the coffin."

"'Seeds of Love'," read Clifford from the CD cover. "Never heard of it."

"Nor me, but they are really adamant that's what they want."

"OK, sweetie, they'll be coming in soon, by the look of it. See you at the other end!"

Neil made his way down the centre of the chapel, which was already quite full of mourners who had taken their seats on either side of the aisle. He carried on through the main door of the chapel so that he could join the small group of mostly family members who were waiting in the porch area to see the hearse make its stately way up the drive to stop in front of the door. He stood beside Joan, Tracey and her brother, Shane, as they watched the bearers take the coffin from the hearse and lift it on to their shoulders. Neil knew that Clifford would take his cue to start the first recording on the CD when he caught sight of Neil taking up his position just in front of the casket. Neil checked to see that his microphone was switched on, then started with these immortal words from John's Gospel to introduce the service:

"'I am the resurrection and the life,' says the Lord. 'Those who believe in me, even though they die, will live, and everyone who lives and believes in me will never die.'"

And with that, Neil set off at a sombre pace to lead the procession down the centre aisle – when suddenly the chapel was filled with music that stopped him dead in his tracks – the opening lines of Tom Jones's hit, "Sex Bomb".

To his astonishment, Neil saw that the expressions on the faces of this congregation of mourners were not at all what he would expect at an occasion like this. Although most of them had their heads down, some were plainly struggling to keep a straight face. They whispered and giggled as the pall-bearers made their slow way down the aisle until they could ceremoniously place the coffin at the front of the chapel, bow their heads and disappear out of a side door. Neil arranged his notes on the lectern, looking out with some trepidation at the congregation who were obviously enjoying and even mouthing the lyrics of the well-known, if totally inappropriate, pop song.

Even George's widow, Joan, was enjoying the music. George must have been a remarkable man, thought Neil, to make people smile just at the thought of him, even after he'd gone! Waiting until the strains of the song had finally faded, Neil continued.

"We brought nothing into the world, and we take nothing out. The Lord gave, and the Lord has taken away; blessed be the name of the Lord."

Hoping that he didn't look as nonplussed as he felt, Neil carried on.

"We have come here today to remember before God our brother George Arthur Davis; to give thanks for his life; to commend him to God our merciful redeemer and judge; to commit his body to be cremated, and to comfort one another in our grief. Lord, look with compassion on your children in their loss; give to troubled hearts the light of hope and strengthen us in the gift of faith, in Jesus Christ our Lord. Amen."

Neil saw with some relief that the mood of the congregation had sobered at these words. Reading carefully from the notes given to him by Tracey and Joan, he went on.

"George's family have specially requested the first hymn, because they feel it sums up his warm-hearted attitude to his friends and neighbours. You'll find the words in the Order of Service."

Knowing that often people find it very hard to sing at funeral services, Neil waited until Clifford had played the introduction before launching loudly into song, in the hope that he was giving a strong melody line which the congregation could follow. Two lines in, Neil realized that he was practically singing a solo. The amusement that had greeted the first piece of music bubbled around the crowd again as the hymn began:

> *He's got the whole world in his hands,*
> *He's got the whole world in his hands!*
> *He's got you and me, sister, in his hands…*
> *He's got the itty, bitty baby in his hands…*

It was a very usual choice of song, Neil realized that – but the response of the mourners was odd, to say the least. He soldiered on, singing enthusiastically until the end, then invited the congregation to sit as he turned to his notes. He felt hot red colour creeping up his neck as he stared out with a definite sense of foreboding at the sea of faces looking in his direction. He made an instant decision that he would not deviate from the facts he'd been given by Joan and the family. No extra comments, however compassionate, would be worth risking when the mood of the mourners was so unpredictable.

He launched into the description of George's early family life, and how he'd gone on to work for a local manufacturer for many years, finally reaching the grade of foreman of the factory. He spoke of George's passion for football. He had played for the local town team as a young man, and later continued his interest by cheering from the sidelines when his son, Shane, started to play. He was a long-standing member of the local Working Men's Club, and as Captain of their Darts Team had enjoyed a measure of success each year in the county league championships.

From here, Neil moved on to the specific wording that the family had asked to be included:

"George was a family man – a husband, father, and grandfather. But he spread his love further than that. He loved one and all, and in fact was such a loving man that some might say he was almost too free with his affection. George was always there for his neighbours, and enjoyed mixing with people from many walks of life. He often spent time with others who were desperate or unable to cope, because he was truly a lover of all men – and women. His neighbourhood will be very quiet without him."

The sound of muffled laughter rippled around the room.

"And he was known to be good with his hands," Neil continued, as beads of sweat coursed between his shoulder-blades. "George wasn't afraid to get stuck in and do whatever dirty work was needed. If he thought it had to be done, George was the first to volunteer."

The sound of the congregation laughing out loud made Neil look up nervously from his notes. Thank goodness that was the end of the piece the family had asked him to read, so he felt on safer ground as he continued with the more formal wording of the service. He moved on to the Prayers of Penitence:

"As children of a loving heavenly Father, let us all now ask his forgiveness." Neil's voice shook slightly as he went on:

"God of mercy, we acknowledge that we are all sinners…"

By this time, the laughter from the congregation was so loud that they could hardly hear the rest of his prayer for forgiveness.

The atmosphere settled as Neil invited everyone to join in prayer, before asking them all to stand for the next hymn requested by the family, "Who Would True Valour See". This hymn was sung unenthusiastically until the line about "hobgoblins" and "foul fiends", when the volume of singing suddenly escalated with those particular words being spat out with gusto. What on earth was going on? Neil's palms felt clammy as he turned once again to his notes, ready to lead the congregation in prayer for the soul of the dear departed George – at least, he knew that George was definitely "departed", but did anyone at his funeral actually think of him as "dear"?

Thankfully, Neil managed to soldier on until the Committal, but wondered with real trepidation how the congregation would react as the curtains closed in front of the coffin to the accompaniment of the CD hymn track chosen by Joan and Tracey. How he wished he were familiar with the hymn! At least then, he would have some idea of what was coming. He froze as the music started with what was obviously its chorus:

> *Sow His seeds of love,*
> *Sow His seeds of love,*

The love of the Father,
Sow His seeds of love!

Tears of laughter rolled down the cheeks of some members of the congregation. Tracey and Joan stood side by side at the front, holding hands, each wearing an expression more of triumph than grief. Neil caught the eye of Clifford on the organ, who looked as confused as Neil felt, but neither had any idea what was really going on. What was clear was that Neil had been duped into playing a central role in what was almost certainly more an act of vengeance than affection.

To Neil's relief, Clifford faded out the CD early, so that Neil could rattle through the final prayers, dismissal and blessing in record time. All he had to worry about now was the final piece of music which they had asked to be played as the congregation left the chapel. He held his breath as Clifford pushed the button on the CD player...

The congregation practically danced out of the chapel to Hank Williams' "Your Cheating Heart". Standing to one side just outside the exit, Neil couldn't think of a thing to say as several of them shook his hand warmly and said what a wonderful and appropriate send-off George had had, and they couldn't ever remember enjoying a funeral service more! Joan and Tracey had ignored him totally as they led the way out to the Garden of Remembrance, but once Tracey noticed that Neil was finally on his own, she made her way over to him, her brother, Shane, at her side.

"You didn't know him, but I can tell you he deserved that."

Neil shook his head as he looked at her. "Surely everyone deserves to be remembered at their own funeral service with some degree of respect?"

"He didn't. He made my Mum's life hell for years. But his last affair was with that tart across the road who had wheedled her way into the Darts Team. Mum finally saw sense and threw him out – and just in case he couldn't remember the way to his floosie's house, Mum marked the route down the street with all the things that were most dear to him. I wonder what his bit of stuff thought when she saw him arrive having picked up his verruca powder, his box of Dinky cars, his haemorrhoid cream and his carrier bag of dirty magazines on the way!"

"Did he want to leave your mother? Had he planned to leave her for this other woman?"

"Mum was beyond caring. He'd already done exactly what he wanted by getting that bimbo pregnant – or at least, she *said* he had. But then she said a lot of things just to get what she wanted. I don't suppose she planned on him having a heart attack when he was in bed with her on that first night, though, did she? Serves them both right!"

Neil's face was flushed as he replied. "You shouldn't have involved me in this way. That wasn't fair or right – not for me, and certainly not for your father."

Tracey peered at him closely.

"This has really upset you, hasn't it? Well, I'm sorry you were dragged into it, but I can't say we're sorry we did it. You were great. Bye, Reverend."

As she moved off, Neil realized that her brother, Shane, was still at his side. When Shane spoke, his voice was barely above a whisper:

"You know what it's like, Vicar. You're a man. You have urges, just like me – just like my Dad. It's just that my Dad didn't know when to stop, and he talked about it too much to too many people. It always got back to Mum. I've seen her crying so many times over the years. She shouldn't have had to go through that."

As Shane moved even closer, Neil realized that there was real sadness in the young man's face.

"You see, I don't think he meant to hurt her. I think he loved Mum a lot, really. She was his rock, his 'brick' – that's what he called her. And I spoke to him that day she finally threw him out. He was really upset and frightened. I don't think he ever thought she would actually go that far. I don't blame her, of course. You couldn't, could you? But she wasn't always the easiest woman to live with either, and sometimes I felt really sorry for the way Mum and Tracey bossed him about. I think he was a broken man. I think his heart was broken, and that's why he died. And I think he'd cry his eyes out if he knew what happened at his funeral, and that he was remembered this way."

"I'm sure he would. He'd be devastated."

"Anyway, I just wanted you to know. Don't judge my Dad by what happened today."

"I won't."

"Don't judge my Mum and Tracey either."

"I'll try not to. Thank you for explaining, Shane."

The young man looked at Neil for a second or two, then moved off to disappear among other members of the family.

The mourners didn't hang around. Within five minutes, the courtyard where flowers were displayed was eerily silent. Looking down at the blooms, Neil noticed the card on one wreath of white roses.

"Rest in peace, George," it read.

And as Neil was reading, a teardrop of rain fell on to the writing, making the ink run. Surprised, Neil looked up, expecting to see dark clouds.

The sky was clear and blue.

* * *

"A group of us are going bowling on Wednesday night. Do you fancy coming?"

Neil turned to find Wendy beside him as he gathered up music books at the end of the choir rehearsal.

"I'd love to!" he replied with a smile. "I'm not busy that night – well, not unless you'd call preparing my sermon for Sunday a hot date!"

"Oh, if you feel you need to work…" Wendy's expression was cheekily wistful.

"No! I'm hopeless at sermons, as you know…"

"I don't agree with that at all."

"Well, I feel hopeless at them, so actually I spend all week worrying about them – so, a night out would be wonderful. Who else is going?"

"Your friend Graham…"

"Great!"

"And Debs. Just the four of us so far."

"That sounds like good company to me. What time?"

"I've booked a couple of games at eight, and the plan is that we go for a pizza afterwards. That all right with you?"

"Perfect!" agreed Neil. "Would you like me to drive?"

"Thanks for the offer, but don't worry. I'm not much of a drinker. I'm happy to stay teetotal for the night. I'll pick you up about half seven, OK?"

"I'll look forward to it. Thanks, Wendy."

She blushed prettily, then turned away to join Debs, who was packing away the music stands. A discreet thumbs-up from Wendy brought a broad grin across Debs' face. Linking arms with her friend, Wendy pulled her away from any listening ears.

"So…" she started.

"… the big question is, what are you going to wear?" finished Debs.

"Come on, fashion expert, you know my wardrobe as well as I do!"

"Your new black leggings, the shiny ones – and that silky white top of yours. You look good in that."

"Demure and yet saucily sweet?"

Debs grinned. "Exactly. It's perfect."

"And you? What sort of outfit might Graham actually notice you in?"

"Honestly, I don't think Graham would even think about looking in my direction unless I turned up wearing nothing at all!"

Wendy laughed. "Well, that's one idea. I do like you in your turquoise top, though. That really brings out the colour of your eyes."

"Graham just never sees me like that. I'm the girl next door. I have to accept he really doesn't think of me as anything but an irritating kid sister."

"Why is it that men are so thick?"

"Good question!" agreed Debs with a chuckle.

"Never mind," said Wendy, giving her friend a hug. "You'll get your man – and so will I!"

* * *

"Sad news, I'm afraid," said Margaret when Neil met her at the Church Centre the next day. "Lily passed away last night."

"I'm so sorry to hear that! How's Elsie taking it – do we know?"

"Well, it was their great-niece who called me this morning. Apparently, Lily fell asleep in her chair after tea, just as she always does – but when Elsie tried to wake her a bit later because the carer had come to help her into bed, they couldn't rouse her. She'd just drifted away in her sleep. Not a bad way to go, really."

As Neil took this in, he saw again in his mind's eye Lily's face, the calm and steady faith shining from her eyes. He couldn't imagine either of the sisters having the slightest fear of dying. For them, it would be a homecoming, a longed-for meeting with the Lord they had loved and faithfully served all their lives. His only sadness was that Lily hadn't made it to her hundredth birthday after all. And Elsie? He was sad for Elsie. She would be so lonely, left behind.

"I feel for Elsie," said Margaret, echoing his thoughts. "This will hit her hard."

"Will she manage in the flat on her own, do you think?"

"Her great-niece and the rest of their family are already considering that."

"And?"

"And they think she should go into residential care now. She's not as sprightly as she was. Her hips are painful, and she's very unsteady on her pins nowadays."

"But she's always active, isn't she? Just think of all that baking she does, and she's got a good circle of friends."

"Yes, but at the end of the day, she'll be living alone. Suppose she takes a tumble? Suppose she's ill, or feeling low without Lily? That's what the family are worried about."

"Has anyone asked Elsie what *she* would like?"

"Well," she replied, "I've spoken to her about this possibility on several occasions. She knew Lily could go at any time. She's not daft, and she knows her own mind. She most definitely does not want to leave her home. They've been there for years. She wants to die there."

"But if she's not safe? It's easy to see both points of view here."

"Look," said Margaret, "as much as I'd love to, I simply can't manage to get over there this morning, not with the Rural Dean due to arrive at any moment. I'll pop across later this afternoon, of course, but would you mind going straightaway? She's taken quite a shine to you during our visits, so I think she'd be glad to see you."

Fifteen minutes later, as Neil sat holding Elsie's hand on the sisters' comfy old sofa, he realized that she was indeed very pleased to see him. She wasn't alone, with several people pottering round the house, not all of whom Neil recognized. He knew Alison, Elsie's great-niece, from past visits, but the others were less familiar.

"They all feel they need to be here," whispered Elsie so that only he could hear. "They're trying to be kind, of course – and I know they genuinely loved Lily and are shocked by what's happened – but honestly, I could do with a bit of peace at the moment. I'd like the two of us to pray, really. That's what Lily would want."

Neil squeezed her hand in total understanding, before getting up to find Alison busying herself in the kitchen. He explained that Elsie had requested some quiet time for prayer, and knowing how important that would be for her great-aunt, Alison took the point that perhaps it was time for the rest of the family to give Elsie a little privacy, knowing that Neil was there to keep an eye on her.

"I'm going to stay, though," finished Alison. "I want to do some sorting out in Lily's bedroom."

"You're not clearing things out already, are you?"

"Of course not – well, not really. I just thought I would put away some of Lily's personal bits and pieces – the plastic cup she put her teeth in overnight, her glasses and night things – bits and pieces like that."

"I wonder if Elsie might take comfort in things remaining the same for a few days," suggested Neil gently, remembering how important that had felt to him when his own father died. "She hasn't had a chance to say her goodbyes yet. She might like to sit in Lily's room to do that."

There was a sudden hardness in Alison's expression. "I know my aunt very well. Elsie doesn't like clutter. She'll appreciate me taking over the jobs that might upset her. I'll be in Lily's room when you've finished. Come and find me, because we'll need to talk about the funeral."

Recognising that he'd been dismissed, Neil returned to the front room, closing the door behind him as he went to join Elsie on the sofa. Soft, silent tears were shining on her cheeks. He reached out to take her hand, and the two of them sat quietly together, both with their own memories of Lily.

"Alison wants me to go into a home."

"What do you want?"

"Nothing." The old lady turned to look directly into his eyes. "I just want to be left alone. I've been used to doing most of the housework by myself for quite a long time now, so why shouldn't I carry on doing what I've always done? I don't understand why they're making such a fuss."

"They're concerned for you, Elsie. You know they only mean well."

"Do I? Why doesn't it feel that way? I'm not an idiot. Why are they suddenly treating me as if I am?"

"I am sure they mean nothing but the best for you. And you're wise enough to recognize that things become more difficult as you get on in years, especially if there's no one else living with you at all. It's not just what becomes hard physically. It's also the challenge of living on your own, with no one to talk to. I expect Alison and the family are thinking about all those things, because they love you and they don't like the idea of you being distressed or in difficulty on your own."

"Maybe. Maybe not."

Neil gave her hand an extra squeeze. "Let's not think about it now. There'll be time enough for that. Shall we pray for Lily?"

With a smile, Elsie closed her eyes and dropped her head as Neil began to lead them both in prayer.

By the time they'd finished about a quarter of an hour later, it was clear that Elsie was starting to tire. Neil plumped up her cushions and helped her to settle back comfortably. Her eyes fluttered for a while before she fell into a deep sleep. Looking down at her fondly, he tucked a blanket around her before closing the door quietly behind him. He found Alison in Lily's room, sitting on the bed with her nose buried in her aunt's nightgown, her eyes sad and gleaming with tears.

"This smells of her."

Neil sat down on the chair opposite her. "Lily was a wonderful lady. What a life she had!"

"I've never known a day which didn't have Lily and Elsie in it," said Alison. "They'd come back from Africa by the time I was born, so to me they were just the aunts around the corner. I remember so much – how there was always the smell of lavender around them; how they were never too busy to sit down and listen to all my troubles; how Lily grew vegetables that were so delicious, I even *liked* her Brussels sprouts; how their hugs made the world go away; how Elsie's chocolate cake made everything and everyone seem better and kinder somehow."

That brought a smile to Neil's face. "Ah, Elsie's cakes…"

"She's such a wonderful cook…"

"And there's no reason why she can't go on baking cakes as she always has done, is there?"

Alison's eyes were sad as she replied. "I know what you're saying. She belongs here. If I love her, why make her move?"

Neil nodded in agreement, allowing Alison to continue thinking out loud.

"But she needs to move, because she'll be unsafe here on her own. What if something happens? What if she falls? What if she has a stroke or heart attack, and she's alone and frightened?"

"She doesn't come across as frightened at the prospect of being here on her own," said Neil. "Quite the opposite. What seems to scare the daylights out of her is the thought that she will be forced to live in a home that's full of people who won't allow her to be what she is – where she can't nip into the kitchen and bake a cake when she feels like it; where the treasures of her lifetime have to be given away so that her life can be squeezed into one tiny room; where her individuality and freedom are curtailed; where her deep faith may not be valued and allowed for…"

"But that might also be the place where she has lovely meals cooked for her; where she gets to know new friends who are also living there; where we can be certain she'll take her medicine, have a proper balanced diet, and be safe if her health takes a turn for the worse."

"And that's understandably reassuring for you and the family – but what about Elsie? Isn't her peace of mind important in all of this?"

"Of course it is! Of course I want Elsie to be content and settled, especially now her life-long companion has gone.

It's all so difficult. I'm not the wicked witch, even if Elsie is beginning to think I am."

"I know," agreed Neil. "There's no easy answer here. It's a balancing act between what you and the family feel is most sensible, and what Elsie herself wants and needs."

"That's exactly it, and although I'm probably the family member who's closest to Elsie, I can't make this decision on my own. We've decided that when the whole family is gathered together for the funeral, we will talk it through with Elsie and make a considered decision."

"That seems sensible."

"You see, I hear what Elsie is saying, but I can also see that she can't bear the thought of any more change. Coping without Lily's company is change enough, so she wants everything else to stay the same. That's so understandable, but it also means that she's not necessarily the best judge of her practical and medical needs."

Alison wrapped the silky material of Lily's nightdress around her fingers as she spoke.

"Isn't it a bit like someone who's spent years banging their head against a brick wall? It's not until they actually stop doing it that they realize life can be so much easier and more comfortable. Life *could* be very pleasant for Elsie, especially in the place that we've taken her to see. It's run by a Christian organization. They're all really caring, skilled people on the staff. The meals looked OK. The room she could have is very nice – not huge, but how much space does a ninety-six year-old need?"

"Well, you must be exhausted after the day you've had," said Neil. "You could probably do with a bit of TLC at the moment."

"You're probably right. I've done my best to be organized today. There's so much to get done. Maybe the one thing I've not allowed time for is my own grief."

"I'll stay here with Elsie if you'd like to go home for a while."

Alison's smile was grateful. "No need for you to stay. My husband, Phil, is going to be here in a little while. They've always got on well, those two. He makes her laugh. Maybe not today – but she likes his company."

"And Margaret is planning to pop in this afternoon."

"Oh, that's another thing. We need to see her so that we can get our thoughts together about the funeral."

"Well, be gentle with yourself today," said Neil, noticing the shadows of fatigue etched across Alison's face. "Let Margaret just be with Elsie this afternoon, then you can talk to her about other arrangements tomorrow, when you're a little less exhausted."

And as Alison went down to the kitchen to collect her coat and handbag, Neil took one last peep at the sleeping Elsie before quietly letting himself out the front door.

⇒ CHAPTER 10 ⇐

On Wednesday night, Neil was sitting at the head of the bowling alley on which the four of them were playing. He was trying hard to keep his attention on the score screen in front of him, but it was very difficult not to be distracted by Wendy, who was looking particularly fetching that night in her shiny black leggings which shimmered tightly around her long, slender legs. She seemed oblivious to him as she concentrated on sending the bowling ball down the centre of the alley.

He felt a nudge on his left shoulder, and managed to drag himself away from the scene to find Graham laughing beside him.

"She really likes you. Debs told me."

Neil's eyes widened. "She does?"

Graham was still grinning widely as he nodded. "She definitely does – so make your move, if you like her too. Tonight's your chance!"

"What about you? Any luck with the internet dating yet?"

"Well, I'm having some deeply meaningful conversations online with about three women at the moment, but…"

"But?"

"… one of them sounds a bit intense. The other one looks

as if she's about fifty if she's a day, in spite of her putting her age down as under thirty. And the one I like…"

"You like one? Are you going to meet her?"

"That's what she's suggesting."

"So you'll go then, won't you?"

Graham sat down heavily on the seat beside Neil, his expression suddenly vulnerable and uncertain.

"That's the problem, isn't it? She thinks I'm athletic and sporty – and that I'm a bit of an intellectual."

"Why? Why didn't you just tell her about you as you really are?"

"Because, just look at me! Thirty-one years old when she thinks I'm twenty-eight, a flabby fifteen stone when she thinks I'm a muscular god – and I told her I'm a great cook, when actually the highlight of my week is Sunday lunch back home with Mum."

Neil nodded gravely, trying hard not to laugh. "That will teach you not to tell fibs!"

The two men looked up at the sound of skittles being knocked down. Wendy whooped with delight to see that six of them in the middle had been hit, which meant she had to decide which side to aim for to pick up another couple of points on her second bowl.

"I suppose you wouldn't consider coming clean? You're a great bloke, Graham. You just don't believe anyone could be interested in you as you are."

"Based on past experience, women *aren't* interested in me just as I am."

"But it sounds as if she's not been completely truthful either."

Graham's eyes opened wide with horror.

"Well, that would be very unfair!"

Neil laughed out loud. "OK, I give in. You are destined to a life of lonely celibacy."

Graham buried his head in his arms and groaned, just as Debs came up behind him to slap him on the back.

"OK, boys. I know we girls are out-playing you, but there's no need to take it so hard. We'll go easy on you, let you catch up a bit!"

At that moment, Wendy came skipping back to the desk, clapping in delight at her score of eight. In fact, she'd had several scores which were even higher, but every success was greeted as a delightful surprise, complete with jubilant, girly squeals and giggles.

"Your go, Graham."

Neil realized, as he turned to prompt Graham, that he was already up and selecting his bowling ball – but in that split second, Neil caught sight of Debs' face as she watched her childhood friend take up his position at the head of the alley. In her expression, Neil could see affection, indulgence and longing – but so much more too. With a flash of understanding, Neil saw the real situation at last. Debs didn't think of Graham as just "the boy next door". She loved him. Even Neil could see that – Neil, who accepted he was sadly lacking in intuition and experience where women were concerned. If Neil could see the obvious, then why hadn't Graham clocked what was happening under his nose? He was searching for the perfect partner – when there she was, standing right beside him all the time.

Neil glanced up to see that Wendy was watching his expression with interest, as if she could read his thoughts. Gracefully, she slid into the seat beside him.

"The trouble is," she whispered in his ear, "Graham is too thick to realize how much Debs cares about him."

The two of them watched Debs go up and throw her arms around Graham as he scored a strike.

"They look perfect together," agreed Neil. "But if Graham has known her for so long and never made a move, perhaps he will never be interested in her in a different way?"

"Who knows? I get the feeling he'd be grateful for any woman to take him even half seriously."

Neil laughed. "You may be right – but if you have a platonic affection for someone you know really well, can those feelings change to become romantic? Don't ask me! I'm hopeless at things like this."

"What do you mean – hopeless?" Wendy's face was disarmingly near his, and she smelt fresh and flowery and her lips looked soft and very pink.

"Well, I'm not very good at this relationship business."

"Why ever not? You're clever, kind – quite good-looking in an individual sort of way."

"Thanks a lot," mumbled Neil.

"So why wouldn't women be attracted to you?"

"Oh, it's me, I suppose. Perhaps because I'm an only child? I've never had sisters or even cousins to practise on. I'm just not very used to having girls around."

"But you must have had girlfriends?" Wendy's eyes were wide and disbelieving.

"Of course, yes!" Neil looked flustered, before adding, "Well, I was in a crowd at university where there were quite a few girls. I got on all right with them."

"There you are, then! All you need is a bit more confidence – and a woman with patience and experience to draw out your sensual side."

Neil blushed scarlet. "Not a lot of those around," he stammered.

"Oh, I don't know..."

And as if in slow motion, Wendy leaned forward to plant the lightest of kisses on his half-open mouth. Her eyes were open and staring into his as she increased the pressure in a way that sent bolts of pleasure coursing through him. He meant to pull away. He meant to extricate himself so that they could share the joke of the moment together – but from the intensity of her gaze, he realized with surprise that she didn't look as if she was joking. With a small groan, Neil closed his eyes, giving himself up to the warm feeling that was spreading to every part of his willing body.

"Break it up, you two!" interrupted Graham. "You'll get us all thrown out – and I'm just on a winning streak! Come on, partner, we've been gentlemanly enough to let these girls win up to now..."

This was greeted with indignant complaint by the girls.

"... so put that woman down, and show them how it's done!"

Neil's feet did actually move as he stood up to take his place, but his mind was in a complete daze. Wendy had kissed him – and he had kissed her back. They had stepped across the threshold of the positions they held in each other's lives – she a valued volunteer at the church, and he a priest. Where did that leave them now? This changed things in so many ways, most of them completely wonderful. His Mum would be pleased, for a start!

The feeling obviously did him good, because he scored a strike straight away, followed by another. By the end of their time at the bowling alley, Neil and Graham had "allowed" (so they said!) the girls to win the first match, although the men thoroughly thrashed their opponents in their last game. Exhilarated and in good spirits, the four of them tumbled into the pizza restaurant which stood just across the way from the bowling alley. They sat in couples on either side of a long table, with Wendy's knees brushing against Neil's leg throughout the whole meal. As the meal progressed, they all mellowed into the warm, companionable atmosphere, as they chatted and laughed their way through three courses followed by coffee all round. It was getting late when they realized they were the last to leave the restaurant as they headed out to find Wendy's car. Graham threw a friendly arm around Debs' shoulders as they walked, while Neil felt Wendy slip her small hand into his as they walked across the car park.

Debs and Graham got in the back because they were the first to be dropped off, as their houses were practically back to back. Once they were gone, in a flurry of hugs and goodbyes, Neil and Wendy suddenly found themselves alone in the silence of the car. Neil couldn't think of a word to say, although the atmosphere was charged with what remained unspoken. Wendy, on the other hand, seemed completely cool as she skilfully navigated her way across town towards Vicarage Gardens.

"I'd invite you in for a coffee…" Neil began when they were parked.

"That would be nice."

"But that probably wouldn't be a good idea."

"Oh, I don't know."

"But…"

"You're my priest."

"Exactly!"

"And my friend?"

"Of course!"

"Well, my dear Neil, I think you and I are on the verge of becoming extremely good friends."

"You do?"

"I do."

She leaned across the car and, with the lightest of touches, placed her hand on his chest. He watched in fascinated anticipation as she allowed her fingers to walk up his chest until, cupping his face in her hand, she drew him to her so that their lips joined in a deep, satisfying kiss that left him reeling.

"Right then," he finally managed to say as he gathered his jacket up from the back seat. "It's been lovely."

"It certainly has."

"See you, then."

"To be continued…" A soft smile played on her lips. "Good night, Neil."

"Good night, Wendy. Thank you."

And Neil stumbled out of her car and into the house, where he collapsed on to the bottom stair with air whistling through his teeth in a mixture of delight and disbelief.

* * *

The knocking on his front door early the following morning wasn't especially loud, but it was certainly insistent. Thursday was his day off, so it was in bare feet and dressing gown that Neil tumbled sleepily down the stairs to open the door. He was greeted by a cupcake – held out to him by Sam, who was grinning with excitement.

"This is for you! Mummy helped Uncle Harry and me make them for her birthday! She's twenty-seven today."

"Sam! You promised not to tell anyone that. It's not polite to tell people how old a lady is!"

Claire's head appeared around the corner of the front porch to join Sam, who was frowning.

"But you are old, Mummy."

In spite of being half asleep, Neil caught Claire's grimace and they both laughed.

"Happy birthday!" he smiled. "You're a dark horse. You didn't mention that was coming up."

She shrugged. "I'm not really into birthdays, at least not mine – but for Sam, birthdays are a *big* occasion. He loves cakes, so we did some baking together last night. He thought you'd like the one with purple, green *and* yellow icing."

"How right he is," commented Neil, looking uncertainly at the multicoloured blob.

"It tastes all right – honest!"

Neil struggled to keep a straight face as he looked down at Sam to say thank you. It was clear, though, that the small boy still had the earlier conversation about his Mum's very old age on his mind.

"Mummy, were you in the Ark?"

Claire tried to look indignant but had to stifle a chuckle as she answered, "No, Sam, I wasn't."

"Oh." Sam looked puzzled. "Why didn't you drown, then?"

The two grown-ups roared with laughter while a perplexed Sam looked on. Neil stretched out to ruffle the boy's hair.

"I see you were listening when Grandad brought you to Sunday School then, when I was telling you about Noah."

"Come on, Sam, you'll be late for school unless we get a move on. Sorry we got you up so early, Neil. I should have remembered this is your day off."

"No problem. I ought to be surfacing anyway. What are you doing to celebrate your birthday tonight, by the way?"

"Eating cupcakes, lots of them."

"Come to tea! Come to tea!" squealed Sam.

"Neil's probably busy," interjected Claire. "And it's his day off."

"I'll show you the beans I'm growing in a jar in the kitchen. They're *huge!*"

"Beans, eh? Now you're talking!"

"We can eat them!"

"When the plants are a bit bigger and they've had a chance to grow in the garden, yes, we can." Claire put her hand on her son's shoulder so that she could guide him away from the door and off to school.

"You're welcome, if you'd like to come."

"I'd love to."

"But you're busy… Please don't feel you have to."

"What time?"

"About five? Will that be OK?"

"I promise to be completely awake by then."

Claire's face softened into a warm smile. "Thank you. Sam will love it if you come."

"Bye then, birthday girl. See you later." And Neil waited at the door until Sam got so far down the road that he had to stop looking backwards to wave to Neil, and start watching where he was going.

Coffee. That's what Neil needed. Coffee to clear his head and sort out his muddled thoughts. He switched on the kettle, then sat down abruptly as he remembered that last kiss he'd shared with Wendy. Leaning forward, he folded his arms on the kitchen table so that he could lay down his aching head. The problem was, what to do next? How ethical was it for a young man of the cloth to get involved with a member of his flock? More importantly, how did he feel about the possibility of being in a relationship with Wendy? He recognized that, whatever happened, he must be up front and honest about his feelings. He couldn't be seen to be playing with her affections. Then again, was she playing with his? How serious was she about him? Was this just a bit of fun for her?

His mother thought Wendy was wonderful, and for once Neil had to agree with her. Wendy was bright, beautiful and charming, an asset on the arm of any man. So, was she "the One"? And was he ready to find that "someone special" right now? He looked round at his house, which was neat as a pin with everything in its place. He was definitely a bit set in his ways, he knew that. He also recognized that a woman's touch, both on his home and on him, might do a great deal of good.

He sighed. Relationships had never come easy to him. Was that because he was an only child, as he had explained to Wendy the evening before? Was it because his parents' marriage had always seemed functional and unemotional to him, to the degree that he had begun to doubt whether close relationships could ever really work without one or the other partner feeling they were compromised? Was he capable of promising himself to one person for the whole of his lifetime? How daunting a prospect was that!

Oh, for heaven's sake, he thought suddenly, how could he possibly be thinking about promising himself to one person for life when all Wendy and he had shared until now was a kiss? How much could that mean – even if one of the friends was a minister? And, who knows, perhaps Wendy too might be thinking better of their liaison in the cold light of morning?

Before he knew it, his questions gradually became prayers, as he opened his heart to share the challenges and blessings of his life with the Lord. And as he prayed, his head still on his arms on the kitchen table, he must have nodded off again, because that was where he woke up, stiff-necked and uncomfortable, two hours later.

* * *

It was just a few minutes past five when Neil's knock resulted in Claire's door being yanked open by a very excited Sam.

"She's in the kitchen!" Sam caught sight of the bag Neil was carrying. "Have you brought presents? Mum, Neil's brought presents!"

"You didn't need to do that," smiled Claire, as she came through with a smudge of something that could have been butter amongst the freckles which were dotted across the bridge of her nose. "I told you I don't make much of birthdays."

Neil looked down at Sam who was bouncing at his side, trying to take the carrier bag from him.

"He does, though! Actually, I have to own up and say I'm not very good at this present business, so if you think this is really inappropriate, please say so. I won't be offended!"

"I'm just thrilled that you thought to do anything," grinned Claire.

"Right, Sam, I need your help!" instructed Neil. "Mummy, would you please go back in the kitchen, and then Sam will tell you when you can come into the front room."

Sam was beside himself with excitement as the two of them went through to the lounge, making sure the door was securely shut behind them. Out of the carrier bag, Neil pulled a pot of Ben and Jerry's ice cream.

"That's her favourite! How did you know that's her favourite?"

"I know she likes ice cream. I just hoped she likes *chocolate* ice cream."

"I do!"

"Well, that's all right, then! I know you and Mum have been baking, so there was no point me bringing a cake – but we've got to have something to put candles in, haven't we?"

Sam clapped his hands with glee as Neil opened the box of candles and holders before inviting the small boy to push several of them into the lid of the ice cream tub in a haphazard pattern. Carefully, Neil lit them all, then Sam yelled at the top of his voice that Mummy could come in.

Claire's face was a picture as she laughed with delight to see her ice cream birthday "cake". Neil wished he'd thought to bring a camera to capture forever her expression of pure happiness as she blew out the candles. There was something about the combination of strength and vulnerability in her that touched him deeply. They may have got off to a sticky start, but Neil realized, as he looked at this lovely young woman with her spiky hair and freckled nose, that her friendship had come to mean a lot to him.

"What else have you got in the bag?" Sam demanded to know.

"Well," said Neil, "I thought you might not have had time to make red jelly – and you can't have a birthday without red jelly, can you?" He drew out a covered plastic bowl of jelly which he had plainly picked up at the supermarket, along with another containing a gooey butterscotch mousse.

"Yum!" said Claire. "You certainly know how to treat a girl!"

"And there's this," Neil continued, "but I'm hopeless at wrapping, so I'm sorry it's still in the plastic bag."

Claire peered into the bag, then pulled out a small, pink book, its cover an explosion of the most gorgeous-looking cupcakes.

"You know how to make cupcakes, of course – but this is full of ideas of the different sorts you can conjure up." Neil hesitated. "I hope you like it. I wasn't quite sure…"

Claire's hazel eyes sparkled with delight as she stepped forward to give Neil a hug.

"I love it," she said simply, and she stayed where she was in Neil's arms for several seconds before, with slight embarrassment, she pulled away.

"And," Neil went on, looking down at Sam, "I thought that even though it's Mummy's birthday, you might need an *un*-birthday present."

Sam caught on quickly that this might mean something nice was about to come his way and, full of curiosity, he stood on tiptoes to try to peer into the bag. Neil pulled out a brightly coloured box.

"You like looking after animals, is that right?"

Sam nodded enthusiastically.

"Well, in this box, there are some friends for you to look after. It's a Sea Zoo. Do you know what that is?"

Sam plainly had no idea.

"Well, we have to fill the little aquarium with water, and put the right chemicals in it. And then, in here is a packet of eggs…"

"Are we growing chickens?"

"No," Neil laughed. "These will be tiny little shrimps. Do you know what they are? Look, there's a picture on the side of the box."

Sam studied the illustration with interest.

"How many will there be?"

"I'm not sure. Quite a few, I expect. It depends how well you look after them. You'll have to look very carefully for when they hatch, and count them every day."

Across Sam's head, Claire smiled at him as she silently mouthed, "Thank you."

"Well," she said to Sam, "why don't you and Neil go and

set the Zoo up on the window-sill in your room, and I'll get tea organized."

It was a long time since Neil had enjoyed a meal so much. There were triangular sandwiches filled with old favourites like chocolate spread, sardine-and-tomato paste, cream cheese and Marmite. There were iced gems, cheese straws and sausages on sticks. And, of course, the red jelly, butterscotch mousse and Ben and Jerry's ice cream topped the whole thing off nicely. An hour and a half later, the washing up done, Claire, Harry and Neil sank into the lounge chairs swearing that they'd never eat again!

"Are you as busy as ever in the garden, Harry?" asked Neil. "What does a gardener do at this time of year?"

"Grow vegetables, mainly. The Brussels just need a touch of frost and they'll be great for Christmas. Most of the other vegetable beds have been cleared now, but I have a good stock of onions, carrots and potatoes stored away in the shed."

"And you, Claire? Are everybody else's gardens keeping you busy enough?"

"It's mainly tidying up beds and pruning right now. It's sad to see the last of the summer flowers, but I love all the berries on the trees at this time of year."

"It's a hard job. Don't you ever get tired of it?"

"Tired of nature and how it changes all the time? Bored of the seasons, with their glorious colours and smells? Fed up with the sense of triumph I feel when I plant a small seed that eventually becomes a golden chrysanth or a loaded tomato plant? I could never tire of that – ever!"

Neil smiled. "You sound almost like a Christian talking about creation."

She crinkled her nose to pull a face. "I wouldn't put it in those terms, naturally…"

"Of course not."

"... but I can appreciate what they feel."

"But don't you ever look at the detail on a flower or leaf, or marvel at the rhythm of the seasons and the colours they bring – and wonder how it all got there?"

"Science. Evolution."

"But what created science and evolution? Surely such perfection couldn't have come from nothing? There has to be a power behind it all..."

"Can't see it, myself."

"And I can't look at all of that and see anything but the hand of God."

"There's no such thing. That's just a human need to romanticize what, years ago, they simply couldn't explain any other way."

"And you can only believe what you can see and touch and prove? Is that it?"

"Exactly. The answer lies in the natural evolution of science and nature. That's a proven fact."

"I remember," interrupted Harry, "someone explaining it to me like this. Imagine you are driving a car on a dark night. You have your headlights on, so that you can see everything you need to know in the arc of light ahead of you. You see people and houses and life along the road. But if you can only believe what you can see and prove, what about everything that lies in the darkness alongside and behind the car? Are you saying that because you can't see it, there is nothing there? Doesn't your instinct tell you that there's all sorts of life going on out there in the darkness, whether or not you can see and prove it? That's how faith is for me. I instinctively know that God is there. At the darkest times, when I am at my lowest ebb or my most doubtful, God is still there – beyond my vision, but alongside me, carrying me, caring for me."

Neil nodded in agreement, whilst Claire quietly thought through Harry's argument. Suddenly she smiled.

"My, we've got very deep. Anyone need a cup of tea? Then I really should think about getting Sam to bed. He'll probably be up half the night with his torch, looking for shrimps!"

* * *

Following the gathering for Lily's funeral, her family spent several hours of conversation and soul-searching as they considered the best options for Elsie, now she was on her own following the death of her beloved sister. As a result, it was during the first week of December, just six weeks after Lily's death, that the family gathered again to oversee what they hoped was the sensible decision to move her into Dale Court, an imposing Victorian house in its own grounds which had been extended to provide individual *en suite* rooms for thirty elderly residents. Elsie didn't want to go, but when one family member after another, along with a dizzying collection of doctors, social workers and well-meaning friends, came to the flat to make her see the error of her ways, she finally gave in. Neil, who visited her every other day if he could, often with Margaret, but equally often on his own – not because he had to, but because he really wanted to – watched sadly as the grand old lady's home was packed up around her, with a small pile of boxes labelled to accompany her to her new address, and a roomful of other bits and pieces which were gradually distributed between family members, or destined for the charity shop.

In fact, her new room may not have been the largest at Dale Court, but it had one of the nicest views of the rockery and the imposing chestnut trees that lined the side of the house. Every time after that when Neil visited, he would find Elsie sitting forlornly in a high-backed hi-tech armchair which could be electrically extended in ways which didn't hold any interest for her at all. She sat looking out of the window, not really seeing, locked in her own thoughts and memories. It was as if the life had been sucked out of her. The staff marvelled at how healthy and able she was, especially at the wonderful age of ninety-six, but her physical health was irrelevant to her now. She had nothing to get out of bed for, except to sit in the chair and stare out towards the light beyond the window. She showed little enthusiasm for food. She smiled when visitors came, but played no part in their conversation, so that several who'd visited when she first arrived found excuses not to come again. It was as if, for many people, she had been put safely on the shelf – out of sight, and mostly out of mind. Neil found himself moved to tears every time he saw her.

He soon realized that the only speaking which drew her interest was prayer. Sometimes he would take the Eucharist set with him so that they could break bread and share wine together. Sometimes, they would just sit side by side, each of them occasionally saying something out loud which would be followed by prayerful silence. For Neil, it was an intensely spiritual experience, humbled as he was by the achievements of Elsie and Lily during their long lives devoted to the God they loved. He hoped to be able to show the same devotion throughout his own life. Instinctively Elsie knew that, as she often included a prayer for his ministry in their worship together.

Mostly they were not alone in their devotions. Margaret joined them when she could, and occasionally Val, the palliative care nurse who had known Elsie and Lily through the church for many years, would be with them too, or would pop in at a time later in the day which suited her better. There were occasions when Neil found himself silently praying for Val during his times at Dale Court – for Val and Peter Fellowes, who had found contentment in the company of each other, even though Peter was not a free man, and never could be.

He prayed for his other parishioners too – for the elderly and disabled people whose homes he visited with the Eucharist; for the young mum at the playgroup whose husband was so tragically ill; for the choir and the servers; for the organist and musicians; for the elderly regulars and the young families; for Frank, who worked tirelessly behind the scenes to support Margaret in her role of spiritual leader in the community; for Harry, who missed his wife so much; for Sam, who didn't know his father; and for Claire – brave, capable Claire who faced everything life brought her way by rolling up her sleeves and dealing with it. He prayed for his mother, although he seriously doubted that her soul could ever quite be redeemed – and he prayed for Wendy.

In the weeks that had followed the bowling night, he still felt very muddled. Wendy was much more open about her feelings, often appearing beside him, slipping her hand into his or putting her arm around his waist. His natural shyness made him want to be more reserved when they were in the company of others, but Wendy seemed proud and delighted to be seen at his side. He noticed how the word "we" crept into her vocabulary whenever he was around – and he thought he probably liked that, almost as much as he liked the times they were alone, when the prim music teacher and church group leader transformed into a teasing minx who left his emotions and reactions in turmoil. Not that anything inappropriate had happened between them. The main reason for that, of course, was the faith they shared that required them to wait until marriage before there could be any intimacy between them. His instinct was that he felt stronger about that than Wendy did, because she seemed to enjoy tempting him to waver on his resolve. But Neil also recognized that within himself, he was just not certain enough about what Wendy meant to him, and what he wanted to mean to her. It was all happening so fast, especially as he sensed that some of the congregation were beginning to think of them as a couple – and without a doubt they were, in Wendy's mind at least.

But how did he feel? Was he falling in love with her? That was the important question, of course, because if he wasn't, then he was wrong to let the relationship continue on the course it was inevitably taking. He was allowing her to make assumptions about her role in his life. She was making plans about places they might visit together, friends they could spend time with, holidays they might both enjoy. He felt as if he'd climbed on to one of those moving walkways that helped you travel with your luggage at airports. It seemed to stretch out ahead of him with no easy exit in sight. Was he looking for a way out? Was that what he really wanted?

So the daily quiet time he spent with Elsie became a welcome oasis when he could think, pray and enjoy the company of the elderly lady of whom he was becoming increasingly fond.

His thoughts were broken by the arrival of one of the nursing staff carrying a tray for Elsie. He winced as he listened to the patronizing tone of the conversation that followed.

"Come on, Elsie, it's time for your tea, sweetheart. Let's get you out of that chair now, and over to the table. Come on, darling, it's your favourite – macaroni cheese. You like macaroni cheese, don't you?"

Neil's heart bled for Elsie, the proud and cultured woman who had achieved so much in her life, whose circumstances had been reduced to being spoken to as if she were a naughty five-year-old. He immediately got up and told the nurse he would make sure Elsie got her tea – but he knew that although he was here to save Elsie's dignity today, tomorrow and every day after that, she would be petted and patronized again. He would have a word with the matron on his way out – but would it really make any difference? Elsie was certainly not mistreated – quite the opposite, in that her every need seemed to be catered for. It was the just the loss of her independence that he mourned for on her behalf.

He went over to speak to Elsie and was appalled to see her cheeks were damp with tears. Reaching out, he put his arms around her and held her close to him. Her frail body trembled and he knew she was crying. She said nothing, but then, words weren't needed. He understood her utter despair that a life of purpose and fulfilment should peter out this way. All the nurses saw was an old lady who needed to be looked after. They didn't know what she was, what she always had been, the person within. They were too busy serving tea and changing sheets. They were doing what they were paid to do, nothing less and certainly nothing more.

He stayed with her for as long as he could, then when he could see she was tiring, he took his leave. Deep in thought as he walked down the corridor away from her room, he almost didn't hear the call from one of the rooms.

"Hello, Vicar! Have you heard my news?"

Neil stopped, then back-tracked to put his head around the door of what had probably been the master bedroom in years gone by. It was one of only a couple of rooms which were for double occupancy, suitable for a married couple or, in this case, for Milly and Hetty, two sisters in their late eighties who, from the little Neil knew of them, seemed to have a bit of a love/hate relationship. It was the younger sister, Milly, who hailed him. Hetty was nowhere to be seen.

"I haven't, Milly. What news is that?"

"About my win!"

"What did you win?"

"It was in the paper, something about a new local radio station starting or something. Apparently they've managed to get themselves one of those digital licences and they had a competition in the paper to celebrate. I didn't have to do much, just filled in my name and address on the coupon. I got that nurse, Jessie, to post it off for me – and blow me down if I didn't win!"

"What was the prize?"

"Well, that's the best thing. It's a radio – one of those new-fangled things with buttons that you push to get the stations. It's marvellous!"

"That's great, Milly. Hetty must be pleased too. You both enjoy listening to the radio, don't you?"

"Well, I love it, but I've never had my own radio before. The old one on the shelf that we've always listened to belongs to Hetty. It came from her house when we both moved here. The only thing is that she's never let me to listen to it unless she's in the room, so sometimes I've missed the programmes I especially like."

"So you won't have that problem now, then?"

Milly beckoned to him to come closer.

"Actually," she whispered as he knelt down to her level, "it's very sad, really. Just after the new radio arrived, one of Hetty's books tumbled off the shelf and knocked her radio on to the floor too. It looked all right, but she can't get any sound out of it at all now. She'd had it for years, you know. She cried. Can you believe that? She was so upset, it broke her heart.

She said how wonderful it was that the new radio had arrived just at the right time."

"It certainly was," said Neil.

"Yes," agreed Milly, "because it meant that I was able to say to her, 'Push off and get your own!'"

And throwing her head back, Milly opened her mouth, which seemed to have more gums than teeth, and cackled with laughter.

CHAPTER 11

O ccasionally, when there were too many people and too much going on in the Church Centre, Neil took himself and his computer off to hide. That Saturday morning, with Christmas looming and so many special services to plan, he did exactly that – which meant that he was sitting at the ancient table in the vestry, engrossed in sorting out hymn-sheets and prayers for the local junior school carol service planned for first thing Monday morning, when his train of thought was broken by voices which became louder as the people involved apparently walked down the aisle towards the front of the church. It didn't take long to identify that the insistent tirade came from Glenda Fellowes, whilst the much quieter responses could be deciphered as the voice of her husband Peter.

"That's not fair! I didn't do anything!"

"That's the trouble, though, isn't it Peter? You don't *ever* do anything!"

"How would you know what I do? You spend all the time you can down at that job in London! You're rarely here!"

"May I remind you, Peter, *that* job in London pays the bills? If we had to rely on what you bring in nowadays, we'd be out on the street!"

"Don't be ridiculous! We've got a perfectly good home that's all bought and paid for. The kids have grown up and left. My pension pot is very decent, and I made a tidy sum when I sold the estate agency. We're very comfortable – and at our age, how much more could we possibly need beyond all that?"

"Need? Need!" Glenda spat the word out. "I need a partner who recognizes the value of my position in life! I need a husband who appreciates how exhausting and difficult every day is for me! I need someone who is proud that I am at the top of my career – and still rising! I need someone who encourages and supports me and doesn't drag me down with boring trivialities all the time! If the washing machine is broken, don't bother me with it – get a new one! You do the washing anyway…"

"I wouldn't dream of making such a major purchase without consulting my wife!"

"Well, this wife isn't interested in washing machines or carpet cleaning or the comparative costs of electricity and petrol prices. I haven't got *time* for things like that. I'm *busy*, don't you understand, you very stupid man? I have a *life*! You've given up on your career. I didn't agree with you selling the estate agency, but you sold out anyway – so *live with it*! Stop whingeing, stop bothering me with irrelevant details – and get on with it!"

There was the sound of angry footsteps stomping down the aisle before the church door was opened and left to close with a shudder.

Neil sat glued to his chair, uncertain whether to sit tight or to make his presence known. In the end, a decision wasn't needed because a minute or so later, the vestry door opened and Peter walked in. He was plainly shocked and embarrassed to find that their conversation had been overheard. He pulled out a chair and sat down heavily.

"I'm sorry. You shouldn't have had to listen to that, especially not in the church…"

"It's OK. In some ways, I'm glad I did. I didn't realize you were under so much pressure."

"Am I? Glenda always makes me feel as if I do nothing at all. I'm worthless, capable of nothing."

"You are one of the most efficient and capable people I've ever met. This place would never run so well if it weren't for you."

"Nothing I do here matters to Glenda."

"But it matters to you, Peter, and it matters to everyone who worships here. You must never doubt the value of the contribution you make."

Peter sighed. "I doubt everything. I doubt my worth. I doubt my ability. I doubt my judgment. And I doubt my marriage…"

"How long have you and Glenda been together?"

"We should be celebrating our thirtieth anniversary next year."

"Well, that's a wonderful achievement!"

Peter almost smiled, but there was no warmth in his eyes. "Isn't it! Quite an achievement, bearing in mind the fact that my wife can't stand me!"

"And how do you feel about her?"

"How do I feel about Glenda?" Peter leaned back in his chair to consider the answer. "I suppose I must still love her, because we've lived together for so many years that it must have taken love for me to have stayed with her all that time. But I'm not sure what sort of love that is now. Shouldn't love be based on sharing, mutual respect, support, understanding, caring and, most of all, friendship? If I'm honest, Neil, I'm not sure that our relationship now has any of those qualities. We're not friends. We're not involved or interested in each other's lives. We have so little in common."

"You're parents. You share your children."

"But they've long gone. One's down in Brighton, the other's in Scotland! We don't see much of them, and I'm really rather pleased to know that they're doing well enough not to need us these days."

"What about marriage counselling? Perhaps it would be good for the two of you to go and talk things through with someone?"

"You need to want the marriage to work for that."

"And you don't?"

"I'm not sure."

"And Glenda? What do you think she wants?"

"I haven't really understood what Glenda wants for years – apart from her job and status and admiration from everyone she meets."

"Peter, I'm so sorry. It's awful to see how unhappy you are."

Peter's head dropped, and Neil felt slightly out of his depth as he suspected the older man was crying. Respectfully, Neil sat in silence, uncertain how to continue. Eventually, it was Peter who spoke.

"It could all be so different…"

"With Glenda?"

"No." Peter looked up and into Neil's eyes. "Not with Glenda. With someone else…"

Neil nodded slowly. There was no need to mention Val's name. They both knew who Peter was talking about.

Peter's shoulders slumped. "That's no answer, though. I could never break my vows in that way."

"Have you seriously considered it?"

"Honestly, I think about little else, but there's no point in it. It can't happen. Val and I accept that."

"Does Glenda know how you feel?"

"That would involve her being interested enough to care. No, I don't think she has any idea at all. As far as she's concerned, my life begins and ends with her."

They both sat for a while, considering the hopelessness of the situation.

"I'm not sure how much good it would do, but would you like me to have a quiet word with Glenda?"

Peter smiled grimly. "Thanks, Neil, but there's no such thing as a 'quiet word' where Glenda's concerned. Besides, she'd eat you for breakfast!"

Gulping at the thought, Neil nodded in grateful agreement.

"And she'd be appalled that I had dragged someone else into our problems."

"But that's why I'm here, to be alongside people when they've got problems on their minds. I know I'm new to this – and I can't help but agree with you that Glenda would make mincemeat of me – but have you considered talking things through with Margaret? She's so much more experienced than me."

"Oh, Margaret knows our situation well enough. Val and I have both talked to her quite openly about how we feel. As a wife herself and as our friend, she is sympathetic about our situation – but of course, as our minister, she is committed to support the Christian marriage that Glenda and I both promised to undertake."

Neil nodded with understanding.

"You must think very badly of me," continued Peter.

"Not at all," was Neil's quick reply.

"But don't you find it unforgivable that I, who profess to be a Christian, should have deep feelings for a woman who is not my wife?"

"You're a human being. Humans are fallible. God knows that."

"Every time I hear about sins and sinners in our services, I feel as if it's directed straight at me. I *am* a sinner..."

"But that's the heart of our faith, isn't it, that Christ died for our sins? And as far as I can tell, you haven't actually done anything wrong. You have drawn back from an improper relationship with Val, and you are committed to your marriage. And from what I understand, you have no intention of breaking that commitment, have you?"

Peter's shoulders visibly slumped. "No, I can't do that. Glenda and I are bound together 'until death do us part'. But I have to say, Neil, that I feel overwhelmed with guilt every time I think about how much I'd like to break my wedding vows and choose another life."

"Thoughts aren't actions, Peter. God knows that."

"So thoughts they will have to stay," replied Peter, pushing back his chair to stand up. "I need to sort out those extra chairs for the Women's Institute service this afternoon."

"I'll come and help you. I could do with a bit of exercise!" grinned Neil, and together the two men headed towards the back corner of the church where the spare seats were stacked.

* * *

With just a week and a half to go until Christmas Day, Neil looked around the faces in the church hall as the playgroup nativity play was about to start. Mums, dads, grandparents –

for all of them, this was the highlight of the year, an occasion they would remember forever, even when their children had grown and flown. Many of the faces he now recognized, and several members of the gathering audience had come up to say hello as they arrived. He had been in the hall for a couple of hours helping Barbara and the other playgroup leaders to lay out the chairs and set up the stage, and now the same teachers were leading in a crocodile of children, all of them looking delightfully homely with tea towels on their heads as men of Bethlehem, carrying fluffy toy sheep to show they were shepherds, or wearing wings and a tinsel halo if they were angels. The twins, Jake and Nathan, were looking splendid in crowns and cloaks, each carrying an interesting-looking "precious gift" wrapped in silver foil. Neil looked around for their mother, Linda, thinking that he hadn't had much chance to talk to her in recent weeks, and wondering how she was getting on with her husband, John, as his illness developed. After scanning the hall, he suddenly spotted them just along the row from him, and although their attention was fixed on their sons at that moment, he could see that they were sitting with their hands entwined.

Neil smiled to himself. After all the soul-searching and turmoil they had been through, it seemed that Linda had found it in her heart after all to work around, if not actually forgive, John's affair, and be with him as he battled with cancer. When Neil had last spoken to Linda, she had said that John seemed to be responding to chemotherapy – but at that time, it was very early days not just for his treatment, but also for their badly shaken relationship. John looked pale and thinner than Neil remembered him. There was no denying the battle he was facing. Neil closed his eyes for a moment to offer up a small prayer of thanks, and to ask for further blessing on the family. He had no doubt that prayers had helped so far, and with all they still had to face, Linda and John needed God's blessing more than ever.

Frank slipped into the seat beside him, and they both watched as Margaret joined Barbara to make last-minute adjustments.

"I never tire of watching this," said Frank quietly. "It reminds me of when Margaret and I sat in a hall like this watching our own children when they were small. Where did the years go?"

Neil smiled. "It will be such a special memory for all the parents here right now."

"I expect you'll be one of them some day."

"Be a dad, you mean? I think I've got a while to go yet!"

"Hasn't Wendy got you organized, then? I thought it was only a matter of formality before you two named the day!"

Neil blushed bright red at the thought that he was being discussed that way.

"Heavens, is that what everyone thinks?"

"More important than that, what do you and Wendy think?"

"I can only speak for myself, I suppose," said Neil slowly, "but honestly, I don't feel ready for marriage and children yet. I'm still getting to grips with the whole idea of being in a relationship with Wendy. It still feels a bit new to me."

"That's fair enough. You are twenty-six now though, aren't you? When do you think you might feel ready to settle down?"

"Good question," grinned Neil. "I don't think it's got much to do with how old I am. I just don't feel that I've had enough experience or know enough about myself to risk someone else's happiness and welfare right now."

"Oh," was Frank's cryptic reply. "Does Wendy know that?"

"We've never discussed marriage – and I'm far too scared to bring the subject up, so I've no idea what she thinks."

"But are you being completely honest when you say you have no idea of her intentions towards you?"

Neil thought for a moment, then turned to look at Frank as he answered. "I've not really allowed myself to think about her vision of the future, because I'm not ready to think about it myself. But you could be right. For all I know, in her own mind she may have our wedding completely planned by now."

"And your reaction to that is...?"

"Sheer panic!"

Frank laughed, but quite quickly became serious as he spoke. "Well, that's understandable, but don't allow yourself to be carried along with someone else's idea of your future unless you are completely sure that what they want is what you truly want too. You are a long time married. You need to be absolutely certain that the partner you choose to spend your life with is completely comfortable and right for you. A wrong choice will ruin your chance of fulfilment, contentment and peace of mind. Choose wisely."

"As you did with Margaret?"

"As I most certainly did. I was drawn to her from the first moment I saw her. Why? Well, there's a good question. It wasn't her looks because, even then, I felt her true beauty was much more than skin deep. It definitely wasn't her sense of style, because she would have laughed out loud if I had even suggested she had one! It wasn't just that sense of humour either, even though we were always able to laugh together. If I had to put my finger on it, I think it was her inherent instinct for just the right way to deal with people and situations which drew me to her, rather than anything to do with her academic achievements – although they were impressive too. I suppose it might have been rather appealing and very helpful if she'd been comfortably off for money, but in fact we were both rather glad that we shared the experience of coming from very modest backgrounds. All I can say is that she stood out as a shining star compelling me to be alongside her warmth and goodness."

"Heavens!" breathed Neil. "You old romantic, you!"

"Yes, I suppose I am," smiled Frank. "I love her to bits. Just look at her now! I'm so proud of her."

They both watched as Margaret climbed on to the stage and started to introduce the nativity play. Neil barely listened to what she was saying. His thoughts were still swirling around what Frank had said about the depth and quality of love he plainly felt for his wife. Did Neil feel that way about Wendy? The two of them had never uttered the "love" word, but he now wondered if that was because he was afraid to give his feelings a name. He knew that the spell he seemed to fall under whenever they were together was heady and intoxicating – but was that love, the kind of love with depth and meaning that Frank described? And what about Wendy? How did she truly feel? Did she think of him with a love that was deep and abiding? Was she expecting him to present her with a ring? Is that what everyone was thinking? Why had that notion not really occurred to him until Frank mentioned it? Why did he feel so unprepared for all this?

His attention was suddenly claimed by the miniature Joseph and Mary making their way across the stage towards a makeshift inn door. Sitting behind the door was a rather grumpy-looking four-year-old.

"Joseph took his wife Mary to Bethlehem because everyone had to be counted," read Barbara. "Joseph was very worried because Mary was about to have a baby – so they found the local inn and knocked on the door."

Neil felt his heart burst with unexpected pride, knowing that "Joseph" was Claire's son, Sam. As he crossed the stage, he grinned broadly at the audience, and when the couple finally reached the inn door, he knocked so hard, the flimsy door-frame nearly collapsed. The innkeeper didn't move, so Joseph knocked again.

"The innkeeper opened the door to speak to Joseph," prompted Barbara – but the innkeeper plainly had no intention of doing any such thing.

Barbara tried again.

"The innkeeper opened the door and told Joseph there was no room in the inn – but because Mary was so tired and about to have a baby, they could sleep in the stable instead."

"No!" shouted the innkeeper, rubbing his eyes furiously. He was definitely not budging from his seat behind the door.

"Come on, Darren," encouraged Barbara. "Show them where they can sleep in the stable."

"No!" shouted the innkeeper, even louder this time.

This was all too much for Joseph, who knew exactly how the story should go.

"Darren," he said patiently, "we have *got* to stay here."

"Oh no you haven't!" wailed the innkeeper. "I wanted to be Joseph!"

The hall erupted with laughter. Barbara was instantly on the stage, leading the sobbing innkeeper off to find his mummy – whilst Sam, his arm still protectively around Mary's shoulder, pushed open the precariously swaying door and led her round the stage to the stable scene with a swagger of triumph. From the cardboard box cunningly disguised as a manger, Mary picked up the Baby Jesus doll who was "swaddled" in what looked like a cotton nappy from head to foot, except for the mass of blond curls which escaped to frame his face.

The audience was completely hooked, consumed with every delightful moment, their eyes shining, perhaps from emotion but also from laughter, as the play continued in the best tradition of nursery school nativities. One shepherd forgot his sheep, and called out to his mum to get it for him. The youngest angel yawned all through the first verse of "Away in a Manger", then curled up in a ball, stuck her thumb in her mouth and promptly fell asleep before the carol was over. By the time they got to the last chorus of "We Wish You a Merry Christmas", there wasn't a dry eye in the place – and that included Neil, who burst into cheering applause along with every proud parent and relative there.

It was some time later, as he was stacking up the chairs and putting away the staging, that Claire came over to say goodbye with an obviously exhausted but still excited Sam in her arms.

"You were great, Sam!" said Neil. "The way you sorted out that innkeeper was brilliant!"

"He's taller than me, that's why he thought he should be Joseph," explained Sam seriously, "but I was four before him *and* I've got a bigger voice."

"You certainly have, young fella," said Harry as he came up to join them. "Time to go home, I think."

"You're coming to tea!" said Sam, pointing at Neil.

"Am I?"

"Would you like to? On Christmas Eve?" asked Claire. "Obviously you'll be with Wendy on Christmas Day, but we wondered if you might appreciate a nice meal early on Christmas Eve to keep you going between the Crib Service and Midnight Mass?"

"That's really thoughtful of you. I'd love to, yes!"

For a moment, Neil and Claire stood smiling at each other – then Harry broke the mood by saying goodbye and leading his family towards the door. Neil watched them until the door closed behind them.

***

Neil felt as if his feet rarely touched the ground in those packed days leading up to Christmas. It wasn't only all the special carol services for schools, clubs and other organizations throughout the town. There were also the extra visits he and Margaret divided up between them, so that they could make sure they took Christian fellowship and practical help to the young, old, harassed, nominal, enthusiastic or fallen-away Christians across the area.

By Christmas Eve afternoon, with the Crib Service due to start at four, Neil decided he just had time to nip in and see Elsie in Dale Court Residential Home. He brought her a small plate of mince pies and a slice of Christmas cake made by Beryl, leading light of the cake rota group at St Stephen's and Dunbridge WI Baking Champion, whose reputation for excellent baking was renowned. He'd also made a mammoth effort to wrap in Christmassy paper his own little gift of a book of Celtic prayers written by David Adam who, for many years, was based at the Holy Island of Lindisfarne off the north-east coast of England. Elsie had often spoken of her love for the simplicity and directness of David's prayers, so Neil knew this new collection would be something she could lose herself in whenever her new home surroundings became too much for her.

He found Elsie's mood calm and settled that afternoon, which bore quite a contrast to the quiet despair he'd seen in her so often since her arrival at Dale Court. She greeted him warmly, ringing the bell to organize a cup of tea for them both. As he'd popped in a few times in recent weeks, he'd already brought her many tales of the manic run-up to Christmas which she loved to hear. Today she nudged him into re-telling her favourites, especially the delights of the playgroup nativity play, which had her giggling like a schoolgirl. She listened in rapt interest as he brought her news of the preparations for that afternoon's Crib Service, when the church would be full to brimming, just as it would be for the Midnight Mass, when those able to keep their eyes open would sing carols and worship together as they welcomed in Christmas Day with celebration and thanksgiving.

"I've always loved midnight on Christmas Eve," she said. "I don't think I've ever missed it. Lily and I used to set an alarm to make sure that even if we'd nodded off, we were awake together to mark that wonderful moment when our prayers of anticipation for the coming of Christ become our celebration of God's greatest gift to man – Christ on earth, to live beside us and redeem our sins. Such a joyful time – almost like a homecoming!"

"Will you manage to be awake tonight, do you think?"

"I'm looking forward to it more than ever."

"Well, my very dear Elsie, I will be thinking specially of you at just that moment. As all of us at St Stephen's welcome in Christmas Day, you will be right there in my prayers, I promise you that."

Neil thought for one moment that she was about to cry, and he sensed a sadness in the smile that touched her lips.

"I'm tired now, Neil. I think I'll take a nap."

"Of course," he said as he moved his chair back and bent down to give her a hug goodbye. She felt frail and small in his arms, and when she reached out to draw him closer to her, the two of them remained entwined for a while, neither wanting to break the circle.

"The Lord be with you, Elsie," he whispered in her ear.

"And also with you, Neil, now and always," she replied, her tears on his cheek.

***

Wendy and the music group were superb at the Crib Service. Being a school music teacher, Wendy had suggested songs and interlude music which were just right for the age group of children who came along with other family members for, what all agreed, was probably the most endearing of Christmas services.

"Debs and Graham are going to The Wheatsheaf for a Christmas drink tonight." Wendy was talking to Neil over her shoulder as she collected up the music. "I've said we'd join them as long as we're definitely able to leave in good time for the midnight service. About six thirty OK? We could have a meal there then."

"I'm sorry, Wendy, I can't. I've been invited to tea by Harry. We arranged it days ago."

Wendy's eyebrows lifted with suspicion. "You mean the Harry that lives with Claire and Sam?"

"That's right." Sensing trouble, Neil's voice was deliberately casual.

"So what you're really saying is that Claire has invited you for tea."

"No, what I'm really saying is that Harry, Claire and Sam are my neighbours, and they help me out in so many ways…"

"I bet she does!"

"... and they were thoughtful enough to realize that because today is such a busy one for me, a home-cooked meal would be a bit of a treat."

"Cooked by her own fair hand, no doubt."

"Harry does the cooking, actually."

"Well, you'd know. You go round there often enough!"

"Look, Wendy, my visit will all be over when Sam goes to bed, and with Father Christmas visiting tonight, my guess is that he'll be snoring his head off by half seven. I can come and join you all at the pub, but I won't need to eat, so you lot can start without me."

"Neil, are we – or are we not – a couple?"

"Well, I suppose we are, but…"

"... but you think it's all right, on Christmas Eve of all nights, to leave your partner while you spend time with some other girl?"

Neil laughed out loud. "Not some other girl! I don't think of Claire in that way, and she certainly doesn't see me in that light either. She's an atheist, for heaven's sake! How could that work?"

Wendy's expression softened a little as she came over to wind her arms round his neck. "I'm sorry, darling. It's been so busy leading up to Christmas, and now it's nearly here, I just want *you* to myself at last."

"We'll be together all day tomorrow."

"We will," she said softly, her lips brushing his cheek. "And I have plans for you…"

"You do?" he smiled.

"I most certainly do." She moved back far enough to look into his eyes so that he was in no doubt that he would enjoy her plans for him very much!

"I'll be with you as soon as I possibly can tonight."

"I'll hold you to that…" she said, planting a lingering kiss on his lips.

"For heaven's sake, you two, not here in the church!" Margaret's voice cut through their magic moment, but she was smiling indulgently at them in spite of the telling-off.

"Are you ready to go then, Neil?" she continued. "You'll be back by half ten at the latest though, won't you?"

"I certainly will. And well done for the Crib Service, Margaret. The atmosphere was just right – involving and meaningful – and not just for the children. I reckon the grown-ups enjoyed it most of all. I certainly did!"

"That's because you're a big kid yourself, Neil," teased Wendy. "*My* big kid! See you later…"

And Neil had no idea, as she walked away, that the seductive sway of her hips was deliberately calculated to ensure he was watching her every move.

***

"What do you think, Mummy?" asked Neil. "Can Sam have my present this evening while I'm here to watch him open it?"

Sam's face was a picture of hope and excitement as he waited for Claire's decision.

"Of course he can!"

Her face was flushed from the heat of the kitchen so she looked pink-cheeked in a way that complemented the soft rose-coloured roll-neck jersey she was wearing above her favourite grey jeans. She came across to kneel beside Sam in case he needed help with Neil's rather haphazard wrapping, which seemed to involve more sticky tape than paper! Neil looked on anxiously to see the little boy's reaction to his gift – but he needn't have worried, because the bright red fire engine, complete with firemen figures, had Sam squealing with delight. When Claire looked across to smile at Neil gratefully, he beamed back at her with pleasure and relief.

In spite of his earlier conversation with Wendy, Neil realized that Claire was the cook today, so that Harry could sit with Sam and Neil in the front room, helping to get the fire engine out of its box. Soon the batteries were safely installed and the toy was racing around the room with its siren wailing and lights flashing. Sam loved it – and, honestly, so did the two men as they chased round after the vehicle, whooping and yelling like small boys themselves.

The delicious aroma floating out of the kitchen turned out to be homemade lasagne, which Claire served with spicy baked potatoes, garlic bread and crisp salad, followed by Neil's absolute favourite pudding, lemon meringue pie with a dollop of ice cream. Afterwards he sat back replete and content, thinking how wonderful it would be simply to fall into their comfy settee and nod off in front of the telly for hours. Time was ticking on though, and once the washing up had been done, he realized he should start making tracks to meet up with Wendy, Graham and Debs in The Wheatsheaf.

"Have you seen this, Neil?" demanded Sam, grabbing his hand to drag him back into the lounge. Sam clambered unceremoniously on to Harry's lap, then produced a rather battered piece of mistletoe. Holding it as high as he could, Sam placed a wet kiss on Harry's lips.

"It's for kissing under, isn't it, Grandad?"

He scrambled off Harry's lap and rushed over to push Neil on to a seat so that he could climb up to place the mistletoe over Neil's head and give him a kiss too.

"Now we'll love each other forever!" he announced triumphantly before giving Neil a big, sticky hug.

Laughing, Neil disentangled himself and stood up to take his leave. He shook Harry's hand and wished him all the blessings of Christmas, knowing that the midnight service would be too much for the elderly man, although he would certainly be at the early morning service.

Following Neil out to the front door, Claire stopped beside the stairs and turned to face him.

"Thank you for making this evening so special for Sam. The fire engine is just perfect. He's bouncing so much I'm sure he won't sleep – even though he knows that if he's awake when Father Christmas comes, he might miss out on presents!"

"It must be lovely being a mum on a night like this. I think you're almost as excited as he is!"

"I am. He's such a dear little boy. He makes every day special for me."

Suddenly, Sam came running through from the lounge and charged up the stairs behind them. Then his chubby little hand came through the banisters to dangle the mistletoe above their heads.

"Go on, Mummy! Give Neil a kiss!"

Neil and Claire looked at each other in alarm.

"You've got to! It's lucky!"

"We've got to," said Neil with a shrug.

"It's lucky," agreed Claire.

And their heads tipped towards each other, eyes open as their lips met in the softest of kisses. Then, Neil's eyes closed as the kiss deepened in touch and tenderness. For seconds they stood there, too stunned to move.

"Ooh!" The disapproval in Sam's voice broke the moment.

"You're being soppy. You're not supposed to be soppy!"

And with disgust, he dropped the mistletoe on to the floor beside them and stomped off to his room, leaving Neil and Claire to step apart with guilty embarrassment.

* * *

"Yea, Lord, we greet thee, born this happy morning…"

It was with a sense of euphoria that the churchful of worshippers came to the last verse of "O Come All Ye Faithful", singing the words which were only appropriate on Christmas morning itself.

After the service, although the time was approaching half past midnight, there was real warmth and excitement in the air as the congregation put on their coats and started to make their way home, hugging friends and calling out Christmas greetings as they went.

It was gone one before the church was cleared and re-set ready for the first service on Christmas morning which, Neil remembered wearily, was due to start at eight o'clock. The main family service wasn't until ten, and for that, once again, St Stephen's would be full of worshippers, just as it had been on that day for all the centuries it had stood at the heart of Dunbridge. An image of his father's face drifted into Neil's mind, and he stopped for a while to think of the many occasions in the past when he and his Dad had shared the experience of the Christmas midnight service together. How he missed him – his wealth of knowledge and interest, his dry sense of humour, his quiet, solid love for his shy, sometimes gauche son.

His mind full of his father, Neil looked round to make a final check that everything was ready for the morning, a job he'd volunteered to do so that Margaret could go home as soon as possible once the midnight service was over. She would also have the pleasant duty of leading the two Christmas morning services, a role which he would not be able to fulfil until he was priested the following June. Next year, he may well be leading these important, busy services himself! His mouth felt suddenly dry.

"Are you ready?" asked Wendy, appearing at his side.

Neil glanced around almost guiltily. Since the unexpected kiss under the mistletoe shared with Claire earlier that evening, his mind had been in more turmoil than ever. He still couldn't understand exactly what had happened – why that kiss, which had started out as nothing more than an innocent piece of Christmas fun, had suddenly taken on a deeper dimension that neither of them had expected. It was probably just the sentiment of the season, an expression of care and goodwill between very good friends. No doubt they would laugh about it together when they next saw each other. There was certainly nothing to be embarrassed about – and yet, he felt a blush of guilt spread up his neck and across his cheeks as he turned to look at Wendy.

He marvelled at the calmness of his voice as he spoke. "Yes, let me just switch the vestry lights out and I'll be with you."

It was as he was walking to the vestry that he felt a stirring in his back pocket. Whoever could be ringing his mobile phone at this time of the morning?

"Neil," said a voice he soon recognized. "It's Jean here, from Dale Court. I've got some sad news for you, I'm afraid."

"Elsie?"

"She passed away about an hour ago."

"At midnight?" asked Neil, vaguely aware that his blood had turned cold in his veins.

"Just after. She was the only one of our residents still awake, so I was sitting with her. She'd been fine, very bright, really – but once the clock had struck twelve, she said she was tired and thought she'd go to sleep. She laid back against the pillow, and by the time I'd got across the room to tuck her in, I realized she wasn't breathing. It was as if she'd laid down to die. A nice way to go, I suppose, when you're ninety-six years old."

Neil was unable to speak as tears filled his eyes. Elsie had gone home. That's what she'd been telling him that evening. To her, Christmas was a triumph – and her homecoming to the God she loved would be triumphant too.

"Neil? Are you still there?"

He took a deep breath before speaking. "Yes. Do you need me to come over?"

"Well, I know how close you two had become."

"Do her family know yet?"

"I wondered if it might be better if you told them?"

"And that should be tonight, of course. I'll be right there."

Switching off his phone, Neil stood for a second, his head lowered.

"God bless you, dear Elsie. I hope you are reunited with your beloved Lily, and with the God you both loved so much in life, and are now with for eternity. I will miss you. I will never forget you. Never…"

And rubbing his hand across his eyes, he switched off the lights and hurried to tell Wendy the news.

≈ CHAPTER 12 ≈

The locals said they got off with a particularly mild winter. A wet, dull January gave way to a mild February when carpets of snowdrops and crocuses heralded the Spring. Neil watched the trees in Vicarage Gardens sprout bright green leaves and clouds of blossom that transformed the ordinary-looking cul-de-sac into a fragrant oasis befitting its name.

His working life had fallen into a pattern of services, home calls, school assemblies, visits to hospitals and residential homes, Confirmation classes, staff meetings, ecumenical gatherings and services, weddings, baptisms, various committees, paperwork, study, preparing and clearing up the church and the hall after one kind of event or another – then paperwork, more study and more paperwork.

He also went off for regular training sessions, mostly just for a day or two, but on one occasion for a whole week, with other curates from the diocese. These post-ordination training sessions were affectionately known as "potty training", when students like Neil – who, after three years' study, had been ordained as deacons at a moving ceremony at St Albans Abbey in the summer of the previous year – were able to prepare for the equally important and solemn occasion in July this year, during which they would become fully fledged priests, able to take on all the duties of the role.

Neil enjoyed these ongoing training sessions at which he met up with old friends, some of whom had been his fellow ordination students. Last summer they had left college full of mission and passion, ready to save the world. Not all of the students had gone on to work as curates in local parishes, but the majority of them certainly had, and it soon became clear that the reality of ministry in modern-day communities had knocked the edges off most of them, so that their initial enthusiasm was mellowing with experience.

As the students discussed and analysed their relative postings, Neil listened to some of the situations others had to face and thanked God for the down-to-earth approach of his own vicar, Margaret. In comparison with others, it became clear that she was doing a very good job of protecting and guiding him where he still had much to learn, but that she also allowed him the actual experience he needed in order to take on certain aspects of the role alone. Dunbridge may not be the most exciting parish in the area, but all of life was there.

"Have you decided to give up on this priest business yet?" demanded his mother during one of her all-too-frequent phone calls. "Or have you finally seen sense and worked out that you need to get a proper job?"

"You said you approved of my choice of career when you were here," retorted Neil.

"You have very conveniently forgotten, Neil, the context in which I made that comment. Have you done what I suggested and made sure that you are noticed in high places – by the Bishop, for example?"

"Not really. I've not done anything wrong, which is more than likely how he'd hear of me!"

"But nothing to make you stand out in the crowd either? Typical of you, Neil! If you're not prepared to get yourself noticed so that you can work your way up the tree, you'll do nothing but scrape along the bottom, perhaps for years."

"Sounds good to me," agreed Neil.

"You could have a word with Wendy's father. He may be able to give you a leg up in his accountancy firm. You can't go wrong in a career like that. And if you're thinking about getting married and starting a family…"

"Which I'm not – at least, not yet."

"… you're going to need a decent income and a home of your own. You must have something behind you to offer a girl. Why would she choose you otherwise?"

"Good question," said Neil. "Just as well I'm not considering all of that just yet."

"Why not? Aren't you and Wendy getting on well?"

"Perfectly well, thank you."

"You're not stringing that poor girl along, are you, Neil? Clever girls like Wendy don't come by often, you know. I remember both your sets of grandparents had a stern word with your father, just to make sure he didn't let the best thing in his life slip away."

Neil was silent for a moment while he considered this.

"Me!" Iris added. "Your father would have amounted to nothing without me by his side, encouraging and supporting him."

Remembering how, even as a young boy, it had occurred to him that his poor father seemed constantly hen-pecked, Neil thought it better to say nothing.

"Neil! Are you still there?"

"Sorry, Mum. I've got my eye on the clock because I'm needed at the church in ten minutes. I should go, really."

"Right, I'll ring you tomorrow, then. Give my love to Wendy. Tell her to ring me again. I do so love her calls."

"I'll tell her. Bye, Mum. Take care of yourself!" And switching off his phone, Neil heaved a sigh of relief.

Later that evening, he was making coffee in Margaret and Frank's muddled kitchen, in which he now felt completely at home. He'd even come to an understanding with the ill-tempered Archie. Neil acknowledged that the kitchen was Archie's territory in which two-legged visitors were definitely not welcome – and Archie agreed to stay on the other side of the room from where he could stare threateningly at Neil without completely scaring the wits out of him.

Neil took the tray through to Margaret's equally cluttered office, where she was, as usual, searching through the mound of papers on her desk, looking for one particularly elusive letter.

"It's here somewhere, I know it is!"

"What are you looking for?"

"A letter that came from the insurance company that covers St Stephen's. I want you to read it."

"Why? Do we have a problem?"

"Well, we might have – with our Boy George."

"How could we possibly have a problem with George? He's a treasure!"

"The insurance company might not think so, not when you read how they've worded the future requirements for our cover from now on. Oh, where *is* that blooming letter?"

"How can a man who's rung bells at this church for more than sixty years be a problem?"

"His age. He's eighty-four next birthday. The insurance company, in their wisdom, don't think that anyone over the age of seventy should be in charge of heavy equipment."

"Over seventy? That rules out nearly half of our congregation!"

Margaret looked at him sharply. "One of your many faults, Neil, is that you're prone to exaggeration."

Neil grinned. "Correction! A third of our congregation, maybe, is over seventy – and probably three quarters of our bell ringers. But George? He's evergreen! He's got more energy than the rest of us put together."

"Well, if I can find that blasted bit of paper, you need to read what the insurers say. They're not going to renew our cover unless we comply in every detail – and they're sending an agent along this week… For heaven's sake, where *is* it?"

"It wasn't an email, was it?"

Margaret looked up immediately, then crossed to her PC. Thirty seconds of anxious searching through her inbox brought a whoop of triumph.

"Yes, here it is. Take a look for yourself! It's from their agent, Charlie whatever-his-name-is, who's apparently in this area on Tuesday morning, so he plans to pop in for a visit."

Neil started to read over Margaret's shoulder as she went on.

"That's tomorrow – my day off, of course. And as much as I'd dearly love to do battle with the insurance man, I can't cancel my arrangements this week because Sarah will be so disappointed. This second pregnancy is really laying her low, you know. At times like that, you need your Mum!"

"So you want me to…"

"Meet the man and save the day!"

"Not much, then!"

"Consider it all as part of your training, Neil. St Stephen's has had bells for three centuries. It's your job to keep them ringing."

"Even if that means without Boy George?"

Margaret looked at him scornfully. "Don't be ridiculous! They can't possibly ring without George. You won't have to do much. Just tell that insurance jobsworth what's what. He's got to sort himself out and re-issue our cover."

"Right." Neil sounded very doubtful.

Margaret laughed. "And if he's got any problem with that, I can speak to him the next day. Just remember, we are the customers, and the customer is always right!"

It took several phone calls and a master plan to pull it all together, but by half past ten the following morning, Neil was standing in the porch of St Stephen's, ready to greet Charlie whatever-his-name-is (it was actually Nelson), with the sun shining on the bell tower from which the best peal in St Stephen's repertoire was ringing out across the town. He was getting a little anxious as the church clock clicked round to twenty-five to eleven before a smart, top-of-the-range saloon car purred into the churchyard. Shielding his eyes from the sun as he tried to take a look at the driver, Neil realized that his palms were clammy and his knees shaking. He thought about what was awaiting Mr Nelson inside, and willed his stomach to stop churning in such an alarming way.

At first he saw a pair of shapely legs in very high heels unfold from the car, then he gasped as he saw a tall, blonde woman ease herself elegantly from the seat and look at the church with interest. As her eyes panned the scene, she at last caught sight of Neil, and picking up her leather clipboard from the back seat, she clicked the remote control to lock the car and moved gracefully towards the totally mesmerized Neil.

"Charlotte Nelson." Her voice was attractively husky as she stretched out to offer Neil her hand. "And you don't look like the Reverend *Margaret* Prowse!" she smiled.

"No," he stuttered in reply. "I'm the curate here at St Stephen's, Neil Fisher. I'm terribly sorry that the Vicar can't be with us this morning, but I'm sure I can help with anything you need."

"I'm sure you can, Neil," she said, her vibrantly blue eyes looking him up and down between long shiny lashes. "Shall we begin?"

Neil felt a bit like a puppy bouncing along behind her as she strode away into the church. Suddenly she stopped in her tracks and turned to face him, her clipboard at the ready and her gold pen poised for action.

"Let me start with your details. What's your full name?"

"The Reverend Neil Fisher."

"No middle name?"

"Anthony."

Her lips twitched slightly at the corners.

"So your initials are…?"

"NAF. I know! I don't think that word had any meaning when my parents named me."

"I should hope not!" And turning on her elegant heels, she closed the clipboard and marched into the porch.

"Nice," she commented, her head on one side as she waited for him to catch up and open the church door. "The bells. Nice."

"St Stephen's is known to have one of the best bell-ringing teams in the county."

"Really?" she replied with no more expression in her face than a slightly raised eyebrow.

This isn't going well, thought Neil frantically. *Three hundred years of bells and I'll go down in history as the man who lost them!*

"In fact," he started again, "you happen to have arrived just in time for bell practice. Let me introduce you to the team."

"That won't be necessary. I just need to go through a few forms with you, make sure all the details and conditions are correct, take a look around to see if there are any undeclared hazards – and I'll be on my way!"

"Oh no, you won't, dear!" The homely voice of Beryl, winner of the annual county WI cake baking competition for the past nineteen years, greeted Ms Nelson the moment she stepped into the church. "You've had a long journey. Hospitality to the stranger has been the ethos of St Stephen's for centuries. You just pull up a chair and have a cuppa and a cake or two before you even think about work!"

Neil suppressed a smile as Ms Nelson took in the scene before her. Stretched out in front of them along the back of the pews was a neatly laid table covered in a crisp white linen cloth which formed a backdrop for the most mouth-watering selection of cakes and pastries he had ever seen. Bone china teacups and saucers stood beside fluted-edge plates topped with embroidered napkins. Beryl stood beaming at them from beside the table, whilst a small efficient army of "ladies of the parish" bustled about cutting dainty triangle sandwiches and spooning whipped cream and fresh strawberries into cut-glass dishes beside platters heaped with freshly baked scones.

The insurance agent was so astonished that she gave no resistance as Beryl gently but firmly frogmarched her to a seat.

"And you, Neil!" Beryl ordered. "George and the team will be down presently – so tuck in, do!"

Putting up no objection whatsoever, Ms Nelson plainly forgot any diet she might have been on. Faced with such an array, she was spoilt for choice, selecting first a scone with cream and strawberries, followed by a delicate lemon slice and a fluffy coffee-and-walnut cupcake and two refills of her china teacup. By the time the bell-ringers came down from the tower ten minutes later, she was already chatting animatedly to the circle of ladies who sat around her discussing recipes, memories of teatime favourites from childhood and the scandalous prices in shops today!

Room was made at the table for the six bell-ringers, three men and three women with a combined age of nearly four centuries – and it was the most dapper and articulate of them who immediately took the seat right next to Charlie. Boy George had pulled out all the stops. He was dressed smartly in grey trousers with a razor-sharp crease down the front, a starched white shirt and his British Legion blazer. Neil guessed he'd even put an extra dollop of wax on his neatly curled moustache. His eyes twinkled dangerously as he planted a reverential kiss on Charlie's hand. He hadn't got to his eighties without knowing how to win over a lady!

"George Sanderson at your service, dear lady. How kind of you to come!"

He's good, thought Neil with relief. He must have been as surprised as any of them that Charlie Nelson had actually turned out to be a woman – but for an old charmer like George, that only made the challenge more of a delight.

"Neil tells me that you'd like to know something about bell-ringing?"

"Well," started Charlie, looking uncertainly in Neil's direction, "I only need to know the bare facts, just for the paperwork…"

"The bare facts, dear madam, are that when English bells ring, angels sing – but I don't suppose your paperwork has a box for that. No, there's only one thing for it! You must come up to the bell-tower with me and I can show you how beautiful the whole experience is."

"Oh, thank you, but I really haven't got time for all that. I just want to…"

"Have you ever been in a bell-tower – or tried ringing a bell?"

"Well, no, I haven't, but…"

"And Neil also tells me that you are concerned that bell-ringing might be too much of a health hazard at my age for insurance cover?"

"That's a distinct possibility, yes…"

"Well, that's nonsense and you can prove it for yourself. Eat up your fairy cake, and we'll get going!"

As obediently as a recently ticked-off child, Charlie finished the last two mouthfuls of cake in silence, aware that all eyes were on her.

"OK, team!" ordered George. "Tea break is over. Back to the bells!"

Like a well-trained dance troupe, the bell-ringers stood up and headed for the tower. George lingered at the back of Charlie's chair, making it quite clear that he was ready to pull it out as soon as she moved. She hesitated – but he was the picture of gracious patience – in spite of his deliberate glance at her stilettos which he plainly considered unsuitable for bell-tower climbing. In the end, she stood up to join him, recognizing that she had no choice in the matter.

The ringing-room was too small for Neil to accompany them, so he paced the floor down below for the next half hour, which really dragged by. Finally Charlie and George descended from the bell-tower. It wasn't until after she'd climbed back into her car and zoomed back to her office that George and the team laughed and guffawed through the story of what had happened.

George had sprung up the tiny spiral staircase to the

bell-chamber like a spring chicken, leaving Charlie to totter precariously behind him on stairs that were nowhere near wide enough for her fashionable footwear. She stepped from the dark staircase into the lit bell-chamber with her eyes like saucers, especially when George leaned towards her in a very gentlemanly manner and picked a cobweb out of her hair and a blob of pigeon droppings from her suit jacket. The team had arranged themselves around the circle of bell ropes, leaving the heaviest for George. Carefully taking off his blazer and rolling up the crisp linen of his shirtsleeves, he spat on each palm and stepped forward to clasp the rope.

Anyone who has ever been in a bell-chamber when ringing is in full swing cannot help but be moved by it – and Charlie was no exception. Trying to follow the intricacies of the peal, she recognized that this was a very competent team indeed. *Mind you,* she thought, *it can't be that hard if even old people like this can manage it…*

"Right, young lady!" boomed George once their first peal was finished. "Your turn!"

With horror, Charlie realized that Madge, who was in charge of the rope opposite George, had stood back to allow the newcomer to take over.

"Oh no, I couldn't!"

"But you *will*, my dear lady. We all had to learn – and here at St Stephen's, we learn properly!"

A light suddenly gleamed in Charlie's eyes. Whipping off her smart suit jacket, she kicked off her shoes and gave a determined grin as she stepped forward to take the rope. She listened closely to the dire warnings of how she could disappear up into the bell-chamber, never to be seen again, if she forgot to let go of the rope after every pull – and then, spitting on her palms just as George had, she stood braced for action.

By the time the peal finished five minutes later, she had overcome her initial panic and bad timing, and was fitting in quite nicely. It was she who asked if they could try the same peal again. Then she suggested they might have a go at a different peal. Finally she asked for a more complicated one. She was absorbed, breathless and completely hooked. It was a smiling, chattering, bare-footed young girl who came down the steps instead of the sophisticated, slightly officious young business woman who had gone up in the first place.

There was no question that bell-ringing wasn't safe, or that the age group of the ringers was unsuitable. The only query Charlie had was whether they needed any more volunteers, because she wouldn't mind joining them every now and then? She took the large box of cream cakes and chocolate eclairs Beryl handed her, hugged everyone in the room – including Neil – and, waving and beeping the horn as she left, she headed back to work a changed woman!

* * *

Easter came at the end of March that year, which was when Neil always thought it should be. It wasn't that he didn't understand the ancient reasons that explained why Easter bobbed around each year across the weeks of March and April. It was simply that the daffodils were safely out and nature was springing into glorious colour at the end of March, so that it felt right to celebrate Easter just then.

It was one of the busiest times of the year for Claire, as she cleared away the winter debris from the churchyard and all the gardens she cared for. She combined that with a routine of pruning, trimming and planting to ensure the shape and colour needed for the summer months ahead.

Neil was very aware that neither of them had ever mentioned their unexpected kiss on Christmas Eve, almost as though, if it weren't discussed, perhaps it had never happened. Not speaking about it didn't mean that Neil didn't think about it, wondering why on earth, when he was settling into a relationship with Wendy, he should feel so affected by a traditional Christmas kiss under the mistletoe. It wasn't as if he and Claire were attracted to each other, he thought to himself. They were so different! They had different interests, different ethics, different points of view in so many ways. That made for some heated debates, which they both relished as Christian versus atheist. There was no moving her. She said she was too much of a scientist to see evolution and the glories of the world in any other way. He respected her opinion, perhaps more than he felt she respected his – but he did enjoy the challenge of the argument, knowing that their discussions would always end in good humour.

Their paths crossed often, either because she was working at the church or in his garden, or because he sometimes popped in to see Harry and Sam on his way back home to Number 96. It didn't take long to discover that her quirky sense of humour was similar to his own, and he enjoyed seeing her laugh, especially as he knew her life was far from easy. She was down-to-earth and practical, not afraid to roll her sleeves up to tackle any problem – and yet she could be so soft and tender when she spoke to Sam or Harry.

If that kiss had made any impression on her, she didn't show it. They were friends, good friends. The kiss was forgotten, irrelevant.

Except Neil couldn't quite forget. On all levels, as a man and as a Christian minister, he was torn with guilt that such a thing could happen when he was in a relationship with another girl – and it was certainly true that he found his life becoming more and more entwined with Wendy's. Within the church circle, they were increasingly thought of as a couple, and her parents treated him as if he were already part of the family. Prompted by constant hints from all who knew them that an engagement should be imminent, Neil found himself hesitating. It wasn't that Wendy was anything except wonderful in every way. She was smart, attractive and popular – and without question, she cared for him very much. Who else would put up with his tidiness fetish, his shyness at inappropriate moments, his lack of social skills in ways she thought mattered? He was learning a lot from her, and trying hard to catch her vision for how his life, alongside hers, could flourish. Perhaps, he wondered rebelliously, his reticence was because, occasionally, when Wendy was making a point, she sounded unnervingly like his mother!

The period leading up to Easter is particularly busy for all churches, but Margaret had been working with clergy from all the other denominations in the town to set up a series of talks throughout the six weeks of Lent. It had been agreed that, because of its size and location, St Stephen's would be the most convenient venue for the talks, and everyone was looking forward to the chance for fellow worshippers from different churches to discuss and celebrate all that they shared in their Christian faith.

At the start of Lent, Neil spent the afternoon of Shrove Tuesday at Wendy's school, telling the assembled pupils the stories, traditions and Christian reasons for clearing out their cupboards and eating pancakes on that day. Then he sat back to watch Wendy organizing the pancake races, hiding a smile as he watched her firm authority over her class. No child had the nerve to misbehave under her watchful eye – and he chuckled to himself as he thought he never dared to disobey her orders either. The afternoon ended happily as he joined the children for a feast of pancakes with lemon and sugar all round.

Ash Wednesday turned from such jollity towards the sober fasts and reflections of Lent. Neil was setting up the church that afternoon, ready for their Ash Wednesday service during which worshippers would be signed with a cross from the ash left after the Palm Sunday crosses from the previous year had been ceremonially burned. At that moment, his mobile rang. It took him a while to recognize Peter Fellowes' voice. The churchwarden sounded strange, as if he was struggling with his emotions.

"I'm sorry, Neil. I meant to be there to help you this afternoon, but something's come up."

"Are you all right?" asked Neil, worried for this man who had definitely become a friend.

"Sort of. I'm not sure, really."

"Has something happened?"

"Look, I know you're busy, but could you spare five minutes to pop round?"

"I'm finished here. We're all set for later. I'll be with you by the time your kettle's boiled, OK?"

Peter definitely didn't look himself as he opened the door. Without a word, he led Neil into the living room and gestured to a handwritten letter lying on the coffee table. Neil picked it up and turned to the back sheet to see that Glenda's signature was scrawled across the bottom. He read:

Peter, it will come as no surprise to you that I feel stifled, under-valued and trapped within our marriage. It isn't that you aren't a good man, but whereas I am able to see your qualities, you seem unable to see mine or understand how constricted I have felt for years. I am suffocating in our small-town life. I am sinking under the routine, the sameness, the boredom of being in Dunbridge. You were the one who decided to give up the estate agency and retire early, but if you thought for one minute that I was ready to play the little wife at home to a man who has walked away from his purpose in life, then you didn't know me very well, did you?

I am younger than you, of course, by three years. That may not have mattered so much in the past, but recently it has mattered to me a lot. You have become an early-to-bed, slippers-and-cocoa sort of man, whilst I still have a lot of living to do. You want routine. I want challenge and change. You hate leaving this horrible little backwater. I want to travel. Your interest doesn't stretch any further than the parochial little problems of St Stephen's. I find the place small-time, small-town and irrelevant. I'm probably not even a Christian, if I'm honest. I only went along for your benefit, but really there were times when I was so bored with the small-minded people there, I felt like screaming!

I worry this might hurt you (and that's not my intention), but I have to tell you that while you have been sadly lacking when it comes to listening to my needs and understanding the woman you're married to, there is someone else who really appreciates all I am. I am speaking of Roland Branson, my boss, of course. You know what an exceptionally clever and talented man he is – but he makes it clear that without my contribution, support and encouragement, he wouldn't be the hugely successful man he is today. And what is more, he wants me! He says he can't imagine living another day without me by his side. He has asked me to move into the new apartment he's buying in St John's Wood, and I have no hesitation whatsoever in saying I can't wait!

So I'm sorry, Peter, I'm leaving you. I'm reaching out for my life, and looking forward to sharing the rest of my years with my true soul-mate, because that's what I recognize Roland to be. You probably don't have the depth of feeling to understand what I'm saying. You will just be hurt that I have left you, and will probably never completely understand why. After all, if you were capable of that, you would have changed before now, wouldn't you, in order to keep our marriage on track by making at least some effort to understand me and sympathize with what I've been going through?

I looked around this house today before writing this and thought there is nothing at all left here that I want. Even my own clothes and possessions are part of this life that I intend to leave completely behind. I realize too that it would be cruel to clear out this house in order to take my half share immediately, even though, of course, I am perfectly entitled to do so. I hope you appreciate that I have no wish to make this any worse for you than it is.

Once you've got over the shock of this, I am sure you'll agree with me that there is absolutely no reason for bad feeling. Why should there be when I only wish you well? And because I know you to be a man to whom fairness matters, I am sure you wish Roland and me every happiness too.

Have a good life, Peter!

Glenda
xxx

Neil whistled through his teeth in sheer disbelief. He looked anxiously at Peter.

"So how are you? What's your reaction to this?"

"Honestly? A bit bewildered. I didn't see this coming. She's been working with Roland for years, so why has it taken them so long to get to this? I have wondered for some time if they've been having an affair, but I honestly didn't care enough to bother asking. Perhaps they have, and maybe they've now got to the point where they want to share their lives more openly. Whatever the truth, she's welcome to her slimy tie-salesman – and he's most definitely welcome to her!"

"She doesn't mention a divorce in her letter, but do you think that's what she means?"

"If she doesn't, then I do. I have kept my promises to that woman over all the years as she's steadily become more demanding, more full of her own importance, and less aware of the needs and feelings of anyone else near her."

"Especially you."

"She has despised me for so long. She's made no secret of it."

"You don't regret marrying her though, do you?"

Peter thought for a moment before answering. "Believe it or not, when I first met her she was painfully shy, living at home with her overbearing mum. She was really pretty, and so eager to break away from her parents to get married and set up home with me. We were married within eight months of meeting each other."

"Too quickly, do you think?"

"Probably. We certainly didn't know each other very well, and over three decades it's become clear that we have very little in common, especially now the kids have left home. And I suppose we've both noticed the failings in our relationship more now I'm retired and have a lot of time on my hands. My wife is just never there — and when she is, she makes it clear she really doesn't enjoy life with me. This decision of hers is just the culmination of years of unhappiness for us both."

Neil nodded. "How do you think your son and daughter will react to this news? Christine's in Brighton, isn't she?"

"Yes, and John has a family of his own up in Scotland now. I think they'll be quite shocked, really. The cracks between Glenda and me have really started to show since they left, but whenever we see the family now, we've managed to keep our differences under wrap. I wonder if Glenda has been in touch with them yet? I'd better give them a ring."

"Well, don't rush to do anything too quickly. This must be quite a shock for you."

"Not one I'm unhappy about, though, Neil. I know I shouldn't feel like that at the end of a marriage which began in church, but I have to be honest and say I feel deeply relieved. There, I've said it! Do you think badly of me?"

"Of course not. I know you have remained committed to your marriage, and it's not your choice that Glenda has decided to set up home with another man. And as your minister, I must counsel you to allow time for your feelings about all this to settle, and the paperwork to catch up with what's happened."

Peter grinned.

"And as my friend? What's your advice then?

"Well, I think there's a certain charming lady whose life will be changed dramatically by this news."

"I can't wait to tell her!"

"You might want to change out of your slippers and run a razor over your chin — but I think she'll be glad to see you, however you are!"

⇒ CHAPTER 13 ⇐

On the Bank Holiday Monday after Whitsun Neil got an urgent call from Graham.

"I need to meet you! Are you around at lunchtime for a pint?"

"Yes, I reckon so."

"The Wheatsheaf?"

"About one?"

"See you then!"

Unusually, when Neil arrived at the pub bang on time, Graham was already waiting with two pints of real ale on the table in front of him. They took a couple of swigs before Graham put his glass down and stared forlornly into his beer.

"She's seeing someone."

"Who?" asked Neil, deciding it was best to play dumb.

"Debs!"

"Well, that's all right, isn't it? She's a free agent."

"He's been here this weekend."

"Staying overnight?"

"No, as far as I know he was just around for the day."

"So perhaps they're just good friends and he's paying a visit?"

"That's what Debs said, but I know her too well. She just doesn't *do* things like this."

"Why should it matter? You've always said you and Debs are nothing more than good friends yourselves. So if she has found herself a nice bloke, then as her old friend, surely you're pleased for her – aren't you?"

"Well, for a start, he's not her type at all. He's a nerd. A big dumb nerd! A rugby player, so she said, and he's got a bashed-in nose!"

"Well, that doesn't necessarily make him either dumb or a nerd. How did she meet him?"

"At work, apparently."

"Not through the internet, then?"

"I hope not! Heaven knows who she'd meet that way!"

Neil smiled. Irony was plainly lost on Graham.

"So if she met him at work, is he a policeman?"

"He's big enough to be a police van!"

"Graham…?"

Graham sighed. "OK, he's a policeman. Apparently they're based at the same station."

"And how were they? Were they holding hands? Did it look like they were an item?"

"Oh no, they were far too clever for that. But I know. I *know*!"

"But you want Debs to be happy?"

"She'll never be happy with a plank like that. He's totally wrong for her!"

"So who would be right, then?"

Graham looked at Neil as if he were totally stupid.

"Not *him*, that's for sure!"

Graham grabbed for his beer, his face like thunder. Neil picked up his pint too, his expression thoughtful.

"Graham, do you think it's possible that you care for Debs more than you let on?"

"Don't be daft!"

"Just hear me out for a second, because I can't help wondering if you'll never think anyone is right for Debbie – except perhaps *you*?"

Graham took a sharp breath as if he were about to refute such a ridiculous idea – but then he stopped, his face troubled as he digested this thought. Finally, he spoke.

"It would never work. We know each other too well."

"Not much of a learning curve needed between the two of you, then."

"But if we fancied each other, surely we'd have done something about it before now?"

"Do you fancy her?"

"She's great looking – a little on the short side, but nice legs and she looks really good when she laughs – and she laughs a lot…"

"So you *do* fancy her?"

"The question is, could she ever fancy *me*?"

"Well, even I've noticed the way she looks at you when she doesn't think you can see – you know, just like you, with that soppy smile on your face when you think she won't notice."

"No!"

"Yes!"

Graham grabbed his beer again, although it didn't reach his lips as he slumped back in his seat.

"Even if it were true – even if we did fancy each other a bit, and I'm not saying we do – how would we ever change the way we've always been with each other?"

"Ask her."

"What? Tell her all this, do you mean?"

Neil nodded. Graham shook his head.

"She'd laugh. She'd think I'd lost my marbles."

"OK, say nothing. Leave her to Police Van Man."

Graham's reaction was immediate.

"How could I tell her?"

"Go round and see her."

"And say what?"

"Say whatever you really feel. Be honest. You've always said she knows you too well to let you get away with anything but honesty."

"And you don't think she'll tell me to shove it – because if I lost her friendship, I'd hate that…"

"She may. But she might not. She might be very glad to hear what you're feeling. And I think your friendship is strong enough to survive a chat like this. If she doesn't feel the same, you can just laugh it off, pretend you were joking."

Graham stared into his beer. "Perhaps it's this conversation that's the joke. I'm not sure about all this at all."

"Then don't do anything. Just stand back and let Debs get involved with someone from work, if that's what she wants. And be happy for her, Graham. She deserves that from you."

Graham snorted irritably, and the two men continued to drink in silence.

* * *

"How many tickets are you allowed for your ordination?" asked Margaret. "It's only a few weeks away now, and there are quite a few people from St Stephen's who'd like to go and wish you well."

"I think we're each allowed fifteen guests, although I can apply for more tickets if I'd like them. St Albans Abbey is a big place, and there are about twenty students being ordained deacon, and then about eighteen of us deacons who will be priested."

Neil and Margaret were in the church office running off posters for a Flower Festival service they were planning for the last weekend in June. The event always took place across the middle weekend of the famous Wimbledon tennis tournament – and everyone, tennis lover or not, knew it *always* seemed to rain over Wimbledon fortnight! Over the years, it had frequently occurred to the organizing committee at St Stephen's that they should change the date of their celebration weekend, but no one had ever got round to doing anything about it.

"I can't believe it's almost a whole year since I became a deacon," continued Neil. "I started properly here at St Stephen's right after my ordination service – but of course, I'd first been up to meet you several weeks earlier."

"I can never see a pork chop and not think of you!"

He grinned sheepishly.

"So who will be in your party at the Abbey?" she asked.

"Mum, of course. She may disapprove, but she'd never miss an occasion like this. You and Frank, Wendy and her parents, Peter and Val – and Harry. He's really excited about it!"

"So there are six places left. Let me know what thoughts you have about them, because there'll be a waiting list for any tickets going spare."

"That's a nice thought," mused Neil. "They're a lovely lot, the St Stephen's crowd, aren't they?"

Margaret looked across at him. "You've worked your way into their hearts, Neil. You've done well this year."

"Have I?" There was a vulnerability in his face that was so endearing, Margaret couldn't help but smile.

"When I think how you were forever blushing bright red when you first arrived…"

"Don't remind me!"

"And now I know I can rely on your judgment in almost all situations. I'm not saying you haven't still got a lot to learn…"

"Thank goodness we stay curates for three years, at least. I'll probably need a decade or two before I feel I'm really up to the job."

"Well, I will be glad to have you on my team as a priest in your own right next year. You'll be able to do so much more then."

"And hopefully serve this community as I intended to from the start of my journey into priesthood."

"Amen to that," agreed Margaret quietly. "Now, stop yacking and finish that printing before you make us both late!"

* * *

The following weeks passed all too quickly, and by Monday of the week leading up to his ordination ceremony, Neil's bag was packed and standing by the front door, ready for the following evening when he would be going on three days of retreat before his public commitment to priesthood during the service that weekend. He was looking forward to a time of prayer and preparation before taking this huge and important step in his ministry.

Wendy had suggested that she drive him down to the retreat house near St Albans Abbey on Tuesday evening, so that when they next saw each other at the end of the ordination service, he could travel home with her and other members of the St Stephen's congregation who were coming to support him during this moving occasion.

It was in the early hours of that Tuesday morning that Neil woke with a start as his house phone rang in the dead of night. He was so disorientated, he almost didn't recognize what the sound was, but as realization dawned on him, he leaped out of bed with a sense of foreboding at the thought of what could possibly be so urgent that it couldn't wait until the morning. His heart skipped a beat when he not only recognized Claire's voice, but heard the note of panic in it.

"It's Harry! It looks like he's had a heart attack!"

"Have you called an ambulance?"

"They're here now, and I want to go with him to the hospital."

"What about Sam? Do you want me to come over and sit with him?"

"Do you know, I think I'd rather have you sitting with me at the hospital? That may be an odd thing to say, but I don't want to be there on my own."

"Of course, I'll gladly help in any way I can. What about Sam, though?"

"I've rung Jan and Paul and they're already on their way over to take him across to their house."

"Good idea. He gets on well with Beckie and Brendan."

"Yes, best not to worry him too much about Harry until we know how he is…"

Claire's voice faltered.

"Look, I'll be right there. Just hold on."

"Oh Neil, he looks so ill…"

"I'm on my way!"

Minutes later, when Neil reached the house, Jan had already turned up in her dressing-gown to carry the sleeping Sam across to spend the rest of the night with Beckie and Brendan (which, when he woke up, he would love). The ambulance crew had finished their basic examination of Harry, and once they had carried him safely into the ambulance, they wired him up to an array of flashing monitors. Claire climbed into the ambulance to hold Harry's hand on the journey whilst Neil followed behind in his own car. He glanced at the dashboard clock. It was five past four.

Even at that time in the morning, the A&E department was busy with patients ranging from the walking wounded to the really worrying. Harry plainly fell into the latter category because he was instantly whisked away, leaving Neil and Claire to register his details at the desk and sit down in a rather drab, impersonal side room to wait for news. An agonizing half hour later, they had still heard nothing.

"Supposing they can't save him?" Claire's voice trembled as she spoke her most dreaded thought out loud.

"He's a tough old bird, our Harry. And I always thought he seemed really fit for his age."

"So did I," said Claire, her eyes filling with tears. "He's always on the go, doing the garden, sorting out meals, running the house, looking after Sam, busy at the church… He never stops, does he? And I was too tied up in my own life to see that. I've worked him into the ground, haven't I? I did this to him!"

Instinctively Neil reached out to put his arm round her shaking shoulders.

"No, Claire. This isn't anyone's fault – and especially not yours. You and Sam *make* Harry's life. He loves you both so much and he knows real contentment just because you're around."

"So why this? What did he do to deserve this?"

"Nothing – except, I suppose, he's getting on a bit now, and this is just one of those awful conditions that affect people as they get older."

She looked up at him.

"An act of God, do you mean? Don't think much of your God if he lets this happen to someone like Harry, the dearest man in the world!"

At just that moment, the door of the room opened. Claire's eyes were wary and fearful as the consultant walked across to sit down beside her.

"Your uncle is very poorly, I'm afraid."

Neil felt her shoulders tremble as she breathed deeply, unable to reply.

"We very nearly lost him. If you hadn't got the ambulance team on the scene as quickly as you did, I don't think he'd be here."

"Is he…?" Claire seemed unable to form her words. "Is he going to die?"

"Without treatment, yes, I think it's unlikely he'll get through the next twelve hours."

Claire's hand shot to her mouth, and tears began to course their way down her cheeks.

"But," continued the consultant, "I'd like your permission to take him down to the operating theatre as soon as possible. The arteries around his heart are badly clogged. A triple bypass should give him a fighting chance to get through this."

"And in his present condition, is he strong enough for an operation like that?" asked Neil.

"Good question, because honestly we won't know the answer until we try it." The consultant looked at Claire. "He's nearly eighty, isn't he?"

"No!" was her sharp reply. "He's nowhere near eighty. He's

seventy-eight. Don't think you can write him off as an old man! Harry is full of life, always active, always running around doing things for people. He'd never give up on life – never!"

The consultant's eyes softened with understanding and sympathy as he spoke.

"Unfortunately, at his age, however he feels about life, it may be his body rather than his mind that gives up. All I can say is that we'll do our very best for him."

"I'm sorry," mumbled Claire. "I'm so sorry. Will it be you doing the operation?"

"Yes," replied the consultant.

"How long will it take?"

He glanced at his watch. "It's half five. We've only got a skeleton staff here overnight, but the full theatre team will be in at seven. I'd like to wait till then. He can be first on the list."

"And the delay?" asked Claire. "That's an hour and a half of nothing. You said he's very poorly. Will he…?"

"He's wired up so that all the functions necessary for life are being supported – but honestly, in an elderly patient, there's always the risk he'll slip away in spite of our best efforts."

Claire made a gesture of frustration with her hands.

"My advice is that we give your uncle the best possible chance by taking him down for a triple bypass as soon as the theatre team are set and ready to receive him. There's a family room upstairs that you're welcome to wait in, and once there's any news at all, we'll get it to you straight away. I have to say, though, you two look beat. Why don't you go down for a cup of coffee? Or try and get some sleep, maybe?"

"We're fine," said Claire sharply. "Can we sit with him? Until you take him down for the operation, can we be with him?"

"Of course," smiled the consultant. "I'll get the nurse to show you where he is."

Harry looked small and pale in the huge bed surrounded by equipment that blinked and beeped, with flashing lights and a startling array of tubes and wires that were linked up to various parts of his body. Neil pulled up two chairs, and they sat side by side as Claire leaned forward to take Harry's hand in hers.

"Uncle Harry," she whispered, "fight! Stay with us! Sam and I love you so much! Don't let go! Fight your way through this. You know you can!"

"The very first day I met you," said Neil, his voice barely above a whisper, "was also the morning I first met Harry. He told me about Rose, about losing her two years ago."

"He never told her he loved her." Claire's voice was so low that Neil could barely hear her. "I think that's why he is always telling me and Sam how much we mean to him. He lives in constant regret that he never told his darling Rose how much he loved her."

"He hoped she knew – and I think she probably did, don't you?"

She fell silent, looking at Harry, his white face expressionless in sleep, his chest rising and falling as the machine by his side beeped out every beat of his struggling heart.

"Do you think he really wants to join her?" Claire asked.

"I don't think death holds any fear for him," Neil replied, "and he believes that in death he will meet his Rose again."

"Do you believe that?"

"Yes. Yes, I do."

"I'd like to think it's true. I'd like to know she's waiting there for Uncle Harry. I'd like to think, when the time comes, they'll both be waiting there for me too."

Neil looked sideways at her. "Doesn't sound much like the atheist speaking?"

"No, it's the despair of someone who is terrified of losing this wonderful man who is so dear to me; someone who hopes that this life isn't all there is, even though my head tells me that's difficult to believe; someone who at this moment hopes with all her heart there really is something beyond what we can see and touch and prove."

"There is," said Neil.

"God? Your God?"

"Yours too."

"I don't know him. If he does exist, why should he care about the despair of someone who's shown absolutely no interest in him until the chips are down?"

"Because his presence doesn't rely on your loving him, but on his unchanging love for you."

She sighed. "I want to pray. How ridiculous is that, when I've never even thought about praying before?"

"Oh Claire, it's an instinct to pray, as natural to the soul as breathing and sleeping are to the body."

"I don't know how."

Her green eyes shone with tears as she turned to him.

"God will show you. You don't need words. Just open your mind and heart and share it all with God. He understands. He'll listen. He's here for you."

"What shall I pray for? To save Harry's life? Even if perhaps he really wants to go...?"

"Everyone dies some time, Claire. Death is as much a part of life as being born. Perhaps it is Harry's time to go. God alone knows. Perhaps the healing you can hope for in prayer is for yourself and all the rest of us who are left behind, rather than just Harry. We all need comfort and strength to get through this. But if there is one thing I am certain of, it's that prayer has power. Never doubt that for a moment."

"Help me…" she whispered. "Show me how."

And sitting side by side, they both bowed their heads until their faces almost touched as they prayed as one, not just for Harry, but as if their own lives depended on it.

* * *

It was half past seven before the theatre team came to wheel Harry down for surgery. He stirred enough to realize they were there, although he seemed confused and sleepy. Once they'd settled him on to the trolley, Neil stood back as Claire leaned over to kiss her uncle, her lips brushing his ear as she whispered urgently:

"We love you, Harry. Come back to us. And you won't believe this, but I've asked your God to look after you, so this is his chance! Make sure he brings you back to us, please…"

Neil reached out to pull her back towards him so that the porter could manoeuvre the trolley out of the door, and the two of them watched helplessly as Harry was pushed down the corridor and out of sight.

"Coffee?" suggested Neil. "You look all in. How about we grab a sandwich or something?"

"I'm going to wait in the Family Room," said Claire. "If anything happens, they'll know to find me there."

Neil nodded with understanding.

"Look, I'll go and pick up some bits and pieces from the restaurant downstairs. I'll ring Margaret too, to let her know what's happening."

"I'm supposed to be working at the churchyard this morning," said Claire bleakly.

"Don't worry, she'll understand."

"And if I give you the number, could you ring Jan and Paul to make sure Sam is OK? Tell Jan I'll ring her as soon as I can."

"Of course. What about your Mum? Should she be told?"

"I'll send her a text, I think. I checked with the nurse and she's says they don't like us making phone calls from here, but we can send texts if we go in the corridor." She stopped to look at him closely. "Are you all right? You look awful."

Neil ran his fingers through his hair. "Well, it's been a pretty awful night, hasn't it? Harry always seemed so fit and vital. It's a shock to see him like this. It brings you face to face with how fragile life is."

Her face was full of understanding as she stepped towards him and drew him into a hug. Neil's surprise at the gesture was quickly surpassed by an overwhelming sense of comfort and reassurance in the face of the concern for Harry which they shared. For several moments they drew strength from each other – then she stepped back, holding his gaze as she picked up her bag and started walking towards the Family Room.

Desperate for some fresh air, he walked out of main reception and found a bench on which he could sit and make calls. The moment he switched on his phone, a text message flashed up. It was from Graham:

Taking Debs to the Italian tonight! No mention of Police Van Man. Say a prayer for me. I might need it!

In spite of himself, Neil smiled. It looked as if there could be at least one happy ending around after all. He didn't dwell on the thought though, because he immediately rang Jan and Paul's number. Jan picked up the phone straightaway, keen to hear news of Harry.

"Tell Claire we're thinking of her," Jan said once she'd been brought up to date, "and say we're right here if there's anything at all we can do."

"She says she'll ring you later. She just didn't want to leave the room now in case there's any news about Harry."

"Tell her Sam's fine. And could you speak to him? I know he'd like to talk to you."

"Is Grandad ill?" Sam's voice sounded thin and worried when he came to the phone.

"He is, Sam. Not very well at all. Mummy had to call the ambulance, so he's in hospital now."

"Is he going to die, then?"

"Well, they're giving him all the help they can, so we really hope they can make him better."

"My hamster died."

"Did it?"

"We buried him in the garden and planted a bush on top."

"That was a nice thing to do."

"Will we have to bury Harry in the garden?"

"Definitely not. The doctors here are looking after your Grandad really well."

"Doctors make you better. When I had spots all over me, Mummy took me to the doctor and he made me better."

"Oh Sam, you're such a good and brave boy. Are you all right with Beckie and Brendan?"

"They have *chocolate* cereal here! Mummy won't let me have that at our house."

"Well, I don't think she'll mind today. She'll be glad you're enjoying yourself. She sends you lots of love."

"Are you looking after Mummy, then?"

"I'm trying, Sam. I'll do my very best, I promise. Mummy will be back just as soon as she can, OK?"

"OK!" And Neil could hear Sam skip away from the phone, his mind switching instantly from hospitals and hamsters to the possibility of him having a bit more of that chocolate cereal.

It was Frank who picked up the phone at the Vicarage. Neil realized that it was Tuesday, Margaret's day off, so Frank was in the kitchen making a cup of tea to take up to his wife, who was still in bed. Neil quickly relayed to Frank details of the night's events, and Frank promised that he and Margaret would cover any of Neil's duties for the day, and pass the message about Harry on to everyone who would want to know.

"Look, if you need Margaret there, just yell, because she'll be there like a shot. In any case, please tell Claire that she and Harry are in our prayers. You too, Neil. We'll get everyone we can from St Stephen's to start praying for Harry right away."

That call finished, Neil glanced at his watch. It was just gone eight. He might just catch Wendy before she got tied up with whatever the day had in store for her at school.

"Neil?" There was a note of curiosity in Wendy's voice that she should be hearing from him at such an unexpected time in the morning.

"I just wanted to let you know I'm at the hospital…"

"Why? Are you OK? What's happened?"

"It's not me. It's Harry. He's had a heart attack."

"So why are you there? Surely it's Claire's job to be with him?"

"She's here too."

"What do you mean? What time did this all happen?"

"She rang me about a quarter to four, I think."

"And you've been there ever since with her?"

"With Harry and Claire, yes."

"But you're not family! What's she thinking of?"

"I'm a friend of the family, Wendy. They're my neighbours. They've been really good to me. This is the least I can do for them at such a worrying time."

"But you're leaving now, aren't you? You've got a really big day ahead."

"Well, I've just been in touch with the Vicarage. Margaret will cover whatever I was supposed to do today. There's not much on – and they know I'm due to leave for retreat later this evening."

"But you've got to be on time, and in the right frame of mind for that, Neil. This time of retreat is important for you as you prepare for your ordination ceremony. You've been working for years towards this moment when you become a priest. There is nothing more important than that."

"Yes – but I also know it's important I'm here at the moment."

"So you mean to stay there?"

"Until Harry comes up from surgery, definitely."

There was silence from the other end of the line.

"It's my job to be alongside people when they are in times of need, Wendy. That's what a priest does."

"Neil, I understand that completely. I would just remind you, though, that there is a line between being alongside a family, and actually joining it! Are Claire's parents coming down?"

"I'm sure they will. She's contacting them now."

"So where is she at the moment? Obviously not with you."

"No, I came outside to ring you. She wanted to stay up in the Family Room in case there's any news."

"Well, you'd better get back to her, then. Tell her I wish Harry well."

"I will."

There was another awkward silence.

"So, do you still want me to give you a lift to the retreat centre tonight?"

"Of course," replied Neil. "I'd like to share that last journey with you, bearing in mind the next time we are under the same roof it will be during the ordination service."

"Well, there's no point you having your car at the Abbey on Saturday when it will be me who's bringing you home."

"Thank you, Wendy. I appreciate that."

"Take care, Neil. Get some sleep today, if you can. You don't want to be nodding off when you're supposed to be in deep contemplation tonight."

"No," he agreed. "Have a good day yourself. See you later."

Neil sat for a while after the call had cut off. Wendy had questioned his role in being there with Harry and Claire. From the very start, it had never occurred to him that he would be anywhere *but* here with them. Wendy's reaction had shaken him. Was he intruding? Had he allowed the line between professionalism and friendship to become clouded? He shook off the thought immediately. His relationship with Harry and his family had always been more about friendship than professionalism. If anything, he had learned a great deal more from all of them than he had ever given in return. He thought about the genuine, loving affection and welcome they always gave him – and the sudden wave of fondness for them that flooded across him took him by surprise. He slid his phone shut, and headed to the restaurant in the hope that he could find Claire something tempting for breakfast.

When he returned to the Family Room with sandwiches and two cups of coffee, he found Claire stretched out awkwardly across a couple of chairs, her neck at an awkward angle as she slept. Neil saw how her long, auburn lashes were resting on the dark smudges of exhaustion which were etched on her face after the night's events. He gazed at the faint freckles on the bridge of her nose, and the way her lips had parted slightly in sleep. He noticed her soft breathing, and the way her arms were tucked around her, almost as if she was hugging herself for comfort.

He laid down the tray of coffee and sandwiches on a nearby table, then as gently as he could, he lifted her head so that he could slip on to the chair beside her. Without waking, she settled herself against him, looking small and vulnerable as she slumbered. Stroking her forehead as a parent would a child, he watched her as she slept – until his eyelids grew heavy, his head fell forward and sleep claimed him too.

* * *

The early morning noises of the nearby A&E hospital ward eventually became so insistent and intrusive that Claire's lids fluttered for a few seconds before she sat up abruptly with an expression of guilt on her face.

"I fell asleep. I didn't mean to do that. Is there any news? What's happened?"

Arching his back to stretch his aching muscles, Neil glanced at his wristwatch, then shook his head.

"No, nothing so far. It's nearly nine. How long do these operations take, do you think?"

"I suppose," she said, her expression grave, "if anything had gone wrong, they would come and told us."

"Yes, they would, so no news is good news."

"I hope so, Neil. I really hope so."

He looked across at the cold cups of coffee.

"Breakfast?"

She almost smiled. "I don't think I could face that, thanks. I wouldn't mind a glass of water, though – and a splash across my face would feel good too."

"The Ladies is down on the right, I think. Take your time. It's good to stretch your legs. I'll come and find you if I hear anything."

Claire got up and, for a second or two, looked back at Neil as if she wanted to say something. Whatever it was, she thought better of it because she turned instead and headed out the door.

In the end, it was gone ten before a nurse from the theatre team came up to find them.

"So far, so good," she said. "He's come through the operation OK, but the attack last night did quite a bit of damage, and he's not a young man. The next few hours will be crucial."

"Where is he? Can we see him now?"

"He's still out for the count, I'm afraid, so they're taking him to the Intensive Care Unit to keep him as stable as possible. I can take you down there though, if you like."

Weak with a combination of relief and worry, Claire reached for Neil's hand as they followed the nurse through a confusion of corridors and staircases until at last they entered the Intensive Care Unit, where they were instantly struck by the atmosphere of hushed efficiency. There were four rooms off a central nursing area, and the sister in charge took them over so that they could peep in through the window, behind which they could see Harry looking unnaturally pale and expressionless, surrounded by a bank of electronic equipment, wires and tubes.

"Don't be alarmed by everything around him. That's all helping to keep him going while he recovers from the shock of what he's been through."

"Can we go in?"

"Not just yet. It's best if just the team are around him at the moment to keep the risk of infection down."

"How's he doing?" asked Neil.

The sister looked through the window to consider her answer.

"He's got this far, and the bypass operation will really help his heart to start pumping properly again. But he's been through a lot. It's a shock to the system. I would say the next five or six hours are critical. If he gets through that, he's got a very good chance of recovery."

Claire, who had never let go of Neil's hand, tightened her grip.

The ward sister smiled kindly at them. "Look, it will be no good him waking up if the two of you are wrecked by the time he comes round. Why don't you take a break? Go and get a bite to eat and a breath of fresh air. Nothing's going to happen for a while, I can promise you that. And I can take your mobile number and give you a ring instantly if there's any change."

Claire looked uncertainly at Neil. "I'm not sure…"

Neil lightly touched the side of her face. "You do look all in. Come on, a breath of fresh air will do us both good. Harry's in the best possible hands. They'll take care of him – and we won't be long."

"Your husband's right," added the sister. "Half an hour won't hurt. It's unlikely that there'll be a change in your uncle's condition in that time."

It looked as if Claire was about to object, but when Neil guided her gently back out of the ward, she went without a murmur.

They found a bench in a small memorial garden at the back of the hospital. Amongst a rather wind-blown selection of shrubs and thinning clumps of bedding plants, Claire tipped her face up to feel the rays of morning sun.

"This garden could do with your magic touch," smiled Neil.

Opening her eyes to look around, she smiled too without comment.

They sat in companionable silence for a while, hearing the bustle of cars, voices and hospital life at a distance from this small garden oasis.

"He's holding on, isn't he? He's still with us," Claire said at last. "Does that mean the worst is over? Could we lose him even now?"

"I don't know, Claire. I really don't know, but the signs are good. He's survived the operation, and that must mean something."

"Do you think it means he's fighting to live? That perhaps Rose can wait for a while…?"

"He's got a lot to live for – you, Sam…"

"… and his garden," added Claire. "Everything he's planted is about to be at its very best, and he's put so much work into it. He won't want to miss that!"

"Or Sam going to school in September? He was telling me how much he's looking forward to meeting him at the school gate in the afternoons…"

"And church?" Claire added, her face thoughtful as she turned to face Neil. "What happened last night, Neil? You got me praying. Me! I can't believe I did that."

"How did it feel?"

She considered a while before answering. "It felt good, as if in a situation when I felt totally useless, I finally found something I could do that had a purpose."

"And he's come through the operation…"

"Yes, he has."

"It's a great hospital, this," said Neil. "I don't think he could have been in better hands last night."

"But was it more than that? Was it just good medicine and treatment that brought him through?"

"I don't think so," said Neil quietly. "Prayer has power, Claire. I know that without a shadow of doubt. Whether it's the prayer of millions across the country all praying for a common need, or a desperate plea from one frightened and longing person, just as you were last night – prayer has power. God hears and he does respond."

"But people die. Even when someone like me cries out for God to save them, they still die."

"Everyone dies." Neil's words were low and considered. "There is a time for all of us, and eventually we have to die. So sometimes God can only answer our prayers by helping us to find the comfort and strength we need to get through. I believe that God knows us so much better than we know ourselves. He's knows what we are capable of coping with, however lacking we might feel when things are falling apart around us. Perhaps it's only through tough times that we actually find out what we're made of. An easy life doesn't breed character. Challenge does. So maybe we only become what God always intended us to be because of what we go through, and how we deal with the difficulties in life."

"I hate that," retorted Claire. "I hate the suggestion that you find God, then everything becomes instantly rosy."

"And you're right – life's not like that. I worry too when people seem to have an instant conversion just when they need it most, because whatever kick-starts you off on your road to faith, taking that road is destined to be a lifetime's journey. It's not that I don't believe in miracles. They happen all the time, I am sure of that. And I know that some people have a road-to-Damascus experience which changes them, like Paul, from the most outspoken unbeliever to a man of inspirational faith. I envy people who speak of how that's happened to them – the "born again" moment that changes them so dramatically – but that's never been my experience. My faith has grown from a million doubts and questions that have stretched over all the years of my life, and I can't help but think that it's through doubts and questions that you find for yourself what *you* truly believe."

She was silent for a while, mulling over what he'd said, then she simply rested her head against his shoulder.

"So I can take my time, then?"

"Definitely."

"And because I reckon I've got more questions than you ever had, will you promise to stay around to help me out with the answers?"

"I'll do my very best."

She hesitated a moment, uncertain how to continue.

"Do you know what?" she asked finally. "I'm not sure I can believe what I'm about to say."

"Try me."

"I felt something – when I prayed last night. I was desperate, begging almost – but I did feel something – like I wasn't alone, like there was someone listening."

"There was."

"Your God?"

"Yours too."

242

She looked down for a moment, lost in thought – then she grinned up at him.

"Or perhaps it was Auntie Rose telling me to pull myself together?"

He chuckled. "Probably!"

"Neil," she started, her voice hesitant. "I may never get a chance like this again, so I'll say it now. When I discovered Harry last night, and everything was so awful and frightening, you were the first person I thought of. No one else could have been better company. You've been wonderful."

There was real warmth in his eyes as he looked at her.

"So are you."

"And I might regret saying this in the cold light of day…"

Claire looked down, as if she was nervous to hold his gaze.

"… but we've learned a lot about each other tonight, about our weaknesses and our strengths too. I've never felt so inadequate and helpless – and yet there you are, caring and unconditionally supportive. I'll never forget that, never."

"I'm just so glad you didn't try to go through this on your own, that you allowed me to share it with you."

"I'm not good at relationships. I prefer not to let people get too close, especially since…"

"Since Sam's dad?"

She nodded.

"Who can blame you? He let you down badly."

"And it's difficult to trust anyone again after something like that. I've just not bothered with people much."

"You prefer flowers and plants."

"Yes, I do. But that's not right, is it? I need to learn to trust again – and I'm learning that from you, Neil. With your gentleness, your sensitivity – even your nerves and awkwardness…"

"Thanks!" he smiled.

"... you're breaking down my barriers. You're getting through."

"I'm glad."

There was an earnestness in her expression as she looked at him. "Look, just remember, when you think about this later, that I'm tired and emotional right now, and I'll probably regret saying this. In fact, why don't I just shut up, because I'm all over the place at the moment?"

She hesitated. "It's just that…"

"What?" he prompted gently.

"Something happens to me when I'm with you, something warm and comforting and wonderful – and the only word I can think of to describe it is… love."

Surprised at her frankness, he took a sharp intake of breath, staring at her wordlessly as time stood still between them. Then he felt himself move almost in slow motion towards her until their lips met in a kiss of need and want and longing. And when it was over, they pulled back, holding their gaze as if they couldn't believe what was happening or the feeling that had sparked between them. There was no world beyond this, nothing else that mattered. In that moment, it was not just their hands that reached out to touch and hold, but their hearts.

Finally Neil spoke, his voice shaking with emotion.

"Love?" he whispered. "God help us, Claire, but I know what you mean. I feel it too."

* * *

They went back to the Intensive Care Unit and sat close together on the lumpy settee to one side of the central area. Nursing staff constantly went in and out of Harry's room, monitoring and checking his progress. Then, at around two o'clock, the consultant who'd performed the operation came to check on Harry, then crossed to talk to them.

"Well, he seems to be holding his own."

Neil felt the tension drop from Claire as her body slumped against him. "Is he out of danger?"

"The worst is probably over, although he's still a very sick man. The operation went well, though, and if he continues to improve as he has so far, I think he might have a much healthier, more comfortable life ahead."

"Do you mean that he's probably not been well for a while?"

"I think that's probably the case, but he may not have realized why he wasn't really feeling up to par. He might just have put it down to getting older."

"So what happens now?"

"Well, I think we'll be bringing him round quite soon and then, once we're sure he's stable, we can get him down to the normal ward, perhaps tomorrow morning. After that, it's just a question of recuperating, physio and getting him home again."

Tears of relief shone on Claire's cheeks.

"Thank you, doctor. Thank you so much."

"Well, let's see about bringing him back into the land of the living, shall we?"

Calling over one of the nurses, the consultant disappeared once again into Harry's cubicle. The ten minutes that ticked by before anyone appeared again seemed more like ten hours – but eventually the nurse popped her head around the door and beckoned them in.

"You can come in for just a minute, no more," she said, guiding them over to the left-hand side of the bed, since Harry's head was facing that way.

"Uncle Harry?" whispered Claire, bending down until she was level with his face. "Uncle Harry, can you hear me?"

Harry stirred, plainly disorientated and uncertain where he was, but finally his rheumy eyes focused on Claire beside him. A slow smile spread across his face.

"What happened?" His voice sounded raspy and hoarse, probably because of the tubes that had been stuffed down his throat during the operation.

"You had a heart attack. You scared the living daylights out of me."

"How am I doing?"

"I'm delighted to say you'll live! You had a bypass operation this morning, and so far everything looks good."

"That explains it then," he said, closing his eyes.

"Explains what?" asked Claire.

"Why Rose was here nagging me."

Claire stared at him in amazement.

"Sent me back, though – for you and Sam."

"So?" asked Claire softly. "Did you tell her? Did you say what you wanted her to know?"

He gave the slightest of nods. "Told me I was daft. Said she always knew…"

"There! You needn't have worried after all."

"I won't any more," he sighed, closing his eyes again and sinking back into sleep.

* * *

Things moved fast after that. Claire's mum and step-dad arrived after a long and hurried drive down from Scarborough, and Neil looked on gratefully as they engulfed Claire in their love and caring concern. This was his cue to leave. After all, it was an important time for him, the start of his three days of retreat in preparation for his ordination on Saturday. Wendy would be arriving at the house in just two hours' time at five o'clock to drive him down to join the other ordinands at the retreat centre near St Albans. There was a lot to do before then. He knew he needed to go.

Wendy.... Since that moment with Claire earlier in the afternoon, the one that had turned his world completely upside down, he had struggled to keep thoughts of Wendy to the back of his mind. Wonderful, supportive, talented Wendy who loved him so loyally – and trusted him too. What sort of man was he? Untrustworthy, unfaithful? And knowing that, how could he possibly go on to become a priest when his emotions were torn in two directions?

Guilt pricked at his conscience – and yet, he knew that the long and worrying hours Claire and he had just spent together had simply brought to the surface feelings that had probably been there for months. Ever since that kiss at Christmas, he'd wondered – and yet he'd deliberately denied himself the suggestion that Claire might actually care for him in any way beyond friendship – or, even more importantly, that he should care for her in return. After all, they were so different. Their situation, their beliefs, their goals in life were worlds apart. Why, then, had they felt such closeness and empathy there at the hospital? They had spoken of love – and yet what did that mean? What sort of love was this? A love that demanded a lifetime's commitment – or was it simply the deep and enduring love that very dear friends could feel for one another?

As the thoughts tumbled round his exhausted brain, he shook his head, knowing that he couldn't think straight just at the moment. Perhaps after some sleep? But not now – not with Harry ill, Claire's parents there, the ordination looming and Wendy picking him up in two hours' time…

He picked up his jacket and hovered to one side of Claire, hoping to catch her attention as she chatted to her parents. Excusing herself, she followed him round the corner where they could speak privately.

"Harry seems to be holding his own, doesn't he?" started Neil. "After all he's been through…"

"It's such a relief. When I found him last night, I really thought we were going to lose him."

Neil nodded, remembering how shocked he'd been by Harry's almost deathly pale complexion when he'd first seen him the night before.

"Well, we know he's in good hands. I'll hold on to that while I'm on retreat. It will be hard not to hear any news about him until after Saturday. We'll be cut off from the world until then."

"Well, you need to get going. You must have so much to do." Claire's voice became unnaturally business-like. "What time do you leave?"

"Wendy's picking me up in two hours for the drive down to St Albans."

"Good. That's nice of her. She's a lovely person, Neil. I know that. I do understand your situation. You're with Wendy, and that's where you belong."

His face wretched, Neil nodded in silent agreement until finally he put into words the question that hung between them.

"So what happened between us just now?"

Her fingers entwined with his.

"We're both exhausted. It's been an emotional rollercoaster."

He looked closely at her. "The heat of the moment, do you mean? Do you think that's all it was?"

"Do you?"

"No."

"Neither do I."

"Claire, I…"

"Sshh…"

He stopped, recognizing that there was so much to say – but not now. Instead, she tipped her head towards him so that her forehead leaned against his chin.

"I'll be thinking of you on Saturday," she whispered.

He nodded.

"See you when you get back."

"Yes."

"Take care of yourself."

"You too, Claire. Take care of you."

* * *

At exactly five to five, Wendy's red Clio pulled up outside, and Neil opened the front door to let her in. His bag was packed and ready to go, and his robes were hanging in a cover draped over the hall banister. He took one last look around to make sure he'd not forgotten anything.

"Locked the back door?" Wendy asked.

"Yes."

"Got the forms you had to fill in?"

"All done and in my briefcase."

"And you've definitely remembered everything you need to wear on the day?"

"I think so."

"Clean socks?"

"Four pairs, and I'll only be gone three days!"

"Right then, let's go!"

Wendy strode on ahead carrying his robes whilst he dead-locked the door and followed on towards her car.

"Oy!"

Alf had suddenly appeared from nowhere, and was staring accusingly at Wendy who had just climbed into the driving seat and slammed the door.

"She *stood* on my flowers!"

Puzzled, Neil followed Alf's stare, wondering what flowers he was talking about. All he could see were a few small, bedraggled dandelion heads peeping out amongst the grass verge at the edge of the pavement.

"My dandelions! She stood on them!"

"Oh, Alf, we're so sorry. She didn't realize they were there."

Alf continued to look pointedly towards Wendy, saying nothing.

"Anyway, Alf," Neil continued, hoping a change of subject might change his mood, "wish me luck because when you see me again, I'll be a fully fledged priest! I'm going off to my ordination now."

There was no reaction at all from Alf.

"Well, give my regards to Maureen. Is she with you today? I expect so. I'll be off now then, Alf. Goodbye!"

It wasn't until Neil was just bending to climb into the passenger seat that he heard Alf finally shout out an answer.

"And good riddance!"

Neil clambered into the car and slammed the door shut, expecting Wendy to drive off immediately. She did put the key in the ignition, but instead of starting the engine, she turned to look at him, a warm smile on her face.

"You OK?" she asked. "You must be exhausted."

"I am – but I'll be fine. As you say, I've been looking forward to this for so long."

"Well," she said, reaching over to take his hand in hers, "as we won't be able to speak again until after the service, I just want you to know how proud I am of you. You're a special man, Neil, and so very dear to me. I'll be thinking of you and wishing you well while you're away on retreat – and I will be the one praying most and cheering loudest for you on the day. I hope it's a truly moving experience for you."

Tears pricked at Neil's eyes as he looked at her. She understood his vocation and sense of calling so perfectly. She always had. She was right at the heart of the church community which had become his home and family. She supported and encouraged and inspired him… and yet… and yet…

"Right!" she said suddenly, turning back to start the engine. "We'd better get going!"

Wendy checked the mirror as she drew the small car away from the kerb outside his house and drove off down Vicarage Gardens. Number 96 faded behind them as Neil peered beyond Wendy through her driver's window to look at Number 80 as they drove by. How quiet and empty the house must be without Harry, Claire and Sam within its walls. Warmth and love – that's what they brought to the home they shared. Warmth and love, thought Neil as he stared past Wendy's face to look out the window – that's what they'd all brought to *his* life too.

At that moment, Wendy turned towards him, smiling with such sweetness and affection that Neil caught his breath.

"Shall I put the radio on?" she asked, leaning down to select the station. "We're just in time for the News."

They turned left at the top of the road in front of St Stephen's Church, then drove through the Market Square and out of town towards the motorway.

Neil Fisher's misadventures continue in:

CASTING THE NET

Also by Pam Rhodes:

WITH HEARTS AND HYMNS AND VOICES

When the BBC "Songs of Praise" team decides to broadcast a Palm Sunday service from a small idyllic Suffolk village, not everyone is happy.

The vicar, Clive, is amiably absent-minded, but his practical wife Helen gets on well with the television team – perhaps a little too well, where the charming, enigmatic Michael is concerned. Charles, the Parish Council chairman, is deeply opposed and resents the enthusiasm of other villagers – including his wife Betty. As the outside broadcast vehicles roll in, the emotional temperature rises…

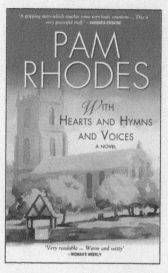

"Very moving, very powerful intimate moments… I really did enjoy it."
– Lynn Parsons, BBC Radio 2

"Very readable … Warm and witty."
– Woman's Weekly

"Ambitions and emotions run high…"
– Family Circle Magazine

"A gripping story which touches some very basic emotions… Captures wonderfully the two extremes of village life… This is very powerful stuff."
– Barbara Erskine

ISBN: 978 1 85424 975 3 | e-ISBN: 978 0 85721 074 6

WITH HEARTS AND HYMNS AND VOICES

When the BBC *Songs of Praise*
team decides to broadcast a *Palm
Sunday* service from a small idyllic
Suffolk village, not everyone is happy.
The vicar, Clive, is amiable,
absent-minded, but his practical wife
Helen gets on well with the television
team – perhaps a little too well, where
the charming cameraman Edward
is concerned. Charles, the Parish
Council chairman, is deeply opposed
and resents the enthusiasm of other
villagers – including his wife Betty. As
the planned broadcast unfolds, rolls in
the emotional temperatures . . .

"Very moving, very powerful: intimate characters . . . I really
did enjoy it."
Lynn Parsons, BBC Radio 2

"Very readable . . . Warm and witty."
Woman's Weekly

"Ambitions and emotions run high."
Family Circle Magazine

"A gripping story which touches some raw basic
emotions. Captures wonderfully the true experience of
village life . . . This is very powerful stuff."
Bygone Britain

ISBN 978 1 84291 673 5 / e-ISBN 978 0 85721 014 8